— Book 1 —
VERITY CHRONICLES

EXILE

T S VALMOND
A K DUBOFF

EXILE
Copyright © 2020 by A.K. DuBoff & T.S. Valmond

The Cadicle˚ Universe is a registered trademark of A.K. DuBoff

www.cadicle.com

Published by Dawnrunner Press
Cover Copyright © 2020 A.K. DuBoff

ISBN-10: 1954344058
ISBN-13: 978-1954344051

0 9 8 7 6 5 4 3

Produced in the United States of America

TABLE OF CONTENTS

Chapter 1 1
Chapter 2 11
Chapter 3 20
Chapter 4 35
Chapter 5 48
Chapter 6 61
Chapter 7 69
Chapter 8 76
Chapter 9 84
Chapter 10.. 99
Chapter 11... 108
Chapter 12... 123
Chapter 13... 134
Chapter 14... 144
Chapter 15... 153
Chapter 16... 171
Chapter 17... 177
Chapter 18... 188
Chapter 19... 195
Chapter 20... 203
Chapter 21... 211
Chapter 22... 220
Chapter 23... 233
Chapter 24... 246
Chapter 25... 257
Chapter 26... 265
Chapter 27... 273
Chapter 28... 286
Chapter 29... 298
Chapter 30... 305
ADDITIONAL READING 313
AUTHORS' NOTES............................... 314
ABOUT THE AUTHORS....................... 316

TABLE OF CONTENTS

ABOUT THE CADICLE UNIVERSE

Tarans are the predominant race in the Cadicle Universe; humans are a Taran sub-race. Most of the Taran sphere falls within the purview of the Taran Empire, governed from the planet Tararia by a council of High Dynasties. Earth is one of several rogue colonies on the outskirts of the Empire, separated so long ago that they have forgotten their Taran ancestry.

The Tararian Guard is the primary military force for the Taran Empire. Its counterpart, the Tararian Selective Service, includes a specialty branch with Agents gifted in telekinetic and telepathic abilities.

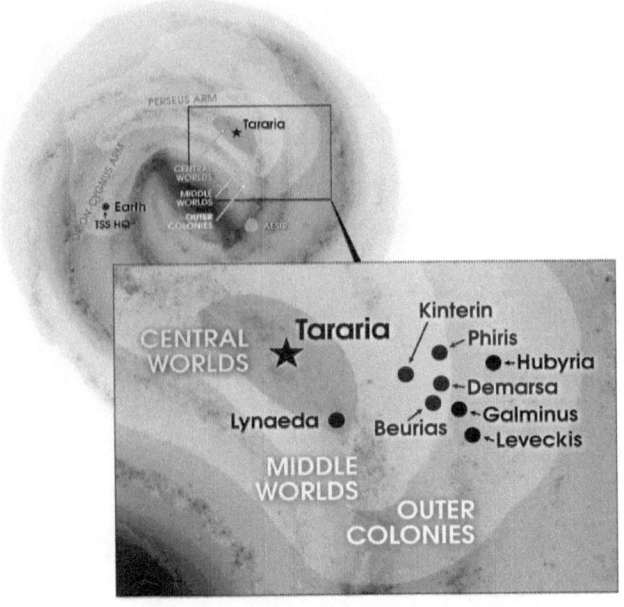

1

As the sea of people flowed along the crowded boulevard, all Iza Sundari saw were potential marks. The oblivious tourists gaped at the colossal, glass-covered buildings, ignoring everything else around them. It would be so easy to relieve any one of them of the credit chips in their pockets.

Seven years ago, she wouldn't have thought twice about pickpocketing. Growing up on the outer edge of the Taran colonies, she'd never enjoyed the comforts available to residents of the inner planets, like these pampered tourists on Kinterin. She'd done whatever she needed to survive, without fear of the consequences. After all, prison wasn't any worse than how she'd spent most of her life; perhaps it was even an upgrade, in some respects. Though still only twenty-two, she'd matured since her tumultuous teenage years, learning to navigate the ways of the Taran Empire to make a living while staying on the correct side of the law. It wasn't an easy life, but she got by.

The smiling and impossibly charming faces of the people on inner planets always made Iza impatient and irritable. Anyone too friendly was either selling something or wanted something. She wasn't in the mood to humor them, so she kept a quick pace. Food was the only thing on her mind; it had been weeks since her last proper meal.

Iza's dark eyes caught sight of a family of four at an outdoor restaurant, reminiscent of a scene in an advertisement. *They don't know how good they have it.*

A throng of tourists stopped abruptly in the middle of the sidewalk in front of her to take a holovideo. In her haste to get around them, she veered to the right.

"Wait, please don't!"

The cry had come from an alley between two tall buildings. A quick peek revealed a middle-aged man at the point of a pulse gun, pleading for his life. He was dressed in the casual clothing of a tourist on holiday—a loud shirt with a busy, white print and matching red pants. The crowd of people on the boulevard pressed forward without noticing his plight.

Iza sighed. *Why do tourists always get themselves into the stupidest situations?*

She knew better than to get involved, but she also recognized that the portly man, now on his knees, wouldn't last the next two minutes if she didn't do something. She flipped her dark, curly hair behind her shoulders. *Here's a clue, tourists: don't walk around flashing your credits for everyone to see.* She hit the button on her handheld to signal for backup before strolling into the alley.

Iza kept her gun sheathed inside her jacket; the last thing she needed was an arrest for a shootout on a public street. As she approached, the desperate man on his knees saw his salvation and began pleading his case again.

"You don't want to do this. I swear, I'm innocent," he said, his bushy eyebrows raised.

His assailant sneered. "That's not the word I'd use. Try neck-deep."

Iza saw her moment and jumped in. "Hey, sorry to

interrupt. Could you help me with some directions?"

The sandy-haired man with the pulse gun jumped at the sight of her, waving his gun in her direction. Closer inspection revealed that he was younger than she'd guessed, no more than eighteen.

"Sorry, Gorgeous, I'm not from here, can't help you. Please leave. This doesn't concern you." The cheeky teenager redirected the pulse gun at the older man. He growled between his teeth and narrowed his hazel eyes. "Where is it?"

"I swear I don't know." The man rose from his knees, the dirt still clinging to his pants as his eyes flew from his captor's face to Iza's.

With her hands raised, Iza took another cautious step toward them. She was in it now and knew that the man's life was in her hands. "Maybe I can help. I'm not from here, either, but if we help each other, I'm sure we can find what it is you're looking for," Iza said. "I'll be honest, though, the way you're waving that gun around is making me more than a little nervous."

She closed the distance between them with another swift stride. In a practiced move learned on the rough streets of the outer colonies, she knocked the gun from the young man's hand with her left fist, simultaneously kicking the back of his right knee cap. Her other knee connected with his ribs, and he let out a screech that made her flinch.

Iza grabbed his arm and lifted it behind his back, stretching it upward until the young man's face was pressed to the rough stone wall of the building, pinning him. No longer in danger, the older victim dashed out the opposite end of the alley.

"Wrong way, brainless!" she called out after him. *Stars, not even a 'thank you'?*

The teenager squirmed as he struggled to turn his head to watch the man run off. "He's getting away! Do you know how long I've been trying to catch that thief?"

He had a distinct accent that Iza was sure she'd never heard outside of the most refined central planets. *Uh oh.*

"I'm sorry, you had a gun. I thought you were robbing that tourist—"

"He's no tourist! He stole from me. Besides, take a good look at me. Why would *I* be robbing *him*?"

Only now did Iza notice that the young man's rumpled clothing, though marred with dirt stains, was expertly tailored from a fine fabric that probably cost more per-meter than all the credits in her pocket. His shoes had lost their luster, but they were also well-made from the soles to the buckles at his ankles.

"Oh, I see," she said and meant it.

"So, can you let me go?"

She looked at where his pulse gun was resting on the ground. "You're not going to try to shoot me, are you?"

He groaned. "No. Even though you've screwed me over, shooting you wouldn't fix it."

There was a sincerity in his tone. Whatever had been going on between the two men, it would seem she had greatly misread the situation. Cautiously, Iza released the grip on his arm.

He hobbled over to pick up his dropped pulse gun, gripping his ribs and swearing as he went. "Months wasted. Father's going to kill me."

"What were you after, anyway?"

Before he could answer, her backup, Trix, arrived. Faster than Iza could see, the almost two-meter-tall brunette android clapped both hands over the young man's ears, rendering him unconscious. He dropped the gun and fell into a crumpled heap on the ground.

"What'd you do that for?" Iza exclaimed.

"You signaled for help. He had a handgun. I deduced that the help you needed was from him. Was I incorrect in that assessment?"

Iza pinched the bridge of her nose in frustration. It wasn't worth explaining. "What took you so long? I thought you were right behind me."

"I could not track the origin of your signal and had to perform a visual search in order to locate you. Someone is jamming all communications in this vicinity. I suggest we leave immediately."

Iza followed her toward the mouth of the alley. Trix stopped short, holding up one hand to indicate Iza needed to duck behind her.

"What's going on?"

Trix tilted her head to one side, indicating that she was listening. "It seems someone has alerted the local Enforcers to a theft in the area. Authorities dispatched patrollers to this area to apprehend someone who fits the description of the young troublemaker."

Iza looked back at the teenager lying in a heap on the ground. He seemed even younger with his face relaxed in unconscious sleep.

He'll never make it with the Enforcers looking for him. She'd messed things up for the young man and felt compelled to give him a chance to set things right. "Pick up our friend. We'll bring him back to the ship."

"You have an odd way of making friends," Trix replied in her monotone lilt.

"Don't start."

"Perhaps it would be wiser to leave him here."

"Wiser maybe, but not right. He's hurt, and he's in trouble."

Trix lifted him over her shoulder with as much effort as it

took most people to lift a bag of fruit.

"What are they saying he stole?" Iza asked.

"Nine thousand credits."

"I smell a bribe."

Trix sniffed at the air. "How do you know he didn't steal the credits?" she asked.

"If he had nine thousand credits, he'd have spent it on a new set of clothes. Someone wants us to think he's after the credits, but it's something else."

"What?"

Iza rolled her eyes and huffed. "I didn't get the chance to ask since you put him to sleep."

"Perhaps we should explain the matter to the authorities and avoid any more misunderstandings."

Iza ignored her, pulling out her pulse handgun from inside her jacket. "When have you ever known Enforcers to accept an explanation? We'd be scooped up and arrested just for talking to them. No, we'll have to make a run for it," she said while they both scanned up and down the busy boulevard for a quick exit. "Where did you park the shuttle?"

"Eighty-Fifth Street and First in the Financial District."

That was at least ten blocks from where they stood. The Guard's Enforcer patrollers, dressed in dark-gray uniforms, were already scouring the streets, checking identification and visitor passes. Trix would immediately draw attention running with the boy, only two centimeters shorter than herself, tossed over one shoulder.

"Can you interface with the shuttle from here and bring it to us?"

"No, not with the signal jammer blocking the connection."

Iza glanced up and got an idea.

Many of the surrounding buildings had exterior stairs for emergency evacuations. Iza eyed the metal staircase on the nearest building to her right, which exited at street-level and wound around the building all the way up to the roof. The height of it weakened her knees.

"Let's go up," she suggested, already moving toward it. "We should be able to cut through the signal jammer from the higher elevation and summon our shuttle to the roof." She pointed upward but quickly had to drop her gaze to the ground when her head started to spin. She centered herself with several slow breaths.

"Are you sure?" Trix's slim eyebrows had drawn together in skepticism.

"I'll be fine. Go."

Trix nodded once and proceeded up the stairs with Iza trailing behind.

"It is a quandary that a starship captain should be afraid of heights," the android commented.

"I'm not afraid of heights. I'm afraid of falling to my death off flimsy stairs attached to the side of a tall building. There's a difference."

The stairs were more manageable than she'd feared, though she had to push herself to keep up with Trix's determined pace. At one of the switchbacks, a wind gust lifted the back of Iza's jacket. She pressed against the side of the building to steady herself, forcing down a wave of nauseating dizziness.

Movement on the street below caught Iza's eye. Enforcers were swarming beneath them. The patrollers pointed upward and then took defensive positions. They opened fire.

Iza ducked behind the stairs leading up to the next level. "Do you have a signal yet?" They were dangerously exposed halfway up the metal stairway, but they could use their shuttle as a distraction if Trix could get it to their position.

"Negative. The jamming field is still preventing

communications."

They had no choice but to keep moving.

The stairs reverberated with the pulse shots as they climbed higher and higher. Hugging the side of the building with the curved stairs at their backs made them difficult targets for the Enforcers, but the rattling of the metal stairs dropped Iza's heart to her belly.

"Trix?"

"Not yet."

Iza let out a slew of curses. They were almost to the top now and, inevitably, Enforcers would be waiting. It didn't take a genius to see they were trapped. Without any idea of what they might have to face, Iza debated whether to grab her sidearm or keep two hands on the railings as she climbed. When another gust of wind whipped under her jacket, knocking her against the side of the building, she made up her mind; she needed to steady herself more than return fire.

The edge of the roof was in sight when Trix paused, turning her head to speak to Iza. "I have a signal. Shuttle ETA in two minutes," she stated.

"Great. Any ideas on how we're going to get to it?"

Trix remained silent.

"We're going to need a diversion. Can you handle that?"

"Affirmative."

Trix cleared the roof's edge first, still carrying the unconscious young man.

"Halt and identify yourselves," a deep male voice called out.

The absence of pulsefire meant the Enforcers wanted them conscious for questioning. It was a good sign. If they'd wanted them dead, they could have taken out Trix immediately.

Iza prepared to climb over the edge, keeping her hands up. "We've got injured!"

Unhurried, Iza took in the scene as she threw her left leg over the rail. Three patio tables were at the center of the rooftop and a green hedge lined the perimeter below the metal railing. A one-story-tall structure on the left of the roof deck housed a small elevator, the only means of accessing the space. Six armed Enforcers were already waiting for them. Behind the patrollers, Iza could just make out the lit numbers indicating the elevator was ascending from the fifth floor, likely carrying reinforcements.

"You have five seconds to identify yourselves." The lead officer, like the others, wore a full-face shield and body armor.

The semicircle of Enforcers around him had pulse rifles aimed at Iza and Trix. They were expecting resistance, and Iza didn't want to disappoint. She nodded to Trix, who lowered the young man to the ground and then imitated Iza's stance, raising both hands.

"Officers, there's been some kind of mistake," Iza said. She attempted to smile in the way obnoxious people were known to do on Kinterin.

Iza watched the elevator behind them as it ascended toward the roof.

Fifteen, sixteen, seventeen.

"There's no mistake. You're under arrest for aiding a known criminal."

Iza put on her most appalled expression and looked down at the young man at their feet. "Oh, you mean *him*? Well, we only just met. To be honest, we didn't even get his name."

Twenty-one, twenty-two, twenty-three.

The next elevator car was going to open at any second. Fortunately, their means of escape was finally in sight.

With the Enforcers' attention on Iza, none of them noticed her small shuttle until it was crashing down on top of them. Trix directed it into a mild tailspin, knocking half of the

Enforcers across the rooftop, unconscious. The rest dove for cover behind large potted shrubbery and the green hedge as the shuttle's weapons powered up.

Trix lifted the young man over her shoulder again while remotely landing the shuttle. The side hatch slid opened and she climbed in.

Iza used her handgun to provide cover fire, aiming at the remaining patrollers. She leaped into the shuttle as the hatch started to close—only a moment before the building elevator doors opened. Another contingent of Enforcers spilled out onto the roof.

"Get us out of here, now!" Iza shouted while the hatch sealed shut behind her.

The sound of gunfire hitting the shields faded as they lifted into the atmosphere of Kinterin.

She scrambled toward the front cockpit. "Are we being followed?"

Trix was already in the pilot's seat, ignoring the manual controls and front viewport in favor of her direct neural link. Her head tilted to one side. "No. They have ceased their pursuit."

"Good. Set a course for Beurias."

Iza peered down at the sleeping form of the young man, where Trix had left him in the cargo area. His features had relaxed into an attractive, though bruised, face.

"Seems our new friend made some powerful enemies. Let's get him patched up and find out exactly why he's so important that they'd send the Guard after him."

IZA RETRIEVED A medkit from underneath the co-pilot's seat and began tending to the cut over the young man's eye. He stirred under her touch, moaning with discomfort. She checked his other injuries, and bruising on his ribs confirmed her suspicion that they'd been broken in the fight. Iza wrapped his ribs to provide temporary relief until the booster nanites from the medkit could complete their work.

As he roused, she placed a light hand on his shoulder to keep him from moving while she smiled down at him. The whites around his hazel irises flashed in alarm at the sight of her.

"Where am I?" He winced at the slight movement.

"Stay still," Iza soothed, keeping her tone soft and light. "You're safe on board my shuttle."

He reached up and touched the top of his head.

"I gave you something for the pain, but I wouldn't recommend any sudden movements."

His hand flew to his pocket, and he seemed to relax when he confirmed something was still there. Iza noticed it, but instead of questioning him, she gave him a reason for her lack of interest.

"We didn't have time to retrieve your handgun. It seems whoever you were mixed up with enlisted the help of Enforcers."

He squirmed.

She blew out a breath of air. "Look, things didn't get off to a great start with us. My name is Iza Sundari." She gave him the customary greeting, holding her palm up.

He carefully eased into a sitting position and did the same. "Braedon Valtteri."

"Well, Braedon, I'm sorry I misread whatever was going on between you and that other man."

"You shouldn't have gotten involved."

"Probably not," she admitted. "But if I hadn't, you might not have had a way off Kinterin and would probably be in a Tararian Guard interrogation room right now."

"The Enforcers wouldn't have been looking for me in the first place if you'd just stayed out of other people's business."

"You were at odds with whoever alerted the Enforcers since well before I showed up. I suspect you would have found yourself in a similar position sooner than later." It was a guess, but Braedon's silence confirmed it. "All the same, I apologize for my part in how things went down."

He looked her over, rubbing his arm that had been twisted behind his back during their altercation. "Why did you take me with you?"

"Seemed like the right thing to do."

He nodded slowly. "Thanks, I guess."

"So, what's your story?" Iza asked him.

"Not a lot to tell."

She arched an eyebrow. "Don't make me regret not leaving you in the alley for the Enforcers to find. Now, how did you come to be on Kinterin with a pulse gun to the head of a man dressed like a tourist?"

Braedon seemed to reason on this and nodded. "All I wanted was to get off-world. I hitched a ride to the first central planet I could." His eyes fell to the floor of the shuttle as if the events were displayed at his feet. "I thought Kinterin was as good a place as any to start. Turns out I was wrong."

"Isn't that long-winded and unhelpful," Iza said, letting the sarcasm through. "Let me rephrase the question. Do I need to be looking over my shoulder while you're on my shuttle?"

Braedon shook his head.

Before she could ask anything else, Trix rose from the pilot's seat and moved to Iza's side. "Iza, would you like me to prepare a meal?"

"No, I'm fine." Truthfully, she was still ravenous, but she'd been looking forward to real food on Kinterin. With that possibility now off the table, she needed time to warm up to the idea of going back to reconstituted nutrient packets.

"Your endorphin levels are elevated. Combined with your muscle fatigue—"

"I said I'm fine," Iza cut Trix off before she could spill the rest of Iza's biometrics to a stranger.

"Is that what I think it is?" Braedon's eyebrows raised as he stared at Trix.

"That's Trix."

"She's Lynaedan." The awe in his voice was evident even without the wide-eyed adoration. "But she's so real."

"Of course, she's real."

"An advanced AI in an android body. Efficient and elegant in every way. Can I touch her?" His hand was already reaching out.

"No, keep your grubby little hands to yourself," Iza said. His hand retracted as if it were on fire. "She helped get you off Kinterin, so a little gratitude is in order, but that's all. She's also my oldest friend, so if you cross the line with either of us, I can't guarantee she won't rip your arms off."

Braedon held up both hands and gaped at Trix with a mix of wonder and worry while she returned to the pilot's chair.

"How did you obtain this model? I've always wanted to invest in a Lynaedan android, myself, but never found the time to do the research required. Though, my father wouldn't permit it, not that it matters. Do you think I could get one, too? I've seen a prototype with male features and the ability to—"

"Trix isn't a 'model' and she's not for sale. She is a sentient person, even though she's not flesh and blood," Iza snapped.

"Oh." He seemed even more intrigued.

"Not to be rude, but we're in a bit of a hurry. Where should we drop you off?" Iza asked.

Braedon tapped the side of his pocket again, making her more curious about what he was keeping in there. His mouth was open to reply when Trix broke in.

"We are coming up to border control at the planetary shield. It appears that our credentials have been revoked."

Iza swore under her breath. *No wonder they didn't bother pursuing us when we took off.*

Braedon leaped up, then winced as his knee gave out. Iza stood up and gave him a hand.

"I can help with that," he said through gritted teeth. He made his way to the co-pilot controls and sat down. "Aww, AS-255, it's so nice to meet you, darling. Can I come in? I promise to be gentle," he said speaking to the console.

"We will encounter the defensive net in twenty seconds," Trix warned.

"Just a minute."

Iza watched with fascination as his hands flew over the console.

"Ten seconds—"

"Done," he said. "Go on through, you'll be fine."

"The net is still active," Trix stated.

Iza's heart was in her throat. The holodisplay showed an intact net, and her ship was about to be fried.

"Don't veer off course, trust me. We're going to slip through like a fish through water."

As promised, the shuttle passed through the net like it wasn't there.

"How?" Iza asked.

"I'm resourceful." Braedon smirked. "You're going to love having me around."

Iza rolled her eyes. She had no intention of keeping him around. He'd been enough trouble for one day.

"I do a little hacking in my spare time. It's just a little trick I picked up while gaming."

"Galactic Dark Net?"

"Sometimes," Braedon shrugged. "What about you, into any VR?"

Iza shook her head. "Waste of hard-earned credits, if you ask me. From the sound of your accent, I'd say you had plenty of credits growing up. You're from a central planet. Tararia?"

Braedon shook his head in the negative but didn't offer his actual homeworld.

"What about your parents?"

"Not exactly interested. Yours?"

"Gone."

Braedon's head snapped up.

"Yeah, well, after my dad died, my mom couldn't take it, so she Left." Not many followed the ancient practice of stepping away from their lives to die on their own terms, especially not young people with families. As a small child, Iza had always understood the practice of Leaving to be for elderly people in failing health. To have her mother walk out on her had caught everyone by surprise, Iza most of all.

"You mean she chose death rather than be a mother to you? Ouch!"

Iza shrugged. "Apparently, she decided she couldn't live without my father. So, to say I have mommy issues is sort of an understatement. I'm just your average colony orphan."

"So, you were a Ward?"

Iza shook her head. "My mom dropped me off with some friends of hers, but their way of life wasn't for me, so I went out on my own."

"How old were you?"

"Ten." Iza squirmed, uncomfortable with where the conversation was turning. She nudged Braedon from the co-pilot's seat and sat down. "Trix, what's our current position?"

Trix brought up the holo overlay showing their location relative to the starscape outside the viewport. "We are currently in transit to our jump point to Beurias. However, there is a problem."

"Another one? What is it?"

"Someone is tracking our movements. They are matching our velocity at a precise distance of five kilometers."

Iza's hands flew over the flat, black panel in front of her. "Is it the local Enforcers or did they call in the military?"

"It is not any branch of the Guard. The ship pursuing us has 'Arvonen One' written on one side."

"Who's that?"

"Perhaps some relation to the Arvonen Dynasty?"

The prospect of dealing with anyone related to the Taran ruling elite was bad enough, but the fact that the ship was charging their weapons made it significantly worse. "Well, they're about to fire on us, so let's get out of here and figure the rest out later. What's the status of our jump drive?" Iza asked.

"The drive is ready. Verifying our course."

Braedon scoffed. "A jump drive? On this bucket?"

"This 'bucket' is keeping you from asphyxiating in the vacuum of space, or would you prefer another run-in with your friends from Kinterin?"

"Sorry, but this is an AS-225. It isn't supposed to have a jump drive."

"This one's had a few modifications," Iza said not bothering to hide her smile. "Prepare to jump." Iza checked their planned travel route along the subspace navigation beacons, as displayed on the SiNavTech console between the pilot seats. The console was still awaiting confirmation of a lock with the entry beacon.

"They have a weapons lock onto the shuttle," Trix said. "Firing."

"Um, Iza?" The tone in Braedon's voice rose with concern.

She cursed the old, slow nav console. She'd need to buy a little extra time before the jump. "We're going to get a closer look at that ship," she said.

Iza veered to the left and then rolled the shuttle to the right to dodge the larger ship's weapons fire. With the initial barrage evaded, she arced over them at a close enough distance to make it difficult for the other ship to use their weapons again. Taking advantage of the opening, Iza altered course so she could peer into the other ship's flight deck through the viewport. She gawked at the men on the other ship, their faces contorted in rage. Trix was right; they weren't Enforcers. Whoever they were, they'd gotten a good look at them, too.

She directed the shuttle away from the larger ship just as the SiNavTech console flashed with a confirmed beacon lock.

"Jumping now." Trix initiated the jump, and a blue-green cloud of shifting light formed around the shuttle.

Iza blew out a breath in relief when she experienced the familiar elongation of time at the moment of transition to subspace.

Braedon slumped down in the seat behind her, breathing hard and holding his chest. "That was too close."

"Yeah, it was," Iza agreed. She watched the ribbons of light swirl around them as the shuttle glided through subspace in a short jump to their new coordinates. The view was still breathtaking, even after all of her travels.

"You're amazing," Braedon said to Iza. "Where did you learn to fly like that?"

Iza shrugged. "I'm resourceful. Hey, Trix, did you happen to record our view of the other ship?"

"Of course." The android displayed the recording on the main holoprojector.

Iza paused the recording on a frame with a clear image of two large men dressed in formal attire, glaring at them through *Arvonen One*'s front viewport. Neither of the men looked pleased to have their images captured.

"Do you recognize those guys?" Iza asked Braedon.

He shook his head.

"It's a mystery, I guess," Iza said. "At least a civilian ship like that shouldn't have the means to track our subspace course, so we should be in the clear when we get to Beurias."

"Why are you going there?" Braedon asked.

"There's talk that Dainetris Galactic Enterprises needs more cargo haulers in the outer colonies. With a down-payment and a contract, they'll give you a cargo ship and a job out of one of their shipping docks. You work off your debt hauling. When your contract is fulfilled, the ship is yours to do with as you please. We're on our way to earn enough credits to get a ship."

"DGE giving out jobs and ships? Sounds too good to be true."

Iza shrugged. "Probably is. But if there's a chance it's legit, I want in."

AGENT JOE ANDERSON had played along when he was asked to participate in Junior Agent training, thinking it was part of the Tararian Selective Service's culture of mentorship and continuous learning. However, it was now clear to him that the Sacon Agent Division Lead, Ian Mandren, was trying to make an example out of Joe by using him to show what *not* to do.

"See, Agent Anderson's mistake was that he underestimated his opponent and made the wrong choice based on his skill set," the older Agent stated, his amber eyes narrowed slightly.

One of the participants in the training session—a Junior Agent in her early-twenties, only a few years younger than Joe—gave him a sympathetic smile.

Great, even the trainees can see what's going on here. Joe wished his superiors would just admit that they made a mistake in graduating him and assign him a nice, quiet desk in a dark corner of TSS Headquarters. Anything would be better than this humiliation.

It hadn't been a fair fight. Mandren had intentionally put Joe up against a final-year Junior Agent with telekinetic strength far superior to Joe's own, as well as a physical size advantage. The entire exercise seemed tailored to call out Joe's shortcomings.

Joe was a graduated Agent. In his mind, that should afford him *some* level of respect beyond having his faults paraded in front of his subordinates. After all, he had been deemed fit for duty. Granted, he'd received a few poor performance evaluations since then, but that was beside the point. Or, maybe that was precisely Mandren's aim—for Joe to recognize his place in the hierarchy. Though Mandren now led the Sacon Agent Division, he'd trained directly under the now-High Commander as a Primus Elite Agent and was in the inner circle of TSS Command.

Maybe I shouldn't have tried to tell Mandren how to do his job, Joe realized. He'd made choice comments here and there, thinking them innocuous enough, but clearly, there'd been a tipping point and now Joe was paying the price.

"It's critical to always keep a cool head and never take your attention off of your surroundings," Mandren continued. "No matter the strength of your opponent, you can always be aware of what's going on and what they are capable of doing to you."

"Well, Agent Mandren, this is a fight I wouldn't have elected to take on," Joe stated. He fixed his topaz-blue eyes in a level gaze at his superior.

The older Agent looked him over with surprise. "Don't tell me you'd submit to a mere Junior Agent?"

Joe felt his face flush to his dark hairline, but he managed to keep his tone calm. "Like you said, know your enemy and fight smart." He hated to say it, but he figured that's what Mandren wanted to hear, and maybe doing so would make the torture end.

Joe had become well-versed in such strategies, with varying degrees of effectiveness in different applications. He'd been at a disadvantage ever since he was recruited into the TSS, being one of the rare humans on Earth to be gifted with telekinetic and telepathic abilities. There were a handful of Earthlings in most training cohorts, mostly falling into the TSS' lowest Trion Agent classification, based on the strength of their abilities. Joe had made the cut for the middle class of Sacon, barely, but outpacing some of the other Agent prospects in raw telekinetic potential hadn't made up for not growing up as a full member of the Taran Empire.

From technology to culture, Joe had constantly felt out of his depth. He'd thought that graduating would be validation that he'd finally 'made it', but the TSS hadn't been able to find a permanent assignment for Joe where he truly excelled. In time, his frustration had made him argumentative, which only created more conflict.

It didn't help his case that Lead Agent Saera Alexri and one of the senior Primus trainers, Michael Andres, were both from Earth. Even though they were of more Taran blood than human, their upbringing was almost identical to Joe's. He had no excuse in their eyes. Since they also happened to be close friends of Mandren's, their comparative accomplishments no doubt factored into his opinions about Joe.

Now, it appeared his chances had run out. *Remedial training as a last-ditch effort to make me into a worthwhile Agent.*

Mandren was still talking, "If you've got the element of control, power, or surprise, you should use it. Let me show you what I mean." He set up the next training exercise, this time inserting himself into the action rather than using Joe for the demonstration.

Joe watched as each of the Junior Agents in the class tried to outsmart Mandren on the exercise. It was fruitless, he knew. He'd seen this particular configuration of moves before, and there was no way to win. That was the point: to present a no-win situation and see which of the two losses you'd take. One for yourself or one against yourself. Psychologically, it was an interesting way of judging if someone is fit for a team or built for being alone.

When Mandren looked his way, Joe rolled his eyes. He already knew the answer and he wouldn't change his approach from what he'd done in the past.

"Don't give it away," Mandren instructed telepathically when he caught Joe's look.

Joe sighed as the students continued to futilely try to gain the upper hand in the impossible situation. When they had thoroughly failed, Mandren instructed them to return to rest positions.

"Good work," the older Agent said. "It may feel like a loss, but there are always lessons in failure. The biggest takeaway you can carry with you is to never give up. Circumstances can change in any moment." He produced two balls from a storage locker. "Now, let's try something else."

Mandren waved Joe forward and also picked out one of the female Junior Agents from the line, Ferrin. She had a reputation for showing off, and Joe would need to be at his best to avoid being upstaged by a subordinate again.

Rather than going up against other people, the opposing side was represented by the two balls, which Mandren controlled telekinetically. He tossed them into the sparring circle, and he directed them to hover in the air at head-height on the other side of the ring.

"You know the drill: score points with a tackle, avoid being hit."

Joe reluctantly stepped into the sparring circle next to Ferrin; he hated the exercise, since it reminded him too much of a diabolical hybrid of dodgeball and football from gym class back on Earth. Careful to keep his thoughts shielded so his movements couldn't be anticipated—one of the skills he *had* mastered—he stretched his arms and waited for the exercise to begin.

"Begin!" Mandren sent the balls flying in opposite directions.

The opening move forced Joe to chase after the first ball as it soared to the other side of the room. He lashed out at it using his own telekinetic skills in an attempt to draw the ball toward him, but Mandren expertly evaded the assault. Knocking the object from the air telekinetically wasn't enough; the exercise demanded physically tackling the ball to show full control of the situation.

Joe's partner raced after him in an attempt to keep their dual defensive positioning, but Joe ignored her, focused on his own target.

Mandren sent the first ball upward, well out of Joe's physical reach. Joe followed it by telekinetically lifting himself up into the air, arms outstretched, but Mandren sped it away at the last second. He was so intent on the target, Joe didn't notice the other ball heading for him until Ferrin had already jumped in front of it to protect him. She sent out a telekinetic blast of energy to deflect the ball, and it careened to the side.

The new path of the second ball put it almost within Joe's reach. He dove for it.

Midair, he wrapped his arms around the ball and brought it to his chest, all of his attention on maintaining control; he needed to land on the ground with it still in his arms. As he fell, he saw the first ball he'd originally been chasing head straight for his partner. He had a split second to react: let go of his prize and save her, or score a point for himself.

After the day he'd had, he wasn't about to let the opportunity to score pass him by.

His shoulder struck the ground just as the other ball smacked into his partner's back. She was sent sprawling across the floor.

The ball in Joe's grasp stopped struggling against him as Mandren released his telekinetic hold. Joe dropped it to the ground when he stood up.

Joe beamed, expecting praise for the scored point. Instead, Mandren turned to the Junior Agent picking herself up off the ground.

"Good job, Ferrin. You put yourself in the line of fire in order to give your partner time to get away. Joe, you let your partner down. No short-term gain is worth sacrificing a teammate." Mandren turned his back to Joe, facing the rest of the class. "Now, let's work on how to take advantage of the element of surprise."

No matter what I do, he won't let me win. Joe had had enough abuse. His right hand curled into a fist. *Oh, I'll show him a surprise.*

—

Joe shoved his minimal possessions into his black TSS standard-issue duffle. His 'reassignment' was a method of getting him out of the way, he had no doubt. *That's what I get for punching one of the High Commander's best friends.*

As he looked over his new civilian clothing one last time, his handheld signaled an incoming video call. It was Emery, one of his former classmates. Joe debated not taking the call but decided that not answering would have more adverse consequences. He propped the device on the table in front of him and dropped his bag at his feet.

Emery's face filled the screen. His dark hair brushed his eyebrows, framing his blue-gray eyes. Most days there was a hint of laughter in them, but not today. His eyebrows furrowed, and his lips pinched together in disappointment.

"I can't believe you're leaving Headquarters," he said. It wasn't uncommon for Emery to skip the pleasantries.

"I'm not leaving, I'm being reassigned."

Emery rolled his eyes toward the ceiling. "For hitting a Primus Elite Agent? I'm surprised Mandren didn't kick your teeth back to Earth and ship your remains in a box."

Joe didn't disagree; he'd been thinking the same thing.

Still, Joe would never forget the satisfying crack of his

knuckles against the older Agent's chin, unleashing all of Joe's frustrations about being belittled in front of others. He hadn't expected the punch to connect, since there was no way Mandren hadn't sensed it coming; for whatever reason, though, the Agent had allowed it. A moment later, Mandren had used his superior telekinetic skills to lift Joe off the ground and remind him exactly who he'd gone up against.

A quick and public apology had gotten Joe reassigned instead of dismissed on the spot. Then again, for Joe, a recon assignment in the outer colonies amounted to the same thing. Having grown up on Earth, Joe had just gotten used to the homogenized Taran culture within the TSS. Now, he'd be living in the outlying colonies, and their disparate customs were a complete mystery to him.

Earth was technologically behind, and it had been a huge adjustment learning about the Taran Empire and humanity's long-lost connection to it. Most people on Earth weren't ready for that kind of advancement. After living in Taran society, however, Joe couldn't help but wonder why any Tarans would choose to leave the comforts of the central planets nowadays. Back when telekinesis was illegal, he could understand why people like him with abilities might have fled to the freer border worlds, but the Gifted were largely accepted now, thanks to the Tararian Selective Service's extensive awareness efforts. When he'd been recruited from Earth to join the TSS, he'd been welcomed into a culture entering a new Golden Age.

Lead Agent Alexri and Agent Andres had done their best to help Joe transition to Taran culture, knowing the trials firsthand. So, when they sat him down for an hour-long lecture on his pitiful TSS career, it was no surprise to see the mutual disappointment on their frowning faces. He was supposed to be a representative for their homeworld, showing why humans were ready to rejoin their Taran brethren. Instead, his rash behavior was an embarrassment.

They were right, of course, but Joe couldn't seem to keep his temper in check.

"How long is your reassignment?" Emery asked.

Joe shrugged. "I don't know. Long enough for Command to forget all about me."

"You'll do your time and then you'll get called back. The High Commander won't leave you out there forever. From what I hear, he's got good reason to want someone out there watching the activity among the colonists."

"You're just trying to make me feel better." Even as an outsider Earthling, Joe knew that the High Commander, Wil Sietinen was a living legend; his skills were so off the chart they couldn't be measured. Joe couldn't help but feel pathetic by comparison, and he doubted he'd be cut any slack.

"Nah, man, you royally messed up—not gonna lie about that. But it doesn't alter the fact that we need people keeping an eye on things in the border worlds."

Joe sighed. "If you say so."

"On the outer rim, there have always been extremists. You have a special gift for observation, it's something to be proud of. Use it to your advantage."

They invested too much time and resources into training me to let it go to waste. This is just a good way to get a return on their investment while keeping me out of the public eye. Maybe Joe would find some threat to Tararia big enough to get him called back early, but he wasn't holding his breath.

"According to the High Commander, my parents would be disappointed that I haven't lived up to my potential, if they'd been alive to see this sorry excuse for a career. Whatever that means."

"I know Wil, and he'd never say that," Emery countered. "He just knows you can do better. You'd make a great Agent if you tried. Why is it that everyone can see it but you?"

Joe didn't argue the point. "Skyler's the child my parents would have wanted, anyway. I'm just a Sacon-level Agent with an attitude problem and issues with authority."

"You can be more if you want to be. I know you've struggled, but trust me, something's waiting for you out there. When you find it, I hope you'll let me know."

Joe's gut tightened. Emery had been the closest thing to a best friend to him. They'd gone in circles over it before. He'd rather talk about anything else.

"Skyler and I want you at our wedding ceremony."

Anything but that. Joe held back a grimace. "No, she doesn't. She tolerates me the way most people do."

"I don't."

"Yeah, but you're a bomaxed idiot."

Emery laughed out loud. Then he grew serious again. "When was the last time you talked to your sister?"

"When you two called to tell me you were getting married."

"That was over a year ago," Emery said, sounding surprised.

"Welcome to the family." Joe shrugged when Emery's expression didn't change. "We've gone longer. You'll get used to it."

At first, Joe's older sister choosing his only friend had floored him. From what Joe understood of the whole thing, there'd been some kind of instant telepathic connection. It'd created an irresistible bond between them. They'd delayed telling him for as long as they'd dared in the hopes it would soften the blow.

It hadn't.

Joe had been with women before, but no one had done it for him in the way they'd described. No fireworks, electricity, or whatever else had drawn them together. He wished they had each found someone else—*anyone* else. Joe just couldn't look at his friend the same way, knowing he was in an intimate relationship with his sister. He'd relied on Emery, but he feared their friendship could never be the same. Skyler hadn't understood why Joe couldn't just be happy for them, and she'd grown distant and resentful. Joe wished he'd been able to explain his feelings properly, but now things were so awkward between them that he'd all but given up broaching the topic.

"I'll talk to her," Emery said.

"There's nothing left to say."

They each looked away for a moment, both staring at something offscreen.

Emery was the first to speak. "Well, I'm not giving up on you. Promise me you'll come back and find a nice woman for yourself." The sparkle was back in his eyes.

"How bad could the women in the outer colonies be?" Joe mirrored the smile on his friend's face, for a moment allowing himself to fall back into their easy banter from when things had been less complicated.

"I'm sure they're more than you can handle. Besides, haven't you broken enough hearts?"

"That joke's getting old."

"So's your game."

It was Joe's turn to laugh out loud—a much needed release of the tension from the terrible day. Even from the beginning, it had impressed him how well Emery had picked up some of Earth's colloquialisms when they'd exchanged cultural tips. He always valued how Emery had gone out of his way to help Joe fit in.

Only now did Joe realize that he'd been a terrible friend in return. He'd let that single friendship be his crutch for too long, an excuse to not build stronger connections with others in the TSS. He couldn't blame anyone but himself. As counselors had told him countless times, Joe's stubbornness was a self-imposed barrier to success. If he wanted to move forward, he'd need to find a way to stand on his own.

"Emery… thank you for always seeing the best in me."

His friend smirked. "You sure make it difficult sometimes."

"I—"

"Hey, relax! I'm just messing with you. That's your problem—you can be so rigid. Sometimes, you just have to take life as it comes," Emery said.

"Thanks, Tips."

"Hey, I'm always happy to share my endless wealth of wisdom over here." Emery's voice went quiet. "Seriously, though, be safe out there. Call me when you're settled."

"Yeah, I will."

As soon as the call ended, Joe was sorry he hadn't asked more about Emery. That's what it meant to be a real friend— you at least acted like you cared about the other person. *He's stuck by me, and I need to do the same for him. Eventually, I need to accept that this wedding is happening and make things right with Skyler.*

Joe took one last look around his room at TSS Headquarters and let out a low groan. Then, slinging his bag over one shoulder, he strolled out the door.

—

The four-hour ride to the public transport hub near Tararia had been uneventful. Joe blinked to avoid rubbing his irritated eyes. The brown contacts blocked the natural luminescence in his irises—indicative of his abilities—from shining through, but they hurt. The doctor had assured him he'd get used to them.

Joe left the TSS transport ship without a backward glance. In seconds, he was swallowed by the crowd on the platform.

He made his way to one of the public transport vehicles leaving for the outer colonies. He didn't pay much attention to the destination since it didn't matter; most border worlds were the same, when it came down to it. He just needed to start somewhere.

Joe held up his new identification for the ID reader.

"Jovani Saletas, cleared for boarding," said the automated system.

He paused a moment longer than usual.

"Is there a problem, Mr. Saletas?" The Enforcer tending the security checkpoint looked from Joe to the machine and back again.

Joe would have to get used to hearing the new name. It had been necessary to create an alias. His real name, though common on Earth, would be a lot harder to explain out here. Joe shook his head at the Enforcer and climbed on board the vessel.

The public transport to Galminus was arduous and slow. He'd been sandwiched between a squalling baby and an elderly Taran man who talked incessantly. It was a welcome relief to disembark. The mother of the irritable baby didn't apologize for spilling half her son's milk over the lap of his brand-new civilian pants as she hurried off. The elderly man in the seat beside him had talked himself to sleep. Joe crept around him and made his way off the ship. He wondered why the old man traveled alone but had already been warned not to interfere with the local happenings. His job was to report his findings first.

The docking platform on Galminus buzzed with activity. He noted a red dust permeated the air, tickling his nose with a spicy scent; it coated everything, from clothing to buildings.

Vendors and consumers shoved each other for better positioning in front of the docked ships. Joe made his way along the platform while looking for a crew where he could blend in.

A boy bumped into him and he felt the distinct flutter of fingers patting him down for credits. He didn't stop him as he had nothing for the boy to take. The handgun holstered at his hip was enough to startle the boy. His brown eyes flew to Joe's face before he drew his hand back as if he'd touched fire and scurried off into the pressing crowd. Two Enforcers monitoring the docks ignored him as they passed.

The Taran worlds were distinct from each other, with their own cultures and idiosyncrasies. It was most notable when one could wander down the docks of a major hub and watch the people going about their business. It reminded Joe of old New York City back on Earth. Their clothing, hairstyles, and attitudes never ceased to amaze him. Despite his fascination, he had limited knowledge of the outlying colonies. He worried he might not recognize trouble before it was too late.

One of the larger crews he passed had more than a dozen crates to load onto their ship. Joe dropped his duffle and lined up with the others to form a chain. He helped the crew load crates until they'd finished. His hopes to ingratiate himself with the ship's captain fell when the man caught him on board. The captain grabbed him by the collar and with more than a few harsh words sent him on his way.

The next few ships he tried garnered similar reactions. The last captain had some particularly coarse language for him. After Joe made some equally insulting remarks about the man's mother, they wound up in a fistfight until he was tossed out by two giants from the man's crew. Still dusting off his pants from the tussle, Joe snatched up his bag to go. He glanced up and caught the eye of an old man with dark skin and a short crop of wooly white hair. The man had an amused smile on his lips and a sparkle in his dark eyes that drew Joe over.

"Sir," Joe said, lifting his hand in formal greeting. When he tried to smile, he could feel the split in his lip crack open and bleed again.

The old man continued to smile at him but shook his head as he spoke. "No."

Joe stopped short six paces from the man's chair. "I'm sorry?"

"You're about to ask if you can board my ship as a

passenger. I'm telling you, no."

Joe staggered back a step. *Can he read me?* He checked his mental blocks; they were still in place. Maybe the old man was only guessing.

"What if I wasn't?" Joe challenged.

"You were. No one who looks like you do roams around down here for a laugh. I'm just trying to save you the trouble."

"Why?"

The old man wheezed with laughter, showing off a full set of bright white teeth. Tears streamed down his face. When he had regained sufficient control of himself, he straightened and looked Joe in the eye.

"Like everybody else here, I don't want no stinking TSS Agent on board."

Joe's eyes widened in surprise. "I'm not an Agent."

"If you're not TSS, then I'm an ignorant old goat!" The old man hissed again with laughter.

"I *was* an Agent, but not anymore," Joe said, remembering to keep his cover as close to the truth as possible. "The TSS decided they had no use for me."

The old man regarded him with open cynicism. His jaw worked as he thought, chewing on something Joe couldn't see. "Where you headed?"

"As far out as I can get." Then as an afterthought, he added, "I can pay."

"I'm sure you can," he said as he looked Joe over. "What's your name, kid?"

"Jovani Saletas."

"I'm Theodus Brenian. Nice to meet you. But I'm not taking you on."

Joe couldn't hide his disappointment. At this rate, he'd never find a crew to use for cover.

"But, I'll give you a piece of advice," Theodus offered.

"Take the shine and polish off of that TSS walk and talk you've got before you make any more offers. You stand out like pearls on a pig and smell just as bad."

Joe looked down at his clothing. He had inadvertently dressed in the color black as was his habit. Worse, the spilled milk on his pants reeked after hours in the heat. He turned away and continued his slog down the docks. Old Theodus cackled behind him.

4

"ARE YOU SURE you want to meet with him alone?" Trix asked Iza when their shuttle touched down at the local DGE shipyard on Beurias.

"I'll be fine. I know how to handle Karter," Iza said.

"Who's Karter?" Braedon asked. "Old friend?"

"Hardly," Iza replied with a glare in his direction as she pulled on her jacket.

"Karter Hyttinen is the manager of Apex Manufacturing Enterprises. He is also a prominent member of the Hyttinen Dynasty, the foremost Lower Dynasty governing Beurias. Iza worked for him in the past. Despite his continued adv—"

"That's enough of a history lesson." Iza did her best to steer clear of the dynastic types, almost uniformly caught up in their egos about being the ruling elite. While the Lower Dynasties didn't carry the same clout as the seven High Dynasties, they made up for it by what seemed like an insatiable need to meddle in others' lives. Karter wasn't an exception.

Iza smiled and raised her hand to wave goodbye to Braedon. "I wish I could say it's been a pleasure."

"I could make myself useful around here," he offered in response.

She ignored the wide-eyed desperation on his face. "Trix, stay put, I'll be back with our new ship."

Iza turned to leave, but Braedon hurried to keep up with her. "I know ships. I could help you get the best deal," he said.

"No, thanks."

"Maybe I can help out around here with repairs."

"I've already got a mechanic."

"You might need someone to hack some codes in the future. It's a valuable skill."

"Goodbye, Braedon."

Braedon gave up at last and she was glad of it. She'd done enough for him. He'd be better off on his own, anyway. She rolled her shoulders back, leaving Braedon and his troubles behind. She'd have to keep her focus if she was going to make the deal of a lifetime.

—

Apex Manufacturing Enterprises was one of the most prestigious and pretentious shipyards in the sector. This particular factory on Beurias had built some of the fastest and most technologically advanced craft for public and private use throughout the Taran Empire, under the stewardship of the Hyttinen Dynasty and their associates. Anyone with credits to spend came to Apex. Most left with a ship. Few left without a debt to pay off. The sprawling compound had two office buildings, a glass-domed showroom, and three factories.

Scattered outside were several shuttles from ships and crews that worked for Karter. Iza spotted the *Herman* and picked up her pace to avoid being spotted. *Please, I don't want to see anyone I know.*

"It's been a long time, Scrap Rat!" Tirkus' unwelcomed arm draped across Iza's shoulders from behind. He'd tortured and teased her relentlessly during her time with the *Herman*'s crew.

Iza had to push down the heat of embarrassment over the name she'd earned as a street kid and been carried over into the two years she'd worked with them. She mentally reminded herself she wasn't a part of their crew and hadn't been for over a year. This time, she wouldn't let him get the best of her. She held her head high and shrugged off his arm.

"Dirt Face, it hasn't been long enough," she said. Iza smiled when he frowned at the nickname.

"Don't call me that." When she didn't stop walking toward the main building, he continued after her. "What are you doing here, anyway? Looking for work? I'll save you the trouble of asking. We don't have any and no one else will take ya."

"I don't need work. I'm here to get a ship."

"You?" Tirkus almost tripped trying to keep up with her while laughing at the same time. "You think you're going to captain your own ship? You're crazy, Scrap Rat."

"Crazy trumps dumb every day of the week."

Tirkus stopped as she drew closer to the shipyard manager's office located inside the showroom building. She'd first come to the shipyard four years ago at eighteen. They'd thought her innocent on first sight, but she'd already served prison time on Sarduvis. By then, she wanted honest work for honest pay. What she got instead were lecherous creeps with an eye for breaking the last of her innocence.

Iza walked in the front door just behind a man dressed in formal wear. She could see the glare of light off the top of his shaved head as he was thirty centimeters shorter than her. Iza shook her head; some people had the weirdest sense of fashion. The familiar large, dome-shaped ceiling let in plenty of the planet's natural light and showed off several modified ships, shuttles, and transports.

The receptionist jumped out of her seat to address the man in front of Iza.

"Mr. Kirken, so good to see you again. Mr. Hyttinen has pulled the top-of-the-line transport vehicles to the floor for your inspection. Becca is already waiting with your favorite drink."

Iza watched the man walk away and then stepped forward to give her name to the receptionist. It seemed since she was not on the list she wouldn't be getting in to see Mr. Hyttinen today.

"I'm so sorry, ma'am."

"Iza Sundari," Iza repeated through her teeth. "Just tell him I'm here."

The insufferable receptionist with the impossibly long legs and severe black bun gave her another tight-lipped smile. She spoke in the tone people reserved for unruly children and senile elderly parents as she scrolled through messages on her handheld. "As I said, he's in a meeting and can't be disturbed. I apologize for the inconvenience. Would you like to make an appointment for tomorrow?"

"No, but a cup of coffee would be great. I haven't had a decent brew in days."

"A cup of coffee?"

"Please." Iza flashed her widest smile at the woman.

The receptionist eyed her with thinly veiled hostility before getting up from the glass desk. She gestured to the line of uncomfortable chairs against the wall. "All right, go ahead and have a seat. I'll be right back with your coffee."

When the receptionist had disappeared through a side door leading away from the main showroom floor, Iza leaped up from her seat and strolled to the office doors. They slid open to either side, sensing her approach.

Karter Hyttinen's office was bigger than an entire cargo

ship. Divided into sections for sitting, eating, and working, she rambled through the seating area toward his massive U-shaped command center. He was in the middle of a holoconference as four 3D images hovered above his desk. Sitting on his make-shift throne before his minions, Karter quizzically raised one of his dark eyebrows when she entered but he didn't stop talking.

"Is that the best we can do, people? I'm sure if we discuss it, we could come up with something better. My assets are pulling in far more revenue than originally projected. Are you going to vacillate now that we're on the cusp of a new venture, just because it hasn't yet proven its value to you?"

The group seemed to be in a heated debate over the issue. She disregarded most of the conversation, as it didn't concern her, and instead took in the room.

Iza sauntered along the far wall of his office until she reached the glass window overlooking the expansive showroom. She knew from previous visits that though she could see out, mirrored glass covered the other side. Karter enjoyed playing the invisible watchdog. Though he rarely lifted a finger himself, he employed the kind of people who did his bidding for him.

Karter put up one finger, signaling for her to wait.

In the meantime, Iza couldn't help but admire the simple but tasteful decorations around the room. Two large potted trees with white bark and small, green leaves sat on either side of the doors she'd entered. The musky smell of the tree reminded her of the cologne Karter wore and made her want to clear her throat of the taste. One large abstract painting in the colors of a Tararian sunset hung on the wall nearest the sitting area and an oversized viewscreen was mounted on the far wall. Near his desk, a tall piece of sculpted metal twisted in elegant lines toward the ceiling. She didn't understand what the sculpture was supposed to represent, but she'd always liked it.

In one smooth gesture, Karter stood up and bowed low to his associates on the call. They all stopped speaking over each other and let him interject.

"Ladies and gentlemen, it's clear we won't agree on anything today. May I suggest that we table the discussion and pick it up again fresh tomorrow?"

As soon as the others agreed, he ended the conference call and turned to Iza with a smirk. Just then, the receptionist came racing into the room.

"I'm so sorry, Mr. Hyttinen, I told her to wait outside. I have security on their way."

"That won't be necessary, Jaen."

"Do you have my coffee?" Iza asked, noting Jaen's empty hands.

The receptionist faltered. "I'll fetch it."

"Sugar and cream, correct?" Karter asked.

Iza smiled as she sat down in one of the pin-striped chairs in front of his desk. "Yes, sugar and cream."

The heat of Jaen's glower burned a hole in her back, but she kept her attention on Karter. Iza listened to the click of Jaen's heels retreating on the marble floor. When the doors slid closed, Karter gave her his winning smile.

"I apologize, your coffee will probably take longer than usual," he said with mock sympathy.

"No doubt, not that it matters. I won't be drinking it, as I'm sure she'll add more than just sugar and cream."

Karter smiled as if she'd just complimented his attire. He moved around the console so he could lean against it and peer down at her. "I have to admit, I'm surprised to see you here. After your last visit—"

The unspoken words hung in the air, forcing her to fill in

the rest from memory. It still made her skin crawl. He'd refused to give her a job in the shipyard and then made an indelicate proposition.

"You shouldn't be. I told you what I wanted the last time I was here, and my goals haven't changed."

Karter watched her like a hunter observing its prey. Then, as if she'd made a sudden joke, he laughed. "You've heard about our plans to provide more jobs for the local people. Well, the contract is extensive, but I don't think it's anything you can't handle. Perhaps we could discuss it over dinner?"

"That won't be necessary. Let's start with a look at your cargo ships," Iza said, standing up as the receptionist, Jaen, returned with the coffee.

A smug smile on her face, Jaen moved to Iza's side and held it out for her. Karter also smiled as if anticipating some kind of reaction from her. Iza shrugged, then sauntered toward the door, ignoring Jaen's offering and shocked expression.

"Shall we?" Iza asked, turning back to wait for Karter.

Karter picked up his handheld and moved to follow her out. He took the coffee from Jaen and moved to drink it.

"Sir—that wasn't meant for you," Jaen stammered.

Karter held the cup to his lips, staring at the woman over the rim. "Is there some reason I shouldn't drink it?"

Jaen's chin dropped to her chest and her shoulders slumped. Karter gestured for her to leave with one hand toward the sliding doors. She led the way, but before she could get to her desk, Karter addressed her.

"Oh, no, you're done here. Becca will gather your personal effects to send to you."

Jaen's mouth fell open in shock. She looked from Karter to Iza and back again.

Iza couldn't hide her surprise. *Is he seriously going to fire her for that?*

Karter spoke into his handheld. "Security, Jaen is leaving us. Can you see her safely out?" He put the coffee down on the reception desk before leading Iza to the showroom floor.

The latest innovations in spacecraft filled the Apex showroom floor from wall to wall, but there was nothing for someone like Iza who just wanted to haul cargo. Before she could say so, Karter headed through another set of doors to a large hangar filled with used transports. The ships, though older models, look a lot better than the beat-up shuttle she currently owned. However, Iza knew, despite their appearance, that these ships were likely already modified.

"I assume you want something for hauling," Karter said and waited for her nod. "I'll show you the ships I have available. Depending on the cargo, they can all be retrofitted to your tastes. Of course, all modifications will be covered under the contract. I'm sure I don't have to warn you to be careful about putting too much money into a transport ship you don't own outright."

Iza rolled her eyes. Karter was so transparent.

He brought her to several models of cargo ships. Iza glanced at each, keeping her expression neutral; she wouldn't begin negotiations with him looking desperate. She walked through the hangar until one caught her eye off in the far corner. Though slightly smaller than the others, if she was right, it was an H3X-Z500—the perfect blend of a passenger vessel and light cargo ship.

What's a beauty like you doing in a place like this? Iza moved to get a better look at it, and Karter did his best to slow her down.

"That's an H3X. It's not a ship designed for hauling."

"It's got a cargo hold, doesn't it?" Iza replied.

"Yes, but it's capable of so much more than that."

She smiled. "I know. What it lacks in a cargo hold, it makes up for in speed and maneuverability."

It wasn't as big as a freighter or standard cargo ship, but it would work for her purposes. "I'm sure it's not cheap, either," she said.

"I won't lie to you, it's in this hangar because the previous owners couldn't make the payment."

"That won't be a problem."

Iza saw the bay door was open, so she walked up the ramp and inside the brightly lit hold. There were far more compartments than she needed. It was a smuggler's dream— tons of invisible storage that wouldn't get underfoot around cargo or crew. There was also plenty of room in the gym area to exercise and train during long runs.

A slender metal staircase led to the upper deck. Karter kept silent as they walked the ship, opting to let her look over everything on her own. Iza appreciated the time to take it all in by herself. If he'd been talking, she probably would have missed the way the stairs opened up into the main corridor leading in three directions.

To her left was the captain's cabin. Karter waited while she imagined herself in the space. The bed was wide and had a plush mattress more luxurious than any she'd seen outside of a hotel. It also had a seating area where she could sit around a wooden table to go over plans with one or two other people on velvety blue seat cushions. The cabin even came complete with stabilized drawer compartments that would secure personal items if the ship got knocked around. It was more than enough for Iza's simple tastes.

Across the corridor from the captain's ample cabin was a fully stocked infirmary—not that she knew the first thing about anything beyond basic patchwork. Next to that was a decent-sized galley and plenty of storage for food. Iza didn't have much of that yet, but with a few jobs under her belt, she figured it wouldn't be long.

"Beyond the infirmary, there are the ship's crew or passenger cabins, half the size of yours," Karter explained. "There are a set of ladders leading to the cargo bay along either side of the upper catwalk."

Beyond the galley was a narrow corridor that led to the flight deck. Iza noted seats for the pilot and a comms tech in front of the captain's chair. On the left and right were places for an engineer to monitor systems and another place for tactical support. Iza imagined faceless people sitting in each seat. Maybe they would even settle into their cabins, decorating them to their own tastes. *But who would want to live on this ship with me?* The idea brought a frown to her face.

"I hope it's not too much ship for you," Karter said with a smirk.

"In your dreams."

They took the forward stairs back down into the cargo bay. Overall, the ship had been well maintained. The stale recycled air would improve with use, she knew. There was even a place for her old shuttle to dock. After touring the entire interior, she knew that she wanted it. To her annoyance, Karter knew it, too.

Karter followed her off of the ship and they stood between the H3X and the other cargo vessels.

"Since I don't plan to haul cargo for the rest of my life, I want a ship that can grow as I do," Iza said. "Let's talk about specs."

Karter pulled out his handheld and began scrolling through for the information needed. "This comes standard with an array of defensive and offensive capabilities, including upgraded shields. Mod capable. Standard cabins for six with double-sized captain's cabin. It's two-hundred-one meters long, has storage for up to fifteen tons, and its antimatter pion drive can reach one-quarter lightspeed. Of course, it has a built-in jump drive with a newly refurbished SiNavTech navigation console." He rattled off a list of other technical specifications about the power systems, comms, and environmental controls.

Iza let him finish without interrupting. "That sounds like a good fit for my needs."

"I think you should consider this other—"

"I've seen the other offerings. This is the one," she stated.

"Are you sure we can't discuss it over dinner?"

Her eyes narrowed. "Let's take a look at the lease terms and get this over with."

He hesitated for just a moment, then smiled. "Very well."

Back in his office, Iza settled into one of the plush chairs across from Karter's desk while he sat in the matching chair beside her to draw up the contract for the H3X. Her heart fluttered. Any minute now, she'd be in a ship of her own. She let her mind wander, thinking about the future and her life in space without any of the cares and stresses of planetside life.

Karter displayed the contract on the touch-surface desktop in front of her. Iza had the distinct feeling she was signing her life away. She looked it over, studying every part of it until she was sure she understood it. Even so, she wanted Trix to read through it for anything she might have missed.

He huffed and crossed his arms as if offended she was taking her time.

"This is business, Karter, relax. I'm sure you don't mind if I get a second set of eyes to look it over." Iza used her handheld to call Trix, "I'm forwarding you a contract to look over. Is there anything outside the normal guidelines for this type of contract?"

After a moment of hesitation, Trix responded. "No, this is a standard spacecraft lease."

Karter uncrossed his arms and the smile filled his face,

reaching the twinkle in his eyes. "I wouldn't cheat an old friend like you. I have nothing but the utmost respect for you."

"However," Trix continued, "it should be noted that failure to make the payment on time to the hour of midnight on the twenty-eighth day of the month in Taran Standard Time will result in an automatic breach of contract and the ship can be repossessed."

Now, his smile dimmed slightly. He held up both hands in defense, but Iza headed him off.

"You'd do that to your friends, huh?" Iza crossed her arms as Trix continued.

"Any desired modifications are permitted and become the property of Apex Manufacturing Enterprises if the ship is repossessed. However, any undesirable modifications to the ship or damage will be counted against the lessee—in this case, you Iza."

"Now I see that utmost respect you mentioned," Iza said.

He bristled. "I'll waive any modification fees. Though, if you destroy the ship, then I'll need a physical or financial replacement."

"That is not equitable," Trix said.

Iza turned back to him and nodded; it was far from equitable, but it was fair enough. "You're right, Trix. Thank you for your help." She disconnected the comm link and turned her attention back to Karter. Shaking her head, she used her palm print to confirm the purchase.

"Excellent, the ship is yours today, if you've got the down payment with you."

"I have your money."

Iza passed him her handheld to accept the credits, and he looked over the amount, frowning.

He rubbed a hand on the back of his neck. "This is embarrassing."

"What?" Iza didn't hide her irritation.

"The down payment for the H3X is substantially more than what you've given me here. I can adjust the agreement for a different ship if you'd prefer."

Iza wanted to strangle him just for the suggestion. He knew she didn't want any other ship, and the fact that he'd offered another was an insult. Now that she'd seen the H3X, no other ship would satisfy her.

"How much more do I need?"

5

"OF ALL THE underhanded, double-crossing, low-down, deceitful—" Iza mumbled as she boarded her shuttle.

Trix was waiting near the hatch for her return. "What happened? Did you procure a ship?"

"No," Iza said. "My down payment wasn't enough."

"How much do you need?"

"Ten thousand more credits."

"What are our options?"

"We get the money."

"We should consider another ship," Trix offered. "A lower-priced vessel may allow us to get more work and sooner."

Iza shook her head. "Karter had no intention of honoring the original down payment price. No matter what I chose, he was planning to up the price. He's such a conniving weasel. Remind me not to underestimate that parasite."

Trix nodded her confirmation.

"We need to make money for the down payment, and fast. We've got one week or he'll give up the ship to the next person who asks."

"That's not a lot of time. This shuttle isn't designed for

large hauls."

"We need to get quick work. Run a high-level search and see if anyone in the vicinity needs any emergency deliveries or odd jobs." Iza kicked at the ground in frustration as she waited for an answer.

After two moments, Trix spoke. "There is a small business in the northern hemisphere requesting an urgent, off-the-books delivery to clients in the southern hemisphere by this afternoon."

"That'll work. Reach out and let them know we're on our way."

"You will no doubt disregard the warning, but I'm going to recommend for the second time that we replace our power cells before taking another job. The cells are showing signs of wear and imminent failure, which is causing significant strain on the other systems."

"You're right, I'm going to ignore you," Iza said with a smirk. She turned to board the shuttle with Trix trailing behind. "After a few jobs, we'll have enough for the H3X down payment. As soon as we can take on bigger work, we'll have the spare credits to get the shuttle repaired. Though, I don't think we'll be using it much."

"You will want the shuttle in peak condition. There are plenty of places a larger ship cannot travel."

Iza shrugged. "Less talk and more walk. Start the engines, we need to—"

Her words were cut off at the shock of seeing Braedon sitting in the co-pilot's seat.

He turned around at the sound of her voice. "Oh, you're back! I thought you'd be bringing a ship with you."

"What are you doing here? What is he doing here?" Iza asked, turning to Trix.

They both started talking at the same time, and in

moments Iza could feel a headache coming on. She pinched the bridge of her nose. "One at a time!"

"Braedon returned with a compelling story about why he could not possibly stay here."

"Compelling?" Iza asked with her arms crossed, facing Braedon.

He hurried to speak, careful to move out of her way when she sat down in the pilot seat.

"Like I told Trix, I would stay on Beurias, but I'm not much of a pilot. I could be stuck here for ages trying to find other work. Besides, the people here aren't that bright or that helpful. I tried to find out if there were any VR tournaments in the area, and it seems the local government has banned all such activities, above or below ground."

"If I drop you off at the next planet, will you promise to stop talking?"

Braedon smiled before pressing a finger to his closed lips. When he winked at Trix, Iza whirled around to stare at the android. Trix stayed as still as stone, like she hadn't noticed a thing. Iza had the distinct feeling they were up to something.

—

The smell of manure still wafted through the small shuttle, burning Iza's eyes as she tightened the bandana over her face, obscuring her words. "How long before we can engage the jump drive?"

"One hour, twelve minutes," Trix answered.

"I don't think we'll get another job with the shuttle smelling like this," Braedon said behind his mask.

"I got paid, and that's what matters. This job plus the last one I took means I'm making progress. That's more than I can say for you. Weren't you supposed to get off back on that last planet?" Iza emphasized each word with a poke to his chest.

"I'm no farmer; I couldn't stay there. You'll save on food, anyway, because I'm pretty sure I lost my appetite for the rest of my life."

"May I point out that if you considered modifications, you would not require food at all?" Trix chimed in. "Supplements would give you the strength and energy you need without the messiness of chewing and digesting your food. However, I would miss preparing your meals."

"At this rate of pay, I'll never have enough money to get the H3X." Iza paced the shuttle. "I need more ideas. There's got to be a way to get more money."

"We could enter a Dark Net tournament that's coming up in a few days. See if we can turn some of our money into profit."

"You mean *my* money. No, I want legal options," Iza said with a significant look at Braedon.

After Iza's statement, the others remained silent.

Guess it's up to me to find something.

It had taken her over a year to get the money she had. Another twenty percent was nearly impossible to get within a week, and Karter knew it.

"If I could figure out a way to get further and faster in the shuttle, we could take on more jobs that way," Iza said as she continued pacing. "We just don't have the time to make the modifications."

Braedon clapped his hands together once. "What if we doubled up on pickups and drops? We could do two jobs at once."

"There is a problem," Trix said.

Iza shook her head. "Good idea, but Trix is right. We don't have the space to accommodate that much of a haul, especially if we're making manure and food supply runs. I seriously doubt Makaris Corp would like us dropping off food and supplements while simultaneously hauling manure."

"That is true," Trix said. "However, that is not the problem to which I was referring. We have entered what looks to be a comet tail composed of dust and gas. The density of the dust particles could compromise our shielding."

"That kind of debris shouldn't be any trouble for our shields to deflect."

"As you will recall, several days ago I mentioned that we needed to repair the power relays to the shields before critical failure. At such time you said, 'Not now, Trix, I'm thinking.' As predicted, our shields will fail."

"Great," Braedon said, rolling his eyes.

"Not a word out of you. So, we'll fix it, right?"

"I am afraid it will not be that easy," Trix replied. "If the shield overloads, it may damage the power relays from the PEM to the other systems."

Iza wasn't much of an engineer, but she knew the PEM was the heart of the ship's engine. The Perpetual Energy Module was a compact zero-point energy device, which powered everything from the jump drive to subspace communications and life support. On their tiny shuttle, there wasn't a backup ion generator. If anything happened to the PEM or power relays, they'd be stranded and have no way to call for help.

She scowled. "What if we—"

A klaxon in the cockpit began to blare and lights flickered before dropping to half-brightness. The shuttle jerked. Instead of falling hard to the deck of the shuttle, Iza bounced against one wall before bumping into Braedon, who looked to be turning green with sick. Iza's own stomach did a flip. The artificial gravity was offline.

"CACI, what's going on with my shuttle?" Iza demanded of the ship's onboard non-sentient AI.

"Voice commands for the central computer are

temporarily offline," Trix stated. "Switching to antimatter reserves."

"No, wait!" Iza cried out when she realized she was going to land on top of Braedon when the artificial gravity reinitiated. However, Trix was efficient and she'd already made the adjustment. Iza came crashing down on top of Braedon who let out a loud *oof.*

Iza rolled off of him, but the damage was done. He lay there clutching his healing ribs, trying to catch his breath, before he crawled on his hands and knees back to the co-pilot chair.

"Can we signal for help?" Iza asked.

"Subspace communication systems are down," Braedon said. "Looks like a power surge fried the comm panel. How far is the nearest nav beacon?"

"We are, unfortunately, thirty-eight hours at maximum sub-light from the nearest nav beacon or planet. We have sufficient antimatter reserves to maneuver at sub-light speeds, but our exhaust port seems to be misaligned. As a result, any attempt to alter our course will only incur further damage to the shuttle."

"Let's focus on getting our life support systems in place; it already feels too hot in here for my taste. Maybe someone will pass by and see we're in trouble."

"There is an eight percent chance of a larger ship spotting us before we lose more systems, including primary life support."

"I knew this ship was old, but I had no idea it was a death trap!" Braedon muttered.

"What do we do first?" Iza asked Trix as she started to pull out the tools she kept in the supply cabinet near the rear hatch.

"Life support systems and shields will require two of us while someone realigns the exhaust port."

"Realigning the exhaust port doesn't sound so bad. I

volunteer for that," Braedon said.

Iza smiled as it solved two problems at once. "Great, suit up."

"Wait, what?"

"The exhaust port is outside the shuttle, of course, so you'll need an EVA suit."

It took Braedon five minutes to get into the suit, his eyebrows drawn together and a frown on his mouth. "I feel like I'm baking in here." Several beads of sweat pooled at his brow.

Iza had already tossed her brown jacket aside and stripped down to her white undershirt to combat the heat. "Don't worry, once you're outside the shuttle you'll cool down quickly."

"Why can't she do it?" Braedon asked with a look to Trix.

"She's the only one who can get our life support systems regulated, and the PEM repairs can't wait." Iza reached for her necklace, rubbing the piece between her finger and thumb. "I'm going to talk you through it while Trix and I begin on the other repairs."

Braedon groaned. "Okay, I'll do it, but you've got to tell me one thing first."

"Sure."

"What's that 'V' symbol on your necklace mean?"

"It's not a 'V'—it's the ancient symbol for truth made from precious metal."

"It must hold some significance, since you reach for it every once in a while. Is it from a lover or something?"

Iza shook her head and sighed. "It's the only thing I ever kept from my parents. I've had it since I was a kid, and I never take it off. Even after my mother died, I couldn't part with it."

Braedon nodded, seeming to understand.

"You never said what you keep in your pocket," Iza countered.

Braedon looked down. Then he patted his pocket through

the spacesuit. "The first credit I ever earned on my own. I keep it with me always."

When they reached the rear hatch, Iza felt a strong desire to reassure him. "You're going to be fine. Don't be nervous."

"I'm not nervous. I've just never done anything like this before."

Suited and ready, Braedon made his way toward the hatch at the back.

"How do you feel?"

"Like a sweaty foot in a sock. Is there enough oxygen in here?"

"The last opportunity we had to refill the oxygen tank was on Kinterin. Due to our haste to leave, we did not have ample opportunity to take advantage of it," Trix said.

That's not going to help.

The worry showed on Braedon's face for the first time as he bit his lower lip and drew his eyebrows together in concern. She missed his confident babbling.

Iza relaxed her face into a grin and nodded. "There should be plenty of air to make the repairs. But if you see any kind of readout on the helmet's HUD in red, let me know. I don't think I have to tell you to be careful out there."

"I realize I'm technically not supposed to be here, but I'd feel a lot better if you pretend that you're going to do whatever it takes to make sure I don't asphyxiate on the outside of this unnamed shuttle."

"Yes, I will risk my own life and limbs to save you," Iza said, attempting to sound bored.

Braedon smiled. "It's so nice to know you care." Then he puckered up his lips and kissed the inside of the helmet.

Was I ever that youthful and silly? Iza secured the tether to the back of his suit and opened the hatch so he could climb into the airlock.

Once he was outside of the shuttle, she checked the comms. "You reading me?"

"Loud and clear."

"Make your way to the junction box. It should be just slightly aft and above your head about a half a meter."

"Will you ever tell him the real reason you didn't go out there?" Trix asked.

Iza killed the comms before Braedon could hear her response.

"My fear of heights is on a need-to-know basis. He doesn't need to know."

Trix paused for a moment. "You have never told anyone else about the necklace. Perhaps you like having him around as much as I do."

"Get back to work. I'd love to see myself on the flight deck of that H3X instead of dying in this old heap."

"If you took better care of the shuttle, it would continue to function long after your natural death," Trix said, her expression neutral.

"No need to be offended. I love this shuttle—it represents my first taste of freedom—but I'm ready for an upgrade."

"I'm at the exhaust port," Braedon said over the comms, "and it looks like it's several centimeters off."

"See if you can line it up."

"Got it."

Iza listened to Braedon's labored breathing as he struggled with it.

"Give it a bit more muscle Braedon, don't be scared of it," she said with half a giggle.

"Come on, I'm giving it everything I have. It's just jammed."

Iza could hear the effort in his voice and waited for him to speak again.

"I felt it budge a little," he said between maneuvers.

"Good. Let me know when you're done and we'll get you inside," Iza said.

Trix had already opened the lower panel of the console and started rerouting their life support systems.

"Where did you grow up?" Braedon asked.

"Nowhere interesting."

"Hey, I'm out here in the cold, silent black of space. I need something to keep my mind off of it! Give me the abridged version at least."

This is hardly the time. Iza sighed. "There's not much more to tell you. I grew up on a backward planet that no one knows or even cares about. As soon as I was old enough, I got out of there. I've been making my own way ever since. It got me in some trouble, but I learned fast that the only person I can trust is myself and that's enough for me."

"Sounds lonely."

Iza shrugged even though he couldn't see her.

He was quiet for another long moment. "My family has always had money. I never wanted for anything other than the freedom to make my own choices in life. I never knew my mom. Sometimes I wonder if she'd have approved of my dramatic escape from a life of privileged tedium."

The lights inside the shuttle pulsed.

"I have augmented life support systems by rerouting from minor systems," Trix broke into the conversation.

There was a rush of cool air on her skin and Iza breathed it in.

"Hear that, Braedon? It looks like we're going to live to see you save the day. You were just about to tell me how a rich kid winds up in the outer colonies."

When he didn't answer, she moved to the viewport. *Where is that bomaxed tether?* There was no sign of him. "Braedon do you read me?"

Silence.

"Trix, do we have a visual on Braedon?"

Trix tilted her head. "Braedon's air supply has been compromised. His life signs appear to be fading. He has less than five minutes of air left."

Her pulse spiked. "What happened? He should have hours of air!"

"There must be a malfunction in the suit."

Stars, we can't leave him out there to die! She forced back her panic. "Will you go and get him, please? Pull him in using the tether, if you can. Whatever you do, don't let go. Without you, we're both dead."

"Affirmative," Trix said with a quick nod then moving to the hatch she secured herself on the other side.

"Braedon, hang on. If you can hear me, we're coming to get you," Iza said into the void.

Iza moved to the hatch viewport to watch while Trix pulled Braedon in by the tether. It wouldn't take her long to get him inside. She did the mental calculations, if he hadn't lost air for long, he'd be okay as long as he didn't have a hole in his suit.

Another alarm went off behind her and she raced to the helm to check the readout.

Something bigger than a pebble was about to run directly into them.

"Trix, we have incoming! Hang on, I need to maneuver us out of the path." Iza hated risking their limited antimatter reserves on the course change, but getting obliterated wouldn't leave them in a better position.

The shuttle lurched to the side, the inertial stabilizers still offline in the low-power mode. To her relief, the short burst was enough to get them out of the debris path.

"Are you okay out there, Trix?" Iza asked while she rushed to the rear hatch.

"I almost have Braedon," the android confirmed.

"Hurry up, he doesn't have long."

At last, Trix pulled Braedon inside the airlock, cradling the young man in her arms. Iza immediately began cycling the airlock.

"Hang on, Braedon." Iza held her hand to the window, counting down the seconds until the airlock would equalize.

The indicator light above the airlock hatch turned blue, and Iza released the inner door. She rushed inside and grabbed for Braedon. He didn't appear to be breathing and Trix was stiff from the brief exposure to space.

"Come on, come on." Iza pulled off Braedon's helmet.

"His heart rate is falling," Trix said after a quick check of his biological systems.

Braedon lay so still she was worried they might be too late.

Iza loosened the suit from around Braedon's neck. She bent down to his mouth and felt no breath coming from him. She put her two fingers where his neck and jaw met. There was a faint thump against her fingers. She pinched his nose and tilted his head back so she could access his airway. Then she breathed into his mouth several times.

When he gasped for breath at last, Iza sighed with relief.

"Stars! If you didn't want to make the repairs, you should have just said so."

Braedon coughed and nodded once. "What happened?" he asked between coughs. He was trembling.

"I don't know yet," Iza said looking over the suit for damage. She found a tear along the backside and cut in the oxygen line. Whatever tiny piece of rogue debris had caused the damaged had missed slicing through Braedon's flesh by mere centimeters. "Braedon, you have all the luck."

He gave her a weak smile, the color slowly returning to his face. "Knowing that, want to reconsider participating in that

Dark Net tournament?"

She smiled shook her head in response. "I'm glad you're okay."

Braedon propped himself up on his arms, still shivering. "I got the exhaust port aligned."

"Nice job. Trix, are you okay?"

"All my systems are functioning within acceptable ranges." Trix closed her hands into fists then released them as if to prove it.

"Can you complete the rest of the EVA repairs, Trix? We need to know if the debris that hit Braedon damaged anything else."

"Yes, I will begin immediately."

Iza turned back to Braedon, who was still staring up at her.

"Maybe I should stick to hacking," he said, wrapping his arms around himself as he continued to shiver. "Not to be dramatic."

"Let's get you out of this suit and under some blankets. Your body is feeling the effects of oxygen deprivation." Braedon gripped her arms, harder than he might have intended. "You'll be fine, I promise," she assured him.

Iza helped him out of his suit and over to her cot. She covered him with thick, gray blankets. Even under the warmth of the covering, he didn't let go of her arm.

"Don't leave," he whispered.

"I won't."

IZA WOKE TO the sound of raised voices in the cockpit.

"You're wrong," Braedon was saying, "there's no way that a backdoor encryption code would work for something like that."

"If you would maintain an open mind, you might distinguish the difference between speculation and fact."

"Whoa, calm down. I didn't think androids could have hurt feelings."

"I am perfectly calm and I do not have hurt feelings," Trix replied, contrary to her sharp tone. "However, I know when someone is being condescending."

After his harrowing experience outside of their dead shuttle, Braedon had recovered and returned to his normal chatty and antagonizing self. He and Trix must have come to some kind of agreement to make Iza's life miserable by arguing about every little thing.

They'd limped to Leveckis on their sub-light antimatter pion drive, operating at a fraction of its normal power output, where they had performed minor repairs to the ship and completed two shipments. Braedon had stayed on because he was still recovering and Iza didn't have the heart to just throw him off. Now, they were on the last leg of their third and final delivery. Iza couldn't wait to get Braedon off of the ship and get some peace at last. She told herself the reason was the bickering and not that if something happened to him it would be on her.

Iza wanted to get to Galminus without losing her mind, which was looking less likely with every ignited debate between her two passengers.

Iza threw back the blanket and crossed to the cockpit. "Knock it off, you two. Where are we?"

"We will arrive on Galminus within the hour."

"When was your last re-charge?" Iza asked her.

"Two days, and eleven minutes ago."

"Why don't you go charge up? I'd like you at peak when we go to get the new ship later today."

While Trix charged, Iza took over the controls. Fortunately, Braedon seemed content to nap, so she got a taste of the quiet she'd been longing for.

Upon reaching Galminus, Iza manually piloted the shuttle setting down to the surface of the planet, landing in a cloud of copper dust. She planned to make good use of their limited time on the world. She'd make the delivery and then contact Karter before the end of the business day. Iza smiled to herself; she might even be able to sleep on the H3X tonight.

First, complete this last job.

Their instructions had been to message their contact upon arrival to arrange delivery, so she sent out the subspace signal with their coordinates and waited for confirmation. The job was by far their most lucrative of the recent run, accounting for over half of the funds she needed for the increased down payment. They'd been lucky to be in the right place and the time to take it on. *The H3X was destined to be mine, and the Universe is looking out for me.*

She didn't notice that she'd started to whistle until Braedon brought it up.

"I'm just excited." Iza swiveled in her seat to face Braedon. "I'm going to have my own ship, and two days early. Karter won't believe it. I can't wait to see the look on his smug face."

"I bet." Braedon looked like he wanted to say something else, but he remained quiet.

No doubt another bid to stay on as a hacker we don't need. Iza nodded at the console. "I'm just waiting for my contact to get back to me. I believe it's time to say goodbye."

Braedon and Trix exchanged a look. Before he could speak, Iza held up a hand.

"I don't like long goodbyes. No excuses, no stories, just have a nice life."

Braedon raised his hand to wave and nodded. Then, with a pat on Trix's shoulder, he turned and exited the shuttle without another word. Iza wanted to believe she preferred the silence, but sitting there all she could think of was how much she already missed the bickering.

—

While sitting in the pilot's seat and counting her total credits, the proximity alert signaled. Iza snapped to attention, thinking her contact must have finally decided to make an appearance. Instead, she looked through the viewport to see armed guards rushing toward them.

"What in the stars...?" She quickly pulled up the communications log, looking for anything that would explain their sudden aggressive action. Her heart sank when she saw her name and face on a bulletin marked 'suspicious activity'. The Enforcers were coming for them.

She rushed past Trix, who was still recharging, and opened

the door before the Enforcers could claim she was resisting. Sure to keep her hands visible, she walked down the ramp out to a dozen guards with their weapons trained on her.

Iza put on her most disarming smile and held up her hands. "There must be some kind of misunderstanding. We have clearance for delivery on Galminus. Let me contact my people and we'll get this all cleared up."

The lead Enforcer moved to stand in front of her while the rest of the team surrounded Iza and the ship.

When the Enforcer lifted her face shield, Iza's heart sank and she let out a quiet curse.

What were the chances?

Bangs and a short, straight bob-cut did little to soften the look of the tall, broad-shouldered woman. Her lips curled into an amused smirk as she raised one of her dark eyebrows. "Well, if it isn't little Miss Iza Sundari. Wait, what did they use to call you... Scrap Rat, was it?"

It beats Mech Neck.

"Desirae," Iza said, making it sound as boring as possible.

"That's Investigator Hyttinen," she bit off the words in a sharp staccato.

Desirae Hyttinen was Karter Hyttinen's cousin and a thorn in Iza's side. Of all the Enforcers to run into, Desirae was the one most likely to make trouble. Unfortunately, she was also the *most* likely to encounter, since she had been Iza's official case manager years before. The Guard liked to keep the same Investigator paired with repeat offenders, since they would have the best inside knowledge. Given that, it set Iza on edge that Desirae was here now; it would suggest that she'd been called to follow up on Iza and this wasn't just a routine port check.

"I wish I could say I'm surprised to see you again," Desirae continued. "However, it seems you often have trouble staying on the right side of the law. It used to be petty theft, and now it seems you've graduated to illegal cargo transport."

Despite Desirae's shrill taunts, Iza kept her tone even and devoid of emotion. "This is a routine run for a Baellas subsidiary, just some textiles. Let me make a few calls and I can get this straightened out."

"Yes, they call themselves Talandis Textiles," she said, glancing down at her handheld. "A shame there's no one there to take your call, since they've all been taken in for questioning."

Iza ground her teeth. The job had come to her via the locally run textiles business operating on behalf of Baellas Corp only a few days ago. She had no idea of their reputation, and she'd been so eager for high-paying work she hadn't checked. How was she to know if they'd been up to their eyeballs in illegal activities when she took the job? Now, she was caught up in it and placed in the vindictive hands of Desirae Hyttinen.

"Are you going to listen to my side, or what?" Iza asked, letting some of the frustration through.

"You're under arrest for transporting illegal goods. I'm doing my duty by getting you criminals off the streets. My superiors can sort out whether or not you're innocent of the charges."

Two Enforcers stepped forward to place stasis cuffs on Iza's wrists.

"Do you have any proof?" Iza asked as she struggled against them. The closest Enforcer placed a firm hand on her shoulder to keep her still. She complied because it was better than a pulse blast to the back.

Desirae sauntered forward and leaned in to hiss in Iza's ear. "I have all the proof I need. Believe me, I'm going to enjoy this so much more than I should." She took a step back and raised her voice for the others to hear. "Impound the shuttle and bring down the cargo."

Six Enforcers rushed past Iza to climb inside the shuttle. Not long after, Iza heard the boots of a patroller returning to report to Desirae.

"There's an android recharging inside, should we bring it?"

"Shut it down and if it's too heavy, dismantle it and bring the pieces back to Sarduvis."

"You can't! She's a person." Iza lunged forward ignoring the pinch of the restraints to reach for Desirae's throat, but the officer stepped back just out of reach.

The Enforcer behind Iza hit her with a pulse from his handgun. The low-level pulse kept her conscious while dropping her to her knees in the dusty ground. Her body curled in on itself for protection. She spat at the ground in front of Desirae's boots, earning a swift kick to the ribs. When the breath returned to her lungs, she glared up at Desirae with all the hate she could muster. The next chance she got, Iza was going to take *her* apart piece by piece.

Desirae put a hand to her mouth as if to stifle a laugh. Her hand dropped away as she turned on one heel, replacing her face shield and stepping out in front of them. She barked out her orders to the other Enforcers. "Load the prisoners and evidence on board my shuttle."

Two Enforcers lifted Iza from the ground, their gloved hands digging into her arms, then dragged her behind Investigator Hyttinen and onto the Enforcer shuttle. Iza was pushed into a metal seat with ankle restraints and a padded vest harness.

Trix was led on a moment later to Iza's relief. She was unrumpled as she walked of her own accord, not attempting to resist in any way. They'd placed an EMP remote-controlled collar on her that would emit a pulse strong enough to render her inert if she became hostile.

"This one's being uncooperative," said the Enforcer behind her.

"What's the problem?" Desirae asked.

"She's lying about the shuttle's identification cards and logs," he said.

"Omission of certain details and lying are not fundamentally the same thing," Trix said.

"We'll get it from her one way or the other. Lock her down for now and prepare for take-off."

"Yes, Investigator."

Trix was placed in the seat adjacent to Iza.

"We'll be on Sarduvis in a matter of minutes," Desirae said moving to stand in front of Iza. "You might view the place a little differently now that you'll be in with the adult population. They're a bit rougher than what you're used to."

"I can handle myself," Iza said under her breath.

"The way you handled my Enforcers?"

"Take off these restraints and I'll show you exactly what I can do," Iza said through gritted teeth. When she bolted forward against the cuffs, Desirae flinched. It was satisfying enough to bring a smile to Iza's lips.

Desirae recovered quickly enough as she smoothed her hands down the front of her dark grey uniform. "No, I like how good those stasis cuffs look on you. It's like they were custom-made for you."

One of her officers moved to join her. He whispered something in her ear that brought a smile to Desirae's face, which could only be bad news. Iza kept her eyes on the Enforcers even as they moved away.

Iza leaned forward to address Trix. "Did you catch any of that?"

"Yes. The officer said, 'the prisoners are to be transferred directly to Sarduvis and under the Investigator's jurisdiction for the time being.' I suspect that means, we can expect to have a lot more time with Investigator Hyttinen."

"It's nothing I haven't dealt with before. She's full of hot air. Just stick to the truth."

"They want to know what happened to our original identification records," Trix said.

"Most haulers have an altered ident. It's not a crime to own one, it's a crime to alter one."

"Should I inform them of that fact?"

Iza gazed over at Trix. She measured the sincerity in android's facial features and calculated the odds of her statements landing them in jail longer than necessary. "On second thought, stick to omission. You're good at that."

7

JOE'S FEET HURT worse than his jaw ever had after a fight. He'd walked the entire dock twice, and no one was interested in letting him board as a worker, a passenger, or even as a toilet bowl cleaner. His options and his patience withering, he stopped off for a bite in the one place he was sure to find food, and maybe information: one of the local bars.

The smell of cooking meat and spilled alcohol hit him in the face as he stepped into the small establishment. It took a moment for his eyes to adjust to the dim ambient lighting.

The six tables and wall to wall bar were near empty in the middle of the day, occupied by a total of three people who had taken respite from work and the sun. A man and woman sat across from each other in silence at a table near the door while another man nursed a short drink at the bar alone. The mirrored wall behind the bar gave the illusion of size.

Joe wondered if the barkeep was also the cook, since he'd been sitting for ten minutes and hadn't seen anyone bring out food or refill drinks. A dimly lit table in the back afforded him a good view of the entire bar. The table's surface, equipped with a virtual interface, allowed for ordering directly from the table.

He input his credit code to get a hot sandwich and an ice-cold fruity drink with what appeared to be frost on the outside of the glass. When a non-verbal robotic server came over half an hour later and placed the food down in front of him, Joe realized he'd come to the wrong place. The sliced meat sandwich was cold and tasted like week-old bologna, and the blended fruit drink was warm. He stretched out his legs, placing both aching feet on the hard seat on the opposite side of the table.

Joe sighed as he pulled out his handheld and made the call he'd been dreading all day. It was hard to admit he was a failure more than once in less than a week. Agent Ian Mandren's face appeared. Joe tensed as he waited for the inevitable reprimand from the Sacon Division Lead for calling over a general subspace channel from a public establishment.

"Agent Saletas, how goes it?" Mandren's joviality took him by surprise.

"Um, well, sir… slow, to be honest. I haven't found anyone willing to let me board their ship." Then he added in case it wasn't obvious, "I had to make this call from a local bar, just so I could sit down for five minutes."

"What are you wearing?" Mandren held up a hand in front of his eyes and backed away from the display. "It's burning my retinas."

Joe looked down at the loud-print shirt and bright-colored pants.

"I'm attempting to blend in here, sir. It's proving to be a challenge."

"Are you serious? Do I have to remind you that your best feature is your ability to read a room? What were you thinking?"

"Someone advised me that the other outfit looked too much like active Agent gear."

Mandren snickered. "What makes you look like an Agent

isn't your clothing, Saletas, it's your demeanor. Lighten up your attitude instead of your clothes. And for the love of all that's good, tone down the loud print."

The resentment bubbled up inside him. It wasn't his idea to go out to the backward planets in search of unrest in the mighty Taran Empire.

"Yes, sir." Joe pulled back his shoulders and continued, "I may not be cut out for this assignment. Is there anything else I can do to appease the TSS?"

Mandren's face sobered. "Joe, I know it's been a difficult three years and we've spent a good deal of time at odds. Contrary to what you might think, I was only trying to help you realize that you can't do everything on your own. But, you haven't taken to any of the teams or my attempts to coach you. That's why we're giving you this chance out on your own, because you're out of options. You may not be the most technically skilled Agent, but you do have an uncanny ability to observe things that others miss—and that lends itself to a solitary endeavor. This is your last assignment for the TSS unless otherwise notified. Make it work or you'll be back on Earth."

Joe's temper flashed before he could bank it. "Is that a threat?"

Mandren paused, letting the question linger in the air between them. Joe knew he'd responded too quickly, and he felt his shoulders fall as his emotions settled.

"Sorry, sir."

When Mandren spoke, his voice was calm and steady. "No, Joe. It's no threat. I know you think this was my idea to send you out there. It wasn't. Do the job or my superiors will be left with no choice but to send you home. Contact me again when you've got something and not before."

The connection cut off abruptly, leaving Joe stewing in frustration. He hadn't meant to be terse with Mandren, but he always felt the need to push back against him, no matter what he said.

How was he supposed to get intel back to the TSS if he couldn't get anyone to talk to him? It was clear he wouldn't get any help from Headquarters. He needed to figure things out on his own. He took another bite of the cold sandwich, wishing he could go back to the kitchen and make one of his own.

If he couldn't board someone else's ship, maybe he could get a ship and take on a crew of his own. A barman came out of the back, carrying various shaped bottles and balancing glasses in front of him. Joe made his move.

"Excuse me, I was hoping you could tell me where I could get a ship."

The man's thick hair poked out from under his cap, while a beard and bushy eyebrows covered the rest of his face. He didn't look up as he answered, instead focusing on stacking his bottles. "DGE is the one making ships these days."

"I'm not looking to buy new, or even pretty. Just something to get me from A to B."

Still keeping his head down, he placed the glasses on a shelf just out of view. "Impound lot's about five kilometers out of town. They've got lots of ships over there, but you'll have to pay."

"Thanks." Joe turned from the bar and back to his table where he saw someone picking the meat off of his sandwich.

The young man with glassy hazel eyes stared boldly back at him with a piece of his sandwich dangling from his mouth. His light brown hair stood up in odd places and his wrinkled clothing with the expensive stitching looked as though he'd slept in them over the past week.

Tempted to remove the smug grin on the thin young man's face with his fist, Joe sat back down in his seat and pulled his plate away and out of reach. He reassembled the sandwich and took another slow bite.

When Joe had swallowed his unhurried mouthful he spoke. "Can I help you?"

"No, but I believe I can help you." The young man leaned forward and his eyes seemed to clear.

Joe glanced up and down at him then raised one questioning eyebrow at him. "Is that right?"

"Yes, you need a ship, right?"

Joe leaned back in his seat. *He must have overheard my conversation with the barkeep.*

Joe didn't like to pry, but he telepathically reached out and found the young man's thoughts were open. His offer was sincere. So Joe answered in kind. "Let's say I do."

"Well, ever see an H3X-Z500?" He didn't wait for Joe to answer. "I happen to have one. I can take you to wherever you want to go for a nominal fee."

"Nominal?"

"Yes, see, I was robbed. The thieves took off with my credits and my ship and I intend to get it back. All I require is a little help. What do you say?"

"What do you need, exactly?"

"All I need is a few credits, plus I haven't eaten all day. Normally, I wouldn't do this, but you've encountered me at a desperate hour."

This might work. Joe nodded thoughtfully. "Let's start with your name."

"I have a better idea. I'd like a plate of whatever you're having."

The young man gave the cold sandwich and warm blended fruit drink a significant glance before he met Joe's eye.

Joe finished his sandwich while he thought over the young man's offer. *I have nothing else to go on. I need to do something.*

He created a duplicate order on the digital system. While waiting for the meal to arrive, Joe began asking questions.

"Your name?"

"Braedon Valtteri."

"Jovani Saletas."

"A pleasure," Braedon said as he reached out to shake his hand. It was so familiar and yet out of character for a Taran that Joe smiled as he took his offered hand. The man's soft hands were unaccustomed to doing hard labor, but not pampered either, he noted. Perhaps he was highborn, but what would he be doing out here?

Once the food arrived, and Braedon was eating like he'd never had food before, Joe spoke again. "Where did you say your ship was?"

"I didn't. It's confiscated, but I can get it back. I just need some credits and we'll need to make one stop," Braedon said around a mouthful of food.

"I thought you said they impounded it."

Braedon shifted a bit in his seat, the smile still on his lips but he appeared uncomfortable with the question. "It is, but it's not in an impound lot. Trust me, we'll be off this planet by tonight."

He didn't know if Braedon was being purposefully evasive or obtuse. "You should know, I have telepathic abilities. I know when you're lying to me."

"Don't all Agents," Braedon said with a snicker.

"I'm not an Agent. The TSS and I parted on a difference of opinion."

"Fair enough. Then you're out of a job. I've got just the thing for you."

"If you don't mind me asking, how does someone dressed like you end up in a place like this?" Joe asked holding out his hands. "Isn't there someone who can come and retrieve you and your things?"

Braedon's smile didn't reach his eyes. "No. My father and

I are hardly on speaking terms. I'm what you might call the disgrace of the family. They should keep out of my personal affairs, if you know what I mean."

Joe thought of his sister. He did know.

"But I have a plan," Braedon continued. "You don't seem like the kind of person who makes friends easily, but you've made one today." Braedon pushed aside his empty plate and drank down the fruit drink.

"What kind of job did you have in mind?"

"Come on, I'll show you," Braedon said as he stood up from the table. "Ever hear of an All Play Dark Net tournament?"

Joe shook his head.

"You don't get out much do you? Well, you'll fit right in. We just need to get you some different clothes. You look too much like an undercover Agent. You do have credits for clothes, don't you?"

Joe peered down again at the loud print on his clothing and rolled his eyes. The merchant had assured him the loud shirt wasn't ridiculous. He should have known the man was only out for his next meal. Joe looked over at Braedon. He'd smoothed down his light brown waves and straightened his clothing. The meal seemed to have revived him.

"Now let's go get us some new clothes."

"Us?"

BRAEDON'S IDEA OF a job was for Joe to pose as private security for him, while he entered an underground high-stakes and highly illegal gambling ring. Joe rolled his eyes when Braedon introduced him as his private guard. Security at the tournament's entrance stored Joe's weapon at the door. His hand kept reflexively searching for it inside his new dark brown jacket, which was paired with a full outfit in similar muted tones.

The virtual reality gambling event took place on the Galactic Dark Net, so the entire fabricated room was kept clean of the red dust using a vacuum air filtration system, so as to not interfere with the computer terminals' operations. As Joe followed Braedon through the archway entry, the remaining film of dust was blown off them.

When they passed the second shiny surface along the columns of the centralized bar, Braedon checked his reflection and adjusted the front curls of his hair. Braedon had picked up another outfit to replace the one he'd been wearing, using credits he promised to pay back. His fitted jacket was worn over a dark blue shirt and new slim, black pants. He'd had his boots shined and now looked the part of a player in a high-stakes virtual gaming room.

The tournament floor tables were lit from above with artificial lights dimmed enough to make gameplay easier on the eyes. Joe watched the players already engaged in virtual games as he and Braedon passed by their way to one of the outer tables. Joe recognized several other men standing about as private security wearing stern and unwelcoming expressions.

Braedon sat down and pulled out his handheld for the tournament master. Joe cursed under his breath when Braedon passed the credits he'd given him to enter. The name he gave the administrator was his virtual alias, BL4CKSH33P. Joe leaned over and whispered in Braedon's ear as he'd seen other guards do on the premises.

"What am I supposed to do here while you gamble away my money?"

Braedon kept a sly smile on his face as he spoke. "You should sit back and watch how easy it is to turn the scraps you gave me into a ship." Braedon reached for his virtual headset.

"You told me you were robbed." Joe's voice rising to compete with the rhythmic music around them.

"In a manner of speaking. Don't worry, I'll get it back and more."

"What are you planning to do once you have your money?"

Braedon got a strange far-off look when he answered, "I only take from those who have more than enough to give, but don't. I give to the ones who no one else will help."

Joe smiled and held out his hand to shake Braedon's. "Nice to meet you, Robin Hood."

Braedon took it, though his brows drew together in confusion. "Who?"

"Never mind." Joe straightened.

Now that his eyes had adjusted to the dim lighting, he took in the rest of the room. Both spectators and guards alike were taking the event seriously, with no one bouncing to the music blaring from all four corners of the space. The communications appeared to be managed through a dish that hung from the cavern ceiling like an intricate chandelier. Joe took note of the dampener throughout the place, which kept the music, shouting, and gaming noise from traveling beyond the walls.

"We have a winner!"

Braedon pumped his fists in the air as they advanced him to the next table.

Over the next two hours, it happened again and again until he'd won himself a seat at the largest table in the room, positioned in the center of the cavern on an elevated platform. The square table had four virtual headsets to accommodate the semi-final winners. The winner of that round of the game received the final prize. They displayed the running total above the table and it ticked higher and higher as each semi-final winner finished.

At the smaller tables, the game was played in VR only. This final version of the game would be on a holodisplay above the table for all the attendees to see—no doubt so they could place bets on their individual favorites and then follow the results.

There were several people already gathered around the table, but the final contestant was still at the semi-final table— a young girl with blue and green hair that went by the name of V1P3R. The intensity grew as she took down her final opponent. She flashed a disarming and bright smile as she was paraded around the room.

Braedon waved Joe over to the table where the final round would take place. He seemed to be in an amorous embrace with two women well above his age and far below his station.

"Sir?" Joe kept his demeanor calm in responding to him. He used no specific title since he'd been warned not to expose the truth about Braedon's past to others.

"I need you to run an errand for me. As soon as this tournament ends, there's a little something I owe you and I'm going to pay you back. But as you'll recall from our previous conversation, there's something I need to pick up, and it's supposed to be waiting outside. Check on it and make sure no one leaves with my ship."

"The H3X-Z500?"

"Yes," he said as one of the women beside him nuzzled his neck.

Joe raised an eyebrow, "Anything else?"

Braedon tilted his head. "Go by the bar and get us a couple of drinks," he said, waving his hand toward the bar.

The entitled pissant.

Joe made his way to the bar. Of the two of them, he'd earned himself a drink.

Joe was about to order something when an announcer came on, signaling the start of the final round of the tournament. He looked back in time to see the girls being ushered away from the roped-off table of final competitors. The last person seated across from Braedon was V1P3R, the young girl with green and blue hair. The other two men, one dark-skinned and the other a lighter complexion, were already settled into their VR headsets on either side of Braedon.

Like the rest of the anxious spectators, Joe forgot to order a drink. He couldn't tear his eyes away from the real-time feed of the virtual game heating up above the center table. Braedon had chosen a dark blue mech soldier with a distinct star on his chest plate. His avatar was battling two other mechs at once— a larger one in dark brown with a gold bandana tied around its head and another with green and black markings. The mechs fought each other with the tools and gifts they'd earned. Joe leaned forward as Braedon took out one competitor and then another.

Braedon was right. They would wind up with more than enough credits and a ship on top of everything else. The crowd pressed in around him, anticipating the final blow. Two competitors were out, leaving only Braedon and V1P3R. Their fingers were rapidly tapping the air, creating different fight combinations to take each other down. Their hands were moving faster than Joe could follow.

A couple of giggling women passed by too close and one lost their drink to Joe's shirt, and he was again covered in something that would stink later. They tried to help clean him up with small towels they retrieved from the bar, but he assured them it was fine. Once they'd moved on, he looked up to see how Braedon was doing.

Wait, he's winning.

Joe was holding his breath. Maybe it was his trained senses, but something made him turn around. That's when something at the back wall caught his eye.

People were moving along the walls all around the room. Before Joe could identify them, cheers broke out and Braedon stood up and threw his fists in the air. Joe started combing through the crowd to reach him, but it seemed everyone had the same idea and he didn't end up making it more than two meters. Whooping with satisfaction, Braedon was carried off the platform and into the crowd.

The kid did it. He won.

There was a distinct change in the room's air as the people along the wall began to close in. Joe realized they weren't spectators at all, but undercover Enforcers.

Joe couldn't afford to be captured along with the rest, so instead of trying to duck beyond the crowd, he joined the ranks of those taking down the illegal facility. They'd formed a perfect, unbreaking circle surrounding the spectators. When he stood up with the other Enforcers, no one questioned him. Why would someone pretend to be an Enforcer? He stepped into the outer circle and reached for his pulse gun at the same time as the others, but he'd checked it at the door. He spread out his hands instead; it was a standard maneuver he'd practiced many times back at TSS Headquarters.

The spectators and competitors didn't know what was happening until it was too late.

"Where's your weapon, Agent?" one of the Enforcers asked.

"Checked at the door. If we're making arrests, I better retrieve it," Joe replied, not needing to remind the officer that he was a weapon unto himself with his telekinetic abilities.

The man still wore a bewildered expression, but Joe turned his back on him. He made it outside without being asked any more questions. He'd worry about that breach in protocol later.

Joe scanned the area for the ship, but when he didn't see it, he wondered if they had already confiscated it.

"Hey," he said to the nearest Enforcer in uniform. "Did they take the H3X already?"

The confused expression on the man's face was enough, but Joe waited for his answer. "No, there wasn't an H3X among the ships we picked up. Did you arrive in one?"

Joe shook his head. "No, a mark I was tailing said he had one waiting for him. He must have been double-crossed."

"Not surprising with this lot, then, is it?"

No, not at all.

Had anything Braedon said been the truth? Not only had all the credits he'd won been seized in the bust, including Joe's loan, but the little weasel had managed to talk an Agent out of his money and then gamble it away before his eyes. Joe wondered if it hadn't been his desperation that had brought him to this point. He should never have given Braedon the credits in the first place.

Joe kept his distance while the Enforcers herded spectators, players, and private guards onto a large cargo ship to be delivered for processing. He couldn't risk getting spotted and mistaken in front of the others for either an Agent or the private security he was pretending to be.

"Where are they bringing them?" he asked the Enforcer.

"The same place we agreed on before we got here." He must have read the confusion on Joe's face because he added, "Sarduvis."

Joe nodded as he realized that Braedon was in real trouble. Sarduvis penitentiary wasn't just a prison for hardened criminals, it was in space. The facility had started out as a prison ship, but as the population in the sector grew, the colossal freighter had been permanently docked to an asteroid. Still bearing the name of its original ship namesake, Sarduvis was known as one of the most secure holding facilities anywhere in Taran space, which could be expanded and retrofitted as needs required. There would be no way to get Braedon out of custody without help. Joe dashed away from the cavern and jumped into the first automated car leaving the area.

Joe wanted to run and never turn back. If caught, he was putting his entire mission at risk. Braedon was trouble. Why hadn't he sensed him lying about the whole thing? He must have believed what he was saying. Joe didn't owe him anything, but perhaps the situation warranted further investigation. If he stayed with the kid, perhaps it might help him reach others who didn't conform to the rules of Taran society.

He'd have to use his real credentials to save Braedon. That would raise questions on both sides, but there was nothing he could do about that. He picked up his handheld and with a groan was about to make another call to Headquarters when a hand came up and snatched the handheld while at the same time pointing a pulse gun at his nose.

"You're not one of us, let's go."

It was the Enforcer who'd asked him about his weapon.

"You're right, I'm not. I'm—" Joe looked around gauging whether or not he should break cover here or on Sarduvis. However, the young Enforcer didn't give him the chance. He pushed him up against the wall intending to put stasis cuffs on him, clearly a misuse of power. Joe wasn't done giving his credentials and pushed back the rage in him shooting from zero to one hundred in the space of a breath. When the other man's fist came at him, Joe was ready with a block and gut-punch of his own. While the man was bent over, two other guards came out from behind and shot him at close range with a pulse gun that dropped him to his knees.

Hands in restraint cuffs, he was dragged off with the rest of the prisoners.

His superiors were not going to like this.

FOUR HOURS LATER, Joe's ears were still ringing from the tongue lashing he got from Mandren for getting arrested and then making the call to be bailed out. TSS Command agreed to help him, but it was made clear that he'd run out of chances and any further calls from prisons would be ignored. Above all else, Mandren reminded Joe to keep his true identity hidden from Braedon or anyone else with whom he came into contact.

They had cleared him to get Braedon released from the penitentiary using his real TSS credentials and that was all. It seemed the young man might be involved in something his superiors thought worthy of further observation.

The underground VR tournament was old news. Local Enforcers had struggled to pin down the group as their ample finances kept their operation well hidden. To succeed, it had required three teams of undercover officers to expose them. Joe had just been swept up in the event. Bad timing, it seemed. His superiors permitted him to make a statement about anything he may have witnessed while undercover at the establishment in exchange for his own freedom. They'd processed the entire crowd by the time Joe arrived on Sarduvis.

The prison was everything one would expect from a

secured lockdown facility with only one way in and out. The layers of security Joe had to pass to reach the major's receptionist bordered on paranoid protective. There were six pairs of grey uniformed Enforcers between the shuttle dock and major's office, not to mention the various patrol officers on board escorting prisoners. The facility received all supplies, prisoners, and guests through the same port. There was no chance of a prisoner escaping through it due to the two shuttles circling the asteroid at all times.

Joe spoke to reception and requested a sit-down with Major Lakonis, who oversaw operations on Sarduvis. Once he explained the situation, he hoped to be on his way. He had just enough credits to get them back to Galminus, and from there they'd have to figure out a legitimate plan for getting a ship. The last thing he wanted to deal with was any more illegal activity that could land them both in Sarduvis.

He stood in the light gray windowless room for over ten minutes waiting to be shown into the Major's office. A team of Enforcers arrived, dragging a young man and woman. The woman, he noted, had skin like smooth silk and the color of burnt sienna. In the muted room, she stood out in vivid color. Her black curls were pulled together in a loose braid that hung past one shoulder. She wore a no-nonsense expression on her face and kept silent as the Enforcer pushed her forward.

"These two are in for processing along with the Talandis Textiles group."

The woman caught Joe staring at her and when their eyes met, Joe's breath caught. The physical response was so quick and so deep he lifted his hand to his chest to make sure his heart was still in place. Her mahogany eyes seemed to reach out grabbing him by the throat. He saw her tear her eyes away before the expression on her face changed. Then she spoke, pulling him out of the temporary trance.

"What's wrong, are your eyeballs stuck on stupid?"

Joe's face grew hot with embarrassment as they dragged her around the corner and out of sight. *What in the world was that?*

The receptionist must have called his name several times because when her voice got through, she'd lost her patience. "Sir!"

Joe turned back to her. "Yes?"

"The major will see you now. Just through those doors on your left, it's the office at the end of the hall."

Joe glanced over his shoulder one last time before turning back to the receptionist. "Hey, what are they in here for?"

She looked down at her display and read the roster. "It appears they were involved in illegal shipping."

"Thank you."

Joe couldn't help wondering why Sarduvis would waste so many resources on an illegal gambling ring and a couple of petty thieves. But, he didn't know the extent of the trouble and was smart enough to keep his mouth shut when speaking to the major. It wasn't wise to criticize when begging for favors; he'd learned that much after his recent dealings with Mandren. Besides, Major Lakonis didn't seem like the type to grant favors or take constructive criticism under the best of circumstances.

"Welcome, Agent Saletas. Have a seat," the older man said without looking up. His silver head was tilted forward as he peered down at the screen integrated into his desk. When he finally looked up, the man's weary eyes and face told Joe he'd been in the job a long time, perhaps too long. "What can I do for you?"

"I'm here for one of your prisoners."

"Weren't *you* brought in as a prisoner?"

Joe cleared his throat feeling the unveiled judgment in the question. "Yes, Major."

"I got a call from your superiors at TSS Headquarters and

they had a few things to say about how you've found yourself shipped off to the outer colonies. Have their standards dropped in recent years, or are you an exception?"

Joe felt the heat of embarrassment rising up his neck and banked his defensive response. "I'm doing my best to improve my image and career."

"Your best? You punched one of my Enforcers. Now you're asking for favors?"

"You don't understand."

The major spread his hands on his desk. "That's where you're wrong. Based on what little I was told, you have a problem with authority, Agent. I suggest you get a handle on it before you come my way again."

Joe forced his closed fists to relax and dropped his shoulders and his head. "You're right. I'm just trying to get out of here and do my job."

"I know what you're doing here." The older man glared at him. "You're a spy. You're working covert operations right under my nose with the permission of the TSS, and the excuses they fed me were a version of the truth to use as a cover story. Well, this is my jurisdiction and I deserve at least the professional courtesy of a call. Not only that, you're doing absolutely nothing to help me and mine."

Joe hadn't considered how his actions might look to local enforcement. There was no way he could justify his actions after the fact, so he remained silent. The air was thick with resentment, but he dug into it. He wasn't leaving without what he came for, and Braedon needed his help and he needed a ship.

Major Lakonis let him stew for a moment before sighing. "Now that I've said my piece, we can get on with the pleasantries. Which inmate are you trying to give a free pass to?" He pulled out his system computer and spoke aloud. "CACI, full roster please."

"The name is Braedon Valtteri."

"CACI, pull up record for Braedon Valtteri."

"There is no such inmate at this time," CACI replied.

"Did he give his real name, perhaps? You've probably got the alias," the major said in the same monotone voice.

Joe didn't press for another name, so if Braedon could have gone by any number of names. He scrambled to remember the alias he'd used when signing up for the tournament. "He was one of the players in the gambling ring from Galminus."

"Oh. That narrows it down a bit. CACI pull only records from today's Dark Net prisoners."

"There are two hundred names, would you like to filter out any other names?"

The major looked over at Joe again, "Anything else you can tell me."

"Male, brown hair, hazel eyes, around eighteen years of age. He used the name BL4CKSH33P during the tournament."

"BL4CKSH33P? Well, we've got a problem, because I have no intention of letting him out of here. His real name is Devyn Arvonen. He's a Lower Dynasty delinquent."

Joe raised an eyebrow. *He's from a dynasty?* That surprised him and did indeed change things. "I have to insist, Major, on behalf of the TSS—"

Major Lakonis raised a weary hand to cut him off. "CACI, pull up the BL4CKSH33P files. Begin reading all charges."

"Dark Net gambling, illegal hauling, shuttle theft, ship theft, petty theft—"

"That's enough CACI," he said cutting her off. "Save me the TSS speech about why you think you might need him. BL4CKSH33P has been on our radar for months. Picking him up was the highlight of my week. The last thing I'm going to do is let him walk out of here with you."

Joe's hands balled into tight fists again as he spoke. "He's involved in an investigation that I'm conducting. The TSS has granted me full authority in the matter, and they'd prefer I not go over your head."

"Over my head?" Major Lakonis laughed as if Joe had told the funniest joke he'd ever heard. The man grabbed his belly and let the tears of laughter fill his eyes before he abruptly sat up straight. "Let's get something clear. No one over my head gives a bomaxed flying flag about what's going on aboard my freighter. If you think you can get someone to call down here and try and move me, you're welcome to try."

The major sat back in his seat with his arms crossed over his chest in challenge. Joe hadn't known the man long, but he knew bitter when he saw it.

"You TSS Agents are all the same."

Joe had to grip the armrest to keep from leaping at him. The man had no respect for the TSS. He wondered angrily how he'd been able to survive the Bakzen war and remain unscathed. Where was he while his own parents were being killed on an outpost in the middle of nowhere? No doubt he'd been sitting at his comfortable desk. Joe gathered himself and spoke in a more measured tone.

"Be careful, Major, the TSS has done a lot for us over the years."

"Yes, and they never let us forget it." He waved a hand in the air when Joe started to say something else. "I'm sorry, Agent Saletas, there's nothing I can do for you."

This man had about as much of a grudge toward authority as himself. Perhaps that could work in Joe's favor. Mandren said he should use his powers of observation and he'd been looking around the room since he'd come in the door.

Three of the walls in the light gray office were bare, with the dark gray tile on the floor. A picture of a lake with a lone fisherman hung on one wall. The picture of his family in a small frame was facing him and away from Joe. There was nothing else in the room to make it comfortable or inviting, and the man wanted to be anywhere else but here. He'd been going at it all wrong.

Joe leaned forward and tested his theory. "When was your last vacation, Major? I don't mean a few days off, I mean a couple of weeks."

Whatever the Major had been expecting, it wasn't this. "I'm not due for another vacation for three months. My wife's sister is getting married in a week and she's dying to attend, but I just can't leave Sarduvis. There are too few men who can monitor the freighter."

Joe had him and he knew all he had to do was figure out a way to make it happen. The man was desperate for a holiday. Joe had no authority to grant or give him what he wanted. He was playing the game without authorization to even be at the table. However, nothing was stopping him from making the call. All Joe needed now were the details.

"What can the TSS do to make this happen?"

—   —   —

Iza's overcrowded cell stank of urine and desperation. It permeated the walls and floor, which mingled with the sweet-smelling floor cleaner, making her dizzy. She stood with her back to one wall, avoiding any eye contact with the other inmates. She breathed in wafts of fresher air through her mouth with her face turned toward the ceiling.

She'd been shoved inside the four-person holding cell along with a dozen others and left to wait for hours. Iza wasn't sure if she'd missed her deadline, only that they confiscated the cargo and she hadn't gotten paid. She'd hoped to explain the misunderstanding, but there was no indication she'd get to speak with anyone of authority beyond Investigator Desirae

Hyttinen. There was only one person to turn to now, and it was doubtful he'd speak on her behalf, but she had to try.

"The Enforcers must be on some kind of rampage today," said the girl with the blue hair leaning on the wall beside her. Iza wondered what she was doing there. She couldn't be more than sixteen.

"What are you in for?"

"Gaming on the Dark Net. Would have won, too, if the other guy hadn't pulled out a cheat move."

That got Iza's attention. The girl must be pretty smart to hack into the Dark Net, but she had no idea what she was talking about. It seemed most of her cellmates were taken from the same Dark Net party.

"I'm Iza," she said with a nod of respect to the short girl.

"Viper."

"That's your real name?"

"It's the only name I answer to. What about you?"

"Complete misunderstanding, that I hope will be cleared up, once I'm allowed to speak with someone in authority."

"Speaking to the authorities never cleared anything up for me. I hope it goes better for you."

Iza nodded again, thinking the girl might be older than she looked.

"It's not right. They haven't let us defend ourselves or contact a rep," the girl continued a bit louder, garnering some approvals and murmurs of agreement.

Iza knew this wasn't in accord with Taran law, but it was rare a colonist got fair treatment out here. Most were beginning to complain more loudly about not getting at least an interview.

"Quiet down in here!" a guard called over the noise. "Iza Sundari!"

Two male Enforcers, one on either side of the prison door,

waited for her.

"Ah, here we go. Perhaps now, I'll get to tell my side of the story," she said to Viper as the crowd parted to let her through. At the door, she turned to the guards, holding out her wrists to one. "Where are you taking me?"

"Interview 1," he said, his tone clipped as he put on the stasis cuffs.

She rolled her eyes. *Won't this be fun?*

Once outside the containment cell, Iza noted the other stuffed cells also held prisoners mostly dressed up in fine clothes. She wondered if any of them were with Talandis Textiles.

She caught the sound of a familiar voice as she passed. The young man was wearing fine clothes like he'd been picked up from a party. The red smudges told the full story as if they'd dragged him through the Galminus dirt before bringing him in. He smiled around whatever he was chewing on.

"Braedon?"

Iza waited for him to turn toward her. "Iza, my gorgeous captain! What are you doing in here?"

"Move it along," the Enforcer said at her back, giving her an unceremonious push. She continued walking and called back over her shoulder.

"Just a misunderstanding!"

The guards led Iza down a series of corridors until they came to a room marked: 'INTERVIEW 1'. Iza pushed down the nagging doubts and skepticism for a system that had never been much help to her. *Maybe this time I'll get a fair chance to tell my side of the story.* She'd said it before, but this time she wanted to believe it. At least, she did until she saw who was waiting for her inside.

Desirae Hyttinen sat at the table inside, drumming her neat nails on the metal tabletop in front of her.

"Oh, come now. Stop acting like you're not thrilled to see

me," Desirae said as she threw her hands up.

"Does it show?"

The guards chained Iza's stasis cuffs to the table and then, with a nod from Desirae, left the room.

"What are you expecting me to do here?" Iza held up her wrists and rattled the chain that connected them to the large metal table.

"Just a pleasant conversation between old friends."

"You have an interesting definition of 'pleasant'. Are you this hospitable with all your friends?" Iza asked with a glance at the blank walls and then back to the cuffs on her wrists.

"Why don't you explain to me exactly what you were doing on Galminus?"

"Like I said, I was making a delivery for Baellas Corp. We got the job from Talandis Textiles. Everything seemed above board and I have all the digital confirmation codes. There's no reason for you to keep us here, we've done nothing wrong."

Desirae stood up and made a show of stepping over a black duffle lying at her feet. She paced the floor dragging her hand along the back wall as she talked. "What would you say if I told you Talandis Textiles is mixed up in some very suspicious activity?"

Iza raised an eyebrow. "I'd say the same thing I said before: I had no idea. My part was legal and documented."

"So, you're saying you took a job and didn't bother to ask too many questions about what they wanted, why they wanted it, or even who they were?"

Iza's mouth clamped closed. It was true, she'd been looking for work and didn't do her due diligence. "Too many questions out here can get you into a lot of trouble," she said.

"However, the same could be said for not asking enough questions," Desirae replied as she continued to pace her side of the table, seemingly preparing to pounce. "You know, there was a time when I thought of you as a threat. We were both younger and less experienced back then. Your time in the Sarduvis juvenile facility was hard on both of us. I'd never arrested a kid before and I thought you were a lost cause."

"Yeah, well, I'm a product of my upbringing."

"That's just the thing. You should have stayed with your benefactors instead of being left to roam the streets getting into trouble. I brought you in for your own good."

Iza rolled her eyes but it still stung to think of the life she'd run from. Through adult eyes, she couldn't be sure it was as bad as she remembered. She'd hardly admit as much to the likes of Desirae.

"Next time I get the chance, I'll send you some flowers."

Desirae ignored the snide comment, lost in her thoughts. "I know how the system failed you, and I recognize my part in it. I only wish we'd gotten to you sooner. Before you became so cynical and bitter."

Is she going to blabber on until I confess or what? "Is there a point somewhere or are you trying to bore me to death with your history lesson?"

Desirae flashed her a wicked smile that made the hairs on Iza's neck stand up before she continued. "You've made an effort to straighten out and I appreciate how hard that must have been. Karter has taken a strong liking to you, though I don't know why."

Uh oh. This is going to get ugly. "I'm supposed to get a call to my representative or someone to speak on my behalf, right?" Iza's voice sound too desperate for her liking.

Desirae rolled her eyes and pulled out her handheld. She passed it to Iza, who kept tight hold of it to keep it from slipping out of her hands and falling to the floor.

"Go right ahead."

"Can I get some privacy?" Iza requested.

"Sorry, we're fully booked."

Iza had to push back her seat and lean forward to put the handheld to her ear. She used the private direct line he'd given her over a year ago and had never planned on using until now.

Karter's voice held a sharp edge as he spoke into the line. "I thought I told you not to call me on this line anymore, Desirae?"

Iza didn't have time to process what it meant, only that she couldn't let him disconnect. "It's me, Iza."

"Oh?" His hesitation and confusion were sincere. "Why are you calling me from my cousin's line?"

"They've arrested me on illegal hauling charges. It seems Talandis Textiles was up to no good in the name of Baellas Corp. I need you to speak with Desirae, or whoever else with the Enforcers, and get me a representative so I can get out of here and get back to work."

There was silence on the line.

"Hello?"

"Yes, I'm here, but I'm afraid I can't help you. If you're smart, you won't let her know you've called me. My cousin is carrying a bit of a torch for me, and I'm afraid you'll reap more trouble if you use my name."

Iza glanced up at Desirae who was pretending not to listen to every word she said. *Too late.*

"I'd be happy to do that, but about the other thing. Can you at least provide some kind of evidence to my character and my current obligations?" Iza said.

"How would it look for a dynastic heir to be seen assisting a known criminal? I'm afraid there's nothing I can do."

"Are you joking? Come on, you have to understand what's at stake here."

"Well, there is one way," Karter left the word hanging there like the last bit of fruit on the last tree on the planet.

"What?"

"There is an offer on the table you've yet to take advantage of. It would allow me to help you legitimately."

"Absolutely not!" Iza's voice rose higher and louder than she'd intended. Desirae's head snapped up, forcing Iza to hiss the rest. "You're out of your mind if you think you're going to blackmail me into that."

"Blackmail? That's such an ugly word. You'd be getting something out of the deal, too. I've made it no secret what I'm after, and despite your many admirers, none of them can offer you what I can."

"No, I won't do it."

"All you have to do is change the nature of our relationship and this whole nightmare disappears."

"Bye!" Iza disconnected the line and placed the handheld on the table.

Desirae snatched it up and tapped a few buttons before she stared down at Iza, smiling.

"Karter? That's who you tried to get to help you?" Desirae let out an incredulous laugh as she slipped it into the pocket of her gray uniform. "You're ridiculous if you thought he'd help someone like you. You're nowhere near his level. A word of advice: if you're going to go through the trouble of blocking your thoughts, don't contact someone I already have in my handheld."

Iza ignored the insult. She wasn't blocking Desirae but didn't have to explain her reasons for contacting Karter. "Yeah, he didn't seem to like the idea of you calling him. Good thing I smoothed things over by telling him it was me before he disconnected the line."

Desirae shook her head and went back to pacing. "I don't get what he sees in you," she said, shaking her head.

Iza was losing her patience with the whole thing.

She sneered at Desirae. "I know what he doesn't see," she gave Desirae a moment to stop pacing in front of her, "a TSS flunkout!"

Desirae leaped around the table so fast Iza didn't see it coming. She hit Iza square in the jaw with a fist. The force of it knocking Iza's head back. Though the hit stunned her, it wasn't the worst punch she'd ever taken. Iza lurched up from the table to retaliate but the cuffs and the chain kept her in place.

"Why don't you tell me what you were really doing on Galminus, or was it the boy with you?" Desirae asked.

"How long are you going to keep us here with no proof or charges?"

"For as long as it takes to get the truth," Desirae said between her teeth.

"So this is how you want to play this?"

"I'd like to give you a break."

Iza kept her mouth clamped shut as she glared at the wall beyond Desirae.

Desirae hefted the bag up from the floor, grunting with the effort. She pushed it into place on the table between them. With slow, deliberate movements, she opened the bag in front of Iza. It was Trix. Or at least she wanted Iza to think the arm and foot belonged to Trix.

A smug smile settled on Desirae's face as if she were reading her mind when she pulled out the head. Her eyes were closed, but there was no mistaking the identity of the android. Trix's head was disconnected from the rest of her body.

Iza wanted to keep her hands steady, but they balled into fists in front of her. She was already planning what she would do once she got free.

"You've programmed her well. I didn't know you could get them to lie," Desirae said as she brushed back Trix's loose hair from her face with exaggerated tenderness.

She's not programmed. She's sentient. Iza's teeth were grinding, but she kept her eyes focused on the speck behind Desirae on the wall, refusing to give her even the satisfaction of eye contact. If Iza didn't get to Desirae first, the Lynaedans certainly would seek retribution for such a crime against one of their own.

Desirae continued when Iza refused to speak. "I suppose that's all for now. Let's get you back to a cell so you can think things over. I'm sure a night in Sarduvis is more than enough to get the truth out of someone like you. Enjoy it though, because the next one will be less comfortable."

Desirae tossed Trix's head into the black bag as the guards dragged Iza back to her cell.

I'm going to enjoy paying you back for this, Mech Neck. You're going to regret this day.

10

THE GUARDS MARCHED Iza back to her cell. Even though she was still fuming, she made a show of tripping forward near the cell where she'd spotted Braedon. He moved to the front of the cell and nodded when she made eye contact with him. He kept her in sight until she was escorted inside her cell on the opposite side. She moved to the corner and waited for the guards to move away before she spoke.

Iza noted the dried blood on his lip and the slight limp as he held his middle. They damaged his ribs again.

"Are you all right? What happened?" she asked him.

"Nothing."

"From what I can see, you got another boot to the ribcage."

He shrugged and then winced.

"You look like you've been doing pretty good for yourself otherwise," she said.

"It's the suit, right? These clothes are ridiculous."

Iza nodded. That's exactly what she thought. "Where'd you get them?"

"I told you, I'm resourceful." His too-charming smile and the dimples in his cheeks would make most girls weak in the knees, but his grin only made Iza roll her eyes.

"So, what are you doing in here?" she asked.

"It's all one big misunderstanding."

Must be going around. "What did you do?"

"Nothing, to be honest with you. I was attempting to get my property back, but the thieves who took it had already sold it. I have a friend working on a way to get me out of here, though I've got no way off Galminus afterward."

"Wish I could help you," Iza said with a smile and feigning her best bored look. She loved watching him squirm. "I'm heading to Beurias to pick up my ship as soon as we get all this straightened out."

"Oh yeah? What kind of ship are you getting, by the way? You never said what it was you put the down payment on."

"It's an H3X, and it will be mine in two days if I can get the rest of the money together."

Braedon stared back with a blank expression as if she'd said something wrong. Iza was on the verge of asking him what she'd said when she heard the guards returning with another prisoner.

When the commotion died down and the guards had left for their regular posts, Braedon continued.

"My friend on the outside will get me out," he said, "We need transportation beyond Galminus. Would you consider taking on passengers?"

"I deal in cargo, not people."

"We can pay."

"We?"

"If you'd consider taking us with you when you get your H3X, we'd be monthly renters. That would be two renters, two rooms. All we ask is to be left alone to take care of our own business—when it coincides with your own, of course. Besides that, you know I'm good for it. My hacking skills are the best."

"Lies!" Viper called out from behind her. "You're a cheat."

Iza looked between the two of them and put it together. *Of course.*

If Braedon had a way off Sarduvis, she'd be an idiot not to take it. With their money for renting two rooms in advance, she could pick up the H3X with no further delays. She'd lost the money from this job, Karter made that clear.

Braedon was trouble, but the money was too good to turn down. Besides, as much as she enjoyed having Trix for company, there were times when even she wanted the sound of something other than her dark thoughts. No one in her life stuck around for that long, anyway.

"I'll want three months upfront if you want a ride off this freighter," she stated.

"Deal."

"What about our friend, Viper, here?"

"What about her?"

"It sounds like you might have done her wrong. You should get her out, too."

"No way, why should I help her? I don't owe her anything. She still owes *me*. I won the tournament!" Braedon shouted.

Viper slammed both hands against the doors. "You're a cheater and liar! I'll prove it."

"Little girl, you have no chance of beating me today or any other day."

"How soon can you get us out of here?" Iza asked, ignoring their bickering as if it hadn't happened.

It was too far to hear him clearly, but Iza was sure he was growling and mumbling something under his breath. "Don't worry I'll do it, but only because you've been there for me," Braedon called out.

When the guards came to retrieve Braedon, he flashed them a wry one-dimpled smile before proceeding down the corridor and away from them.

"Why are you helping me?" Viper asked, her face still red from her burst of anger.

"I was a lot like you once and you shouldn't be here."

Viper's eyebrows were still drawn together in confusion, but she nodded as if she understood. "Thanks."

"You can thank me by staying out of this place in the future."

"Bet."

— — —

Joe's conversation with Agent Mandren the second time in five hours went about as well as he'd expected.

"You promised him what?"

"The man needs a vacation. I had to promise him something or he wouldn't let Braedon go. Don't tell me you're not the least bit interested as to why a Lower Dynasty family member might be roaming around gambling for money."

There was a long pause while Mandren thought about it.

"You are treading on very thin ice, Saletas. I don't have to remind you that this mission was meant to be recon with no interference. You've done too much already." There was a light sigh at the end of his words as if he were too tired to speak.

"Is there something wrong, sir?"

"You mean besides the fact that you're still hitting fellow officers and getting into more trouble than I want to hear about in a day? Yes, there's something wrong but it's nothing for you to worry about. Keep your head down, Saletas, we can't afford to have any more trouble with you."

That was the second time Mandren had hinted that there was something wrong at Headquarters. He wondered what it could be—not that he'd be close enough to help in any way, which only made him more frustrated.

"If that is all, I'll see what I can do," Mandren said.

"Yes, sir." Joe put as much respect into the words as he could muster.

After his conversation with Mandren, he went to wait for the Guard to bring Braedon to the hangar where they could catch a ride on a transport ship back to the planet's surface.

The first words out of Braedon's mouth had Joe cursing the day they'd met.

"We've got a shuttle off Sarduvis. The only catch is the crew is still locked up."

Joe took a calming breath. "What are you talking about?"

"Trust me when I say we're both going to come out ahead in this deal. I ran into an old friend—a captain with a ship—and we're getting on it. The catch is, one of the local Guard Investigators has a personal grudge."

"What does any of that have to do with me?"

Braedon rolled his eyes. "We need to get a few more people out of here and we'll be on the H3X in no time."

A few more people? He'd barely got Braedon out without being sent back to Earth. Joe looked him in the eyes, trying to find a hint of deception but there was none. He believed whatever he was saying.

"No way, you're out of your mind. You have no idea what it took to get you out of here."

"What exactly *did* it take to get us out of here? Do you still have connections to the TSS that I should know about?"

Braedon was getting too close to the truth and Joe tried to read him for any signs that he knew more, but there was nothing except curiosity behind his hazel eyes.

"I have an idea. Let's take the money we've got leftover and we'll find another ship."

"No!" Braedon's voice echoed off the empty hangar. "We can't. It's the H3X. I need to be on that ship."

"Why?"

Braedon's eyes flew to one side of the hangar and then the other as if searching for the answer. "I left something behind and I need to get it back. Besides, weren't you whining to me earlier about wanting to be on a ship and crew but no one would take you? Well, I found a ship *and* a small crew and got us on. You really should be thanking me."

"How much of *my* credits is this little adventure going to cost?"

"I promised her our three months' rent for two rooms."

"Her? And *three* months?"

Braedon continued talking, ignoring the question. "I'll be able to make mine back fast. But you'll need to spot us both for the down payment. I think she might be a little desperate for the money. That'll work in our favor. The best thing about it is with her legitimate business, we won't have any problems with local Enforcers."

"Right, thanks," Joe said letting the sarcasm drip off every word. "Tell me again, how did she end up on Sarduvis?"

"Some kind of misunderstanding."

"I've heard that before."

"I think I forgot to mention she's heart-thumping, gorgeous."

"Fantastic."

Despite his better judgment, Joe agreed to get the woman and her people out of the prison to secure a ship for himself and Braedon.

As it turned out, Major Lakonis was in such a good mood after receiving his vacation approval that Joe could have asked for a dozen inmates. The major cleared them all for immediate release as soon as they reviewed the arrest report.

There were three, including the android. It seemed the captain's story held up. She had the documents to prove she'd taken the hauling job legally and they'd wrongfully imprisoned her. However, it didn't mean she was innocent. Joe wasn't sure yet how he felt about getting on a ship with her.

Joe and Braedon waited and watched as two groups of riders came and went before the captain and her people arrived. When the blast doors opened and she came through, Joe had the gut-punched sensation again at the sight of her.

It was the same woman he'd seen dragged in earlier that day. The thick braid she wore had come loose; strands of curls now framed her face. She didn't appear to be happy about being rescued from imprisonment. The young gamer girl, Viper, was with her.

"Thanks again," Viper said to the other woman.

"You need a ride?" she asked.

"No, I've got my own way off." Viper waved to Braedon. "See you later, Little Lamb. You owe me a re-match."

Braedon leaned forward as if to go after her, but Joe held him back with a light arm across the chest.

The captain turned her attention to Joe. "So, you're his private security?" She looked him up and down.

Joe gave Braedon an exasperated look before turning back to her.

"Um, yes. We recently started working together. My name is Jovani Saletas."

He held up his hand in a respectful greeting and she complied with a nod of approval.

"Iza Sundari, and my mechanic, Trix."

He recognized Trix as an android from Lynaeda—realistic enough to pass as a flesh-and-blood person from a distance, but possessing a distant air that was slightly unnerving when he looked at her up close. She had long auburn hair and wore a yellow and blue jumpsuit common among androids, from what he'd seen about the tech-obsessed Lynaedan culture. He had to look up at Trix due to her significant height, but she didn't seem at all concerned with him or Braedon.

"Braedon says you've agreed to allow us passage on your ship," Joe said.

"Yes, for a price," Iza replied. Her eyebrows furrowed as she stared intently back at him.

Joe's face grew hotter, but he ignored it. "I thought getting you out of here would have been good enough."

Iza glared at him. "This isn't a negotiation. Either you pay us in advance or you can hitch a ride on the next public transport vehicle due in the morning."

"A simple thank you would have been enough."

Iza seemed to bristle at his words. "Thank you for speeding up a slow process, but don't be confused. It's not like you saved us. We were getting out anyway." The frown on her face deepened as she stared at him.

What did I say? "Have I offended you again?" Joe asked.

"No."

"Your endorphin levels are elevated and your pupils are dilated," Trix cut in. "You are either angry or—"

"No more physical stats in public or I'll send you back home," Iza said, raising her voice. "Where's my shuttle?"

Trix tilted her head. Joe heard the shuttle's engines fire in a far corner of the large bay, and within moments it was in front of them. Trix set the shuttle down and remotely opened the entry hatch.

Joe looked over the sad-looking shuttle with no little skepticism. It had more craters than Earth's moon and sputtered like a newborn baby.

"*This* is it?"

"The AS-225 will keep you alive in the vacuum of space. If it is unsatisfactory or not to your taste, you are welcome to find another mode of transport," Trix said in a matter-of-fact tone.

"Careful, Trix is sensitive about our shuttle. It's temporary as long as you've got the credits to pay for your passage once I get the H3X, as promised." Iza gave Braedon a raised eyebrow.

A klaxon alarm sounded as the bay doors opened to space. A thin force field was the only thing separating them from the stars outside.

Joe lowered his voice and spoke to Braedon. "Are you sure this is going to get us where we're going?"

Iza boarded the ship without looking behind her and Trix followed.

"This is going to be fun. Let's go." Braedon rubbed his hands together and leaped on board.

Joe took a deep breath and followed. *This is going to be a huge mistake.*

11

THE STRANGE INTENSITY Joe had felt around Iza the first time was even stronger within the close confines of the shuttle.

There were seats for the pilot and co-pilot and two passenger seats. Most of the shuttle was empty to leave space for cargo above the hold, which could be reached by lifting a hatch in the floor. The inside looked to be in only slightly better condition than the outside. Braedon took his position behind Iza on the right while Joe sat behind Trix on the left.

Iza glanced over her shoulder as Joe squirmed to get comfortable in the seat. He was glad for an unobstructed view of her; it was the only way to catch her stealing glances at him every once in a while, as if she sensed him. He couldn't get a solid read on her in any way, like she had a metal door around her thoughts. She wore a determined look on her face as she issued her orders and took over piloting the ship manually.

After several moments of debating within himself about how to start a normal conversation with someone, she glanced back for the third time and he took the opening. "So, where are you from?"

To his surprise, she turned in her seat to face him. "Let's get something straight. You're a passenger and not entitled to know anything about my past or my future. In exchange for your acceptable behavior, I won't dive into your past or question you about your business. Understood?"

Joe leaned back in his seat. "Yes."

"Sorry, he's from Earth," Braedon said apologetically.

"Earth? No wonder he's so weird. I don't think I've ever met anyone from there. Are the others as annoying as him?" She rolled her eyes and stood up, turning her back on him.

"I hope not." Braedon shrugged when Joe shook his head at him.

"Earth: limited technological advancement, politically divided, and one of the few inhabited planets left in the galaxy that's not part of the Taran Empire," Trix said.

"The planet's not that special." Iza waved a hand in dismissal.

Joe didn't know what he'd done to earn her wrath, but he hoped he could overcome it. He had never been any good at making friends, as Emery could attest. However, if anything happened out here, he'd be at Iza's mercy.

She raised her voice while looking down at the console. "Trix, time to Beurias?"

"Twelve hours and forty minutes."

"That's cutting it close. Do what you can to shave some time off or we'll lose the H3X. I'll be in my cot. See that I'm not disturbed." Iza glared at Joe as she passed.

Her cot was a bench hidden within the starboard side panel of the hold area, just at the edge of Joe's view from his seat. She lifted out the folded blanket and fluffed the small pillow before lying down. Iza turned her head away and pulled the light blanket up to her chin, leaving her boots uncovered. It was a matter of minutes before she was snoring lightly.

With Iza resting, it didn't take long for Braedon to lean over Trix's shoulder. "It's good to be back. There are so many other things I thought to ask you after I left before!" He dove into all manner of annoying questions. For an android, Trix seemed eager to please, answering the inquiries in turn.

"Sorry, Braedon, can I talk to you for a moment?" Joe interrupted, indicating with a hand he should lean back from Trix.

"Sure." He turned in his seat to face Joe and leaned forward expectantly.

Braedon wasn't telepathic, but they needed to speak in private. Joe tapped his temple before speaking.

"I think we might be in over our heads here. This captain seems to have her own agenda."

Braedon's expression didn't change. He seemed comfortable with hearing another's thoughts, as if he'd done it before. Joe wondered who he'd known with telepathic abilities.

"Yes, she does," Braedon agreed. He gave Iza an appreciative glance before turning back to Joe. *"So?"*

"We might want to get our story straight. I'm not able to read her. She's extremely good at blocking me, or maybe it's something else. Do you know what I mean?"

Braedon seemed confused for a moment, then the light of understanding lit his eyes. *"You think if she finds out you're TSS she'll boot you off the ship. Don't worry, I'm not going to tell her."*

"That doesn't matter because I'm not TSS, I only used to be. There's a difference, Devyn."

At the mention of the name, Braedon tensed and his eyes grew wider with surprise. Then, his eyes dropped to the ground and his shoulders fell.

"Not one that matters." Braedon shrugged. *"Look, I'll keep what I think I know about you to myself if you keep what you learned about me to yourself. If the captain doesn't trust me, I won't be free to do what I need to and get us more credits."*

"When you say that, are you talking about illegal activities?

Because I'm not so keen on them myself. Besides, I don't know anything more about you than your real name."

"*That's more than enough.*" Braedon shifted in his seat before meeting his gaze. "*I'm not going to lie to you. I take chances, that's what I do. But it's served me well in the past, and I'm sure it will benefit us both in the future.*"

Joe didn't want to think too hard about what he meant. He didn't have to guess. If he gave Braedon his way, they'd be back on Sarduvis before long.

"*Glad we had this little chat,*" Braedon said as he turned back to Trix at the helm. "I still can hardly believe you managed to cram a jump drive on this little shuttle."

"We Lynaedans are adept at modifying ships like these to suit our purposes, regardless of the inferior base product. Technology is much more central to our lives than most in the Taran Empire."

"What about the back-up life support systems?" he asked Trix.

"The shuttle is equipped with twelve hours of auxiliary life support."

Joe tuned out their conversation, instead choosing to focus on Iza's light snoring. He thought back and remembered how annoyed he'd been at the way his sister snored. Maybe Emery found Skyler's snoring adorable, too.

—   —   —

Iza strolled with purpose through the dome-shaped showroom building of Apex Manufacturing Enterprises, with Trix alongside and Braedon and Jovani trailing behind. Their reflections mirrored in Karter's upper office window overlooking the show floor.

"Wait, here." Iza made her way upstairs.

She ignored the receptionist, Becca, at her desk and strode to Karter's office doors. Out of the corner of her vision, she caught Becca sending a too-late warning to Karter using her handheld.

Iza enjoyed the surprised look on his face as Karter moved from his desk to meet her in the middle of the room.

"Stars, you're a real jerk," she said without preamble.

Karter lifted his splayed hands out at his sides. "I am. However, I hope you'll overlook it to complete our business."

Iza hesitated at his quick agreement with her before letting him direct her to a chair.

"Coffee?" he asked.

"Let's skip the chatter. You know why I'm here and what I've come for."

"Yes, I see you've completed the transfer of funds. There's nothing left but to send over your digital cert and command codes." He used his handheld to send them to her.

She didn't glance down when her handheld pinged, only stood up to leave.

"Wait." Karter caught her by the arm.

Iza stopped and made a slow turn to glare at his hand on her arm and then his face, hard enough for him to understand his mistake. He released her, keeping his open hand raised.

"I can't seem to do anything right when it comes to you. I apologize for what happened on Sarduvis, but it seems everything got cleared up."

"No, it didn't. But now I see you for who you really are."

"A businessman," he said.

"A scammer. I may be making payments on the H3X, but I'm going to make something abundantly clear. You. Don't. Own. Me."

"I'm well aware," Karter said dryly. He smiled, but it never reached his eyes. "You're absolutely right. I took advantage of your desperate situation for my own benefit. I hope you understand it's not personal."

"It's always personal," Iza said. "When I ask you for a favor, I expect to pay you back with a bunch of strings attached. Keep that in mind for when you need a favor from me." Iza whirled on her heel to leave. He didn't speak again until the doors slid open, the whoosh of air making the small leaves on the planted trees on either side rustle. "Rent is due on the twenty-eighth."

Iza didn't bother to turn around. She was still cursing him when she caught up to Trix, Braedon, and Jovani downstairs. *Let it go. He's not worth the energy.*

"Did you get it?" Braedon asked eagerly.

"I did."

Jovani nodded. "We'll meet up with you there shortly." He and Braedon headed for the exit from Apex.

"Don't be long." Iza rolled her shoulders and smiled at Trix. "Let's get my ship."

— — —

Karter watched Iza leave with a mixture of emotions. She was a complicated woman, quick to anger and lacking patience. But, stars, if she didn't curl his toes.

He watched her march across the showroom floor and meet her friends. The way she tossed her hair off her shoulder with one hand while smiling lit up the room. The young men with her obviously adored her. Iza probably didn't notice the devotion in their eyes; she seemed oblivious to that kind of attention. Of course, Karter had tried himself once, but it was clear they were incompatible. It didn't stop him from appreciating the masterpiece that was her, though.

Karter's handheld pinged and he glanced at it. Not a call he could ignore. He tore his gaze away from Iza and sent the call to the holodisplay on his desk.

The older man on the other side of the conference call was sitting uncomfortably close to the camera, blocking out his shoulders and anything else in the room.

"Hello, sir, what can I do for you today?" Karter greeted.

"You promised me five cargo ships."

"Has there been a problem with the shipment?"

"What happened to the H3X?"

"It's been sold."

"What?"

"Sir, an impounded transport vehicle like that won't sit for long. I held it for as long as I could, but the buyer was very insistent. If you're having trouble with the ships I sent you, I'd be happy to allow an exchange."

"I should have known better than to trust someone like you to deal with something of this magnitude."

"Someone like me?"

"A Lower Dynasty brat with a mother who's—"

"Careful, I'm sure you don't want to insult my mother."

The older man cleared his throat. "No, of course not."

"Sir, if I knew what you were working on, I'd be able to assist you in finding the kind of ships that would be the best fit," Karter said.

His attempt at sympathy must have come off as condescending, because the old man fumed and raised his voice an octave. "I specifically asked for the H3X, that's all you need to know. My reasons are my own."

Karter's eyes narrowed. *What is it about this particular ship?* The H3X had amazing features, but there were far better craft available. "Is there, perhaps, something on it you need that I can retrieve it for you?"

"Nice try, Karter. Enough of this banter." He waved a hand in front of him.

"As I said, the ship is sold. I promise you, though, if it is repossessed you will be my first call." Karter didn't add how likely that might be. "In the meantime, if there's anything else I can do to help, I'm at your service."

"Your mother says you're going to be busy with domestic matters soon."

Karter's jaw clenched but he kept his tone neutral. "I have no idea what you mean."

"She's an intelligent and crafty woman, your mother. I wouldn't make her angry if I were you."

Karter could feel his plastered-on smile faltering. "Stick to the things you know. Let me handle her."

The older man sat back in his seat enough to show his torso, and he folded his hands together. There was bright light filtering in through the window behind him, casting his features into silhouette.

"Then get me that H3X-Z500. Not another one, *that* one. Don't fail me again, Karter, or you'll have more to deal with than your mother's wrath." The call disconnected.

Karter let out a calming breath. *It's always something.*

His handheld pinged again and he swore, having no doubt about who it was calling. He'd already sent the last two calls from his mother to Becca. She would hardly let a third one go without some choice words designed to give him grief, so he answered.

"Hello, mother. Now's not a good time."

"Don't 'hello mother' me," she got in before he cut her off again.

"I'm in a very important meeting. I promise, I'll call you right back." He ended the call and sat down on one of his loungers. There was just too much at stake, and that H3X seemed to be at the center of it all. He signaled Becca to bring him a drink.

His eyes were closed when the doors opened.

"That was fast," he said opening his eyes. That's when he saw his mother sweep into the room.

Her black feathered hat and the cloak wrapped around her shoulders fluttered as she walked in. She stared down at him. "You're a disgrace, Karter. You can't keep neglecting your duties. We just don't have the luxury."

Karter sat up in his seat, struggling to hide his shock that she'd actually left the Hyttinen estate for something other than an exclusive gala.

She sat down in front of him and crossed one leg over the other, bouncing her heel with impatience. "I'm sorry, am I interrupting? I thought we were discussing your very precarious future. Would you like to put me on hold again?" She rolled her eyes with exasperation.

Then, she turned her full attention on him. Her face was pinched in annoyance and her nostrils were already flared. To come to his business, she must have been angry from the start. This wasn't going to go well. He had enough to do without worrying about what Taran high society thought of them.

"No, Mother, I'm sorry, go ahead. I think you were about to remind me of my very serious duty of marrying to secure the family name and fortune."

"Don't you dare mock me. Who do you think put you in the luxurious lifestyle you're currently enjoying? Do you think you'll be able to give the same to your children?"

At his silence, she huffed. The breath of air rippled the meticulously combed hair she let hang over her large forehead. "Exactly. You don't *have* any children, and it seems our family line is going to end with you. What a pitiful shame. I had such high hopes for both of you boys when you were young. If your father were here…"

"Stars, what do you want me to do, just marry the next girl

that comes my way?"

"Don't use that gutter language with me. Gifted abilities are re-emerging. Would you deny your children of the privilege just because you're not inclined to marry? You have a real chance to improve our family's standing. Your disinterest is infuriating."

"I'm sorry, but your tactical approach to marriage did nothing for your own life, or my father's. I refuse to be a puppet to serve the whims of this family."

"Don't you dare speak of your father in such a way! Besides, there are plenty of nice girls out there—your second cousin, Desirae, has shown interest. You could do a lot worse."

"You only say that because you don't know her. She's as rigid as a board, and I wouldn't subject our line to the kind of crazy she'd be bringing to it."

"Enough! Find a partner or I'll find one for you."

Her tone was calm, but his mother didn't bluff, which could only mean she was ready to make good on her word. She would prefer to make him uncomfortable rather than risk embarrassment. There were few people more determined than a woman who'd lost a husband and a son scrambling to maintain her delicate position of relevance.

She was still mumbling something about 'plenty of young girls ready and available', but Karter tuned her out while he waited for her to gain control again.

Becca slipped into his office, and he held up a finger to keep her from approaching.

He stood up from his seat. It was the universal signal that their business was concluded, but his mother ignored it and stared up at him as if he'd just had some kind of seizure. "Sorry, Mother, I have some business to attend to. I'll be sure to contact you soon."

He waited for her to rise. She took her time on purpose.

"Well, I'm sure I've never felt so unwelcome. You'll be by for dinner tomorrow night?"

He sighed. "Of course, Mother."

"I've invited guests, so don't be late."

Karter couldn't muster another fake smile for his mother and nodded. He'd no doubt be in for another night of small talk with his mother's current lineup of favorite marriage prospects.

"The cook is preparing your favorite. I'll see you then."

She leaned her face out for him to kiss her cheek. He did so knowing she'd stand there until he did, no matter how long it took. Though she hadn't known his favorite meal since he was ten, he didn't correct her assumptions.

She swept her cloak tight around her shoulders and glided out of the room. Becca was careful to stay out of the older woman's way and kept her head bowed as she passed.

"Sir?" Becca asked when he didn't immediately speak. She held out the drink for him that he'd requested before his mother's unexpected visit.

He took it. "Thank you." He wearily met her eyes. "Becca, I want you to do a little digging for me. Make it your daily priority. Understand?"

"Yes, sir. What can I do for you?"

"In addition to Iza, I want you to look into her passengers, Braedon Valtteri and Jovani Saletas—and even the android, Trix. Who are they and where do they come from? Everything."

Becca nodded before retreating from the room, leaving Karter alone with his thoughts.

When it came to his situation, the sooner he had something he could use, the better. His mother's threats had been toothless in the past, but she wasn't powerless. Should she choose to meddle in his affairs, she could make his business dealings more difficult for him. Better to have another plan in place before things got out of hand.

—   —   —

Trix followed Iza on board the H3X, taking in the interior for the first time. "An H3X-Z500, not the most sophisticated of machines, but I believe I'll be able to sync with the control system," Trix said.

Iza smiled at her friend. "Good. Get the shuttle docked as soon as your integration with the H3X is complete."

Trix nodded her assent and Iza headed toward the flight deck. When she passed by the captain's cabin, she stopped to peer inside. She couldn't wait to have a proper bed again and real privacy—especially with that Jovani around. *What's with him, anyway?*

Every time she turned around, he was there, staring at her like he'd never seen a woman before. He made an excellent security guard. His dark, brooding eyes would intimidate most people but she wasn't afraid of him. There was something else, though, that didn't sit right when he was around.

She'd known physical attraction. There were several boys she'd run around with that got her pulse racing and kept her from thinking straight. This wasn't that. Her skin was almost on fire when Jovani stared at her. It was like he was peeling back the layers of her soul every time they were together. After the first encounter, she thought it would ease up, but it only seemed to get worse the more they were together.

What's he doing to me?

Iza looked down at her handheld and saw a ping for a job come through. Braedon and Jovani hadn't returned from whatever business they were up to yet.

She made her way to the flight deck and tried to reach

Braedon. He didn't answer, so she left a message. "You two better hurry. I've got a job to do so we need to pull out of Apex ASAP." She sighed. *What's taking them so long?*

Trix came onto the flight deck. "Braedon and Jovani are on their way. There was a hiccup," she announced.

"What kind of hiccup?"

Trix tilted her head to one side. "The kind that requires us to wait for them."

Iza rolled her eyes. "Fine, I'll be acquainting myself with the ship. Let me know the minute they're on board."

Iza roamed to the cargo hold, imagining all the places they could keep their hauls. There were so many compartments within compartments, she found herself lost in discovering them all.

Eventually, she found herself well beneath the stairs leading to the flight deck, and she wondered why anyone would use such a hard-to-reach location. Well, a normal person—such a compartment was a smuggler's dream.

Having a hunch that there might be a hidden hidey-hole, she reached inside and felt along the back wall. Sure enough, the panel slid to the side. *Ah ha!*

The spring mechanism seemed to stay in place for the moment before gently closing without a sound. When she was sure she wouldn't lose her fingers, she reached inside to feel how much space there was to work with in the hidden hole.

To her surprise, an object brushed against her hand. It was hard but warm. She found its edges and pulled it out: a small wooden box. It was etched with an intricate design and seemed to hum as she held it in her palms.

Not sure if she was imagining the sound, she lifted it to her ear. *Nope. Maybe I'm losing it.* The fact that the hum was inside of her and not coming from the box didn't concern her in the way she would have expected. It wasn't loud or intrusive, but more like a resonance.

She turned the box over, and there was a satisfying *thunk* of an object sliding around inside—something heavier than a piece of jewelry, possibly made of metal. She inspected the box, looking for a latch or opening. After repeated attempts to twist, tug, poke, and finally hit the box against the side of the metal compartment, it still didn't budge.

Well, aren't you a little mystery?

—

At Trix's signal, Iza came down the stairs from the upper deck to the cargo hold to meet her passengers.

"I told you so, isn't she beautiful?" Braedon's voice echoed in the cargo bay as he boarded with Jovani. "This isn't even half of it. All of these areas can hold cargo, too. Look at all the space."

"Where have you two been?" Iza demanded.

They looked from one to the other then back to her before Braedon spoke. "I believe the rules state that we don't ask about your business in exchange for privacy," he repeated her own words back to her.

Iza nodded. He had a point, but she had work, which meant they needed to move. "Fine, but for future reference, use your handhelds to let someone know to wait for you. Otherwise, I'm leaving when I get work. I can't afford to be late."

Jovani was looking at her again in that way that made her think about the hum in her jacket pocket. It was annoying, so she slowed down and spoke louder for his benefit.

"We've picked up a job. We could leave you here to complete your business if you prefer?"

"Where is it?" Braedon asked, ignoring her tone.

"We're headed to Hubyria, a little mining planet."

"I've heard of it. They supply the materials needed to make the ships here on Beurias," Jovani said.

"You didn't answer my question." She looked at Jovani and then Braedon.

"That'll work for us," Braedon said with a shrug. Jovani nodded his agreement.

"Trix," Iza said into the communications system, "plot a course and get us out of here."

"Yes, Captain."

I like the sound of that.

IZA WAS DREAMING. She knew she was because nothing made sense.

In the first place, she was hand-in-hand with Jovani. In the dream world, it felt right and good and she was smiling like a fool; he was, too. She was wearing a dress and walking uphill without a sweat. The planet was unfamiliar but far too bright and too lush to be one of the outer colonies. The desire to look down at her feet was strong, but something cool on her back made her turn around instead.

A massive ship was blocking the sun in the clear sky, casting a shadow that crawled along the ground and covered her and Jovani. She felt the tug of Jovani's hand in hers as he pulled her upward, but Iza couldn't stop staring up at the ship. It was larger than any freighter she'd ever seen up close. Sarduvis wouldn't come close. It seemed so foreign that she wondered if Tarans were inside or someone—something—else.

By the time she turned back to Jovani, he was screaming, except she couldn't hear the words over the humming. He tried pulling her forward, but the ground shook below them and her hand slipped out of his. Jovani's panicked eyes were the last thing she saw as he reached for her. To her horror, he slipped off the side of the mountain and into the black that swallowed him below.

The pain of the moment ripped through her chest and she couldn't breathe as the world began to spin out of control. Then, it wasn't her dream anymore but the room itself spinning. She must have been screaming out loud because her throat felt raw and dry.

Everything in the room other than her bed had been turned over. The items from her shelf, including the box that she'd found in the cargo hold, were strewn across the floor. With another lurch of the ship, the objects jumped and scattered. She'd have to find a better way to display her things if this was going to be a regular occurrence.

Her heart pounded in her ears. *What in the stars is going on?*

She managed to crawl to the door and release the manual controls. Her cabin, opposite the infirmary, was closest to the front of the ship. Holding her arms outstretched to each side, she stumbled down the main corridor to the flight deck.

Just as the door to the flight deck slid open for her, the H3X jolted back and forth as the ship took a nosedive toward the surface of a planet—Hubyria, from the look of the dark rock and barren landscape.

Jovani was in one of the back seats working at a control station along the side bulkhead, and Trix was lying in the middle of the floor.

"Trix!" Iza shouted to her, but the android was unresponsive. She staggered onto the flight deck. "What happened?"

"I don't know," Jovani replied. "Nothing is responding." His fingers tapped uselessly over the controls, then he dove under another console and started pulling things.

"What are you doing?" Iza snapped.

"I'm trying to re-activate the manual stabilizers."

"What happened to Trix?"

"No idea. At the moment, I'm a little busy trying to keep us from crashing into the ground. I haven't got time to fix your android, too," he growled.

Iza ignored his flash of temper as she was still clinging to the seat in front of her to counter the effects of the ship spinning out of control. She worked her way to the captain's seat and strapped into the flight harness.

After a minute that felt like an eternity, the ship stopped spinning. However, it was still dropping fast.

Iza tugged at the unresponsive controls. "We're going to crash."

"It all depends on how you look at it," Jovani said.

"I look at it like a giant hunk of metal plummeting to the ground!"

Jovani didn't answer her this time; he was too focused on the horrific sight out the viewport of the planet's landscape rushing toward them. Sweat glistened on his brow.

Iza felt the noticeable deceleration as the nose of the ship was pulled up by an invisible force.

The ship rocked and bounced as it grazed the top of a mountain in the range she'd seen a second earlier, then the hard impact with solid ground sent everyone flying. Iza's harness held her back from slamming through the front viewport, digging into her shoulders and hips.

The H3X peeled up dirt until at last it came to a stop, hitting a clump of rocks with a loud crunch.

Iza slumped back in her seat, testing her arms and legs for any serious injuries. All she could see out the viewport was pure black rock.

"What just happened to my ship?" Her hands shook,

though she wasn't sure if it was more from fear or anger.

Jovani stood up to face her. There was a hint of sympathy in his expression Iza didn't expect. He raced forward and lifted her chin with two fingers, turning her head from one side to the other.

"You're hurt," he said, his voice filled with tenderness.

"I'm fine." Iza lifted a hand to pull his away, but there was a buzzing in her ears that made it hard to think when he was this close. Instead, her hand lingered on top of his as he spoke.

"I think we were hit with an EMP," he said. "It's affected all of our electrical systems and probably the android. We're going to need our electrical systems back just to assess all the damage."

Iza's hand dropped away as she pulled away from him. As her eyes dropped down, she realized she was still in her bedclothes.

This couldn't have happened at a worse time. She was on a tight schedule and this not only meant they would have trouble getting to their supplies, but they'd also have to repair the ship and Trix.

Iza unbuckled the flight harness and rolled her shoulders as she rose unsteadily to her feet. She started toward the exit.

"Hey, where are you going?" Jovani asked. His hand was outstretched as if he meant to touch her but her glare stopped him.

"We're dead here. I need to know who shot us out of the sky and why. Plus, I'm getting a headache that's going to make me want to throw up. Would you like to sit around chatting about what's wrong, or do I have your permission to leave my ship and go find help?"

Jovani took a step back.

Good, he won't make that mistake again.

"That might not be a good idea considering that whoever

shot us down might want the ship," he said.

"No one wants a dead ship; it would be far too much work and time to strip it. Besides, we don't have anything on board anyone would want."

He took a deep breath and calmed. "What can we do to help?"

That got her attention. But she shook her head. It was her ship and her problem. She couldn't expect the passengers to help every time she was in trouble. Iza was about to say 'no' to his offer when Braedon appeared behind her.

"What's going on? Why is Trix lying in the middle of the floor?"

"We were hit with some kind of EMP. We're not sure yet who fired," Jovani said, filling him in before Iza had a chance to say anything.

"Do you want me to go for help? I've been on this little backward rock before. Horrible atmosphere, but they've got some darling little shops in their towns. Remind me to tell the story about the young waitress at a place called The Raven. Her father owned the place and made the best meat stew I've ever had. Many of the miners went there for dinners when their days went long. Everyone here is pretty laid back. They could have information on what's going on out here. Since they mine the stuff your ship and our weapons are made of, there might be someone who can get us fixed up."

"I don't think it works like that," Iza replied. "Almost no raw materials are processed where they're mined."

"Even so, we—"

She held up a hand to stop his excited chattering and looked from one to the other. It seemed they were going to get in her way no matter what, so the least she could do was take advantage of the help.

"Fine." Iza turned on her heel. "But I need to get dressed

first."

—

The others were waiting for her in the cargo bay and followed her out into the cool night air.

"You're more than telepathic," she said to Jovani as they walked over the uneven terrain.

He shrugged and she thought she glimpsed a bit of pink on his ears in the moonlight.

"You saved the ship, and though I don't know what your real agenda here is, I appreciate it."

"Jovani's my security. Saving people is his thing," Braedon explained. "It's probably a personality quirk left over from his former days as a TSS Agent."

Ahh, there it is. He's former TSS. That explained the serious guard-like walk and talk he had. She wondered why he left the TSS. Maybe he'd been forced to leave like Desirae; they'd sent her home after the first year. This guy, though, had all the markings of a fully trained guard without the cred.

"We flew over a small settlement a little way back. With the shuttle and the ship down, we're going to have to walk it. Stay close. I'm not sure what we're going to run into out there."

"Hubyria isn't known for its wildlife. If you haven't noticed, not a lot grows here," Braedon said with his arms outstretched.

"I had noticed, but thanks for the insight. I was thinking more along the lines of pirates, thieves, and kidnappers."

Braedon seemed to sober at the thought, then he continued with his incessant chatter. "The minerals here are what they use for the ships and transports all over the Taran colonies. Is that the job you took on, hauling the raw materials? That's backbreaking work. You're going to need a crew for that. Good thing you have us."

Iza didn't answer, though he wasn't wrong. A crew was what she needed and passengers are what she got. She was used to getting by with what she had.

"To tell you the truth, it's probably the best place in the quadrant for a ship to crash. It's definitely a good thing," he said.

Iza stopped to give him a look like thrown daggers at him.

"I didn't mean it was good that we *crashed*—only that we'll have access to all the material we'll need to repair the ship. There might even be mechanics who know what they're doing."

"This isn't a repair dock. It's a mining colony. All the materials here are raw. There's very little chance that they're going to have any of the parts I need for the H3X. Besides, I have a mechanic."

Braedon took a breath then spoke up again. Iza was grinding her teeth before he finished his thought.

"An H3X is the model name, what are you calling the ship?"

"I don't know, and I haven't really thought about it," Iza said, not bothering to hide her superior tone.

"No good can come from flying a ship with no name."

"I don't believe in that superstitious nonsense."

"Did you ever name your shuttle?"

"No."

"Well, not to point out the obvious, but your ship and shuttle seem to have a bit of trouble staying in the air. It could be because you haven't named them."

"Then there's Trix," Jovani chimed in, sharing a knowing look with Braedon.

"What about her?"

"She's a lot less animated than most of her kind. She's like a robot."

"She's not a robot and take care to remember that. She's a sentient and complex individual." Iza couldn't help the rise in her voice as she defended her friend. "She had to make choices in her behavior to suit her original circumstances, so leave her alone."

Both of them raised their hands in unison.

"No offense, but if you want me to tweak her personality programming a bit, I might be able to do something for her."

Iza stopped short and stabbed a finger into his chest. "Don't even think about it."

She marched on with purpose, ignoring Braedon; he talked far too much for her taste. If Jovani stared less, he'd be almost perfect company. While he spoke up, it was only when he had something worth saying. She wondered if he'd learned that assertiveness from the TSS.

The dark gray and black ridges of the mountains seemed endless, broken up only by patches of lichen and similarly low-profile plant-life. It was no wonder this planet was mostly used for its rock. It was everywhere. She knew from previous study that Hubyria's system only had one dwarf star and it didn't stay up in the sky for very long. Fortunately, the reflection off the large moon gave them plenty of light to walk by.

"There, I see smoke. That must be a town," Braedon clapped his hands together and rubbed them.

The smoke he'd pointed out was still a ways off, but they'd probably make it within the hour.

"We should stop at the pub, assuming they have one," he added. "It might be a nice little spot to find warm food and unlimited drinks."

The chill in the air started to get to all of them, and Iza soon found herself rubbing her hands down the front of her pants for warmth. The thought of warm food made her stomach growl, but to her relief, their hike over the rocky terrain masked the sound.

The temperature on Hubyria swung thirty degrees in difference between night and day. Compared to the other planets they'd been to recently, it was at least ten degrees cooler. Iza kept her coat zipped, which had the added benefit of keeping both her handheld and pulse-gun out of view.

It was strange that there were no signs of life—no trees, no grass. Not even an insect. She'd lived on a backward planet herself, but this one would have been much worse. She touched the chain at her neck as she thought about her parents. It seemed there would have been worse places to have been left behind.

Angry voices sounded on the other side of the ridge. Iza and the others slowed their pace, and Iza's hand instinctively gravitated toward her pulse gun. She led them over the ridge to the back of a rock face. The voices were closer.

"Stay down," she whispered before slowly creeping out from behind the rock face.

Up ahead was a dilapidated settlement, where a large bonfire was burning in the center of a group of fifty people. Iza couldn't make out what they were saying. Before she could take another step closer to investigate, Jovani's hand reached out across the front of her body to prevent her from moving forward.

"We better find a way around all of this," he advised.

She scowled at his hand. "I need to find out who took down my ship and where I can get help."

"I believe we already have our answer." Jovani pointed toward the crowd.

Iza scanned the group to find what he meant. Then, her eyes caught the metal glint of a large EMP cannon. It was surrounded by people holding all manner of weapons, large and small. They were chanting something, their fists raised in the air but she couldn't make it out. She gaped at Jovani, unsure how to proceed. "Can you tell what's going on from here?"

He squinted at the crowd gathered. "They're shouting something about 'miners matter'."

"Sounds like the workers are on strike," Braedon said.

And they're shooting down ships in protest? Iza frowned. "Maybe we should go back. We're not going to get any help out here tonight—especially not from the people who shot us down."

"Let's go into the town and find a pub where we can ask questions without drawing too much attention," Braedon urged. He brushed a hand through the waves of his golden hair made black by the lack of light.

"You go ahead, I'm not finished here yet." Iza resumed moving toward the group of people gathered around the fire. If she handled it right, she figured she might get some answers out of some willing miner over drinks.

Jovani and Braedon were arguing about something behind her, but she tuned them out while she tried to make out the other conversations. As she got closer, she noticed an illuminated structure that could be a pub, standing alongside several other structures of varying sizes and states of repair. The windows in most buildings were already darkened; most of the shop owners it seemed had gone home for the night.

A shout broke through the cool night. "Hey, it's the TSS! Get him!"

Iza turned in time to see the crowd around the fire rushing toward Jovani. She was already too far away to reach him before they descended.

To his credit, Jovani didn't run or reach for his weapon. They had him surrounded in seconds, and all Iza could do was watch.

Braedon was nowhere to be seen. *Did he run back to the*

ship? Iza could only hope Braedon had gotten away safely as she watched the crowd engulf Jovani, dragging him away from the fire and toward one of the lit buildings beyond.

I don't have time for any of this. This was the reason she didn't like taking on passengers; normal cargo didn't wander off and get nabbed by the locals. The clock was running on this haul and she needed the money to make her ship rental payment on time.

Can nothing go according to plan today? Maybe Braedon was right about needing to name the ship. At the very least, it couldn't hurt.

13

IZA SKIRTED THE edge of the settlement, trying to blend in with the people still warming themselves on the fire. Thankfully, her clothing and style meant she couldn't be mistaken for a TSS Agent like Jovani. *Does he have to continue to wear such dark colors all the time? He's going to get us all killed.*

Most of the mob had gone into the building after him, leaving only a few malcontents standing around. She passed close enough to hear their conversation.

"Serves them right. TalEx sending people here to haul away our goods and leave us with a quarter of the profits… They've been getting away with it for too long."

Something was going on here and they'd just crash-landed in the middle of it. The miners were taking down the ships, just as Jovani said. But hers hadn't been the first. Perhaps there was even another crew stranded there ahead of her.

Interesting coincidence? Doubtful.

Hauling the cargo was going to be hard enough without a working ship, but maybe she could convince the miners to work with her. It was a longshot, especially since they were holding Jovani. She debated about leaving him, but it just didn't sit well with her. She'd come to an agreement with

Braedon and she wasn't going to go back on her word. Not to mention, if something happened to him because of her, it might keep her up at night. She was losing enough sleep as it was.

She pressed on toward the buildings at the center of the settlement, walking down the main street between the aged, prefab buildings. An antique shop with the lights on seemed like a promising place to start. It boasted rare gems and jewelry made from the durable raw material mined on the planet. The café next door would require a purchase to get any information, but the jewelers might be more willing to engage in small talk.

As she walked into the shop, a motion monitor signaled her entry.

"Be right with you!" The shop owner sounded like an older woman.

Iza did her best to look interested in the many kinds of rocks on display, though they all looked the same to her.

After a minute, a woman came out from the back wearing a green smock over a striped shirt and pants that were rolled twice from the bottom in large cuffs, which still rested almost to the floor over her black boots. "What can I do for you?"

"I've just arrived, and I was hoping to get some information."

The woman tossed her head and sniffed. "We close in five minutes." She twisted her silver hair into a bun and secured it with four polished wooden sticks, then turned away to return to the back room.

Iza made to follow her. "Look, it's been a really bad day and I'm short on time. The miners outside appear to be dropping ships like flies. Do you know why?"

The woman gave her a slow once over before shaking her head. "I don't know anything."

"That's not true," Iza said.

"What are you, some kind of telepath?"

Iza let out a laugh. How many times had she wished for that little gift? "No, simple observation. You're the last one open on a street where everyone else has closed up early. I bet you're the first to open your door in the morning, too."

She gave an agreeable nod but kept her lips pursed in disapproval.

"You've been here longer than anyone else, and I suspect you know exactly what's going on here."

The woman shrugged. "TalEx Corporation wants to lay off half the miners on Hubyria."

"Half? That's a big number. Why would they do that?"

"Why does the Talsari Dynasty do anything? They're looking out for themselves—never mind the people here who need the work and food to feed their families."

Iza knew from experience that the High Dynasties tended to operate in their own interests, despite the recent political rumblings about the core services that their corporations provided being so fundamental that they should be regarded as public services rather than private businesses. The DGE contract under which she received her ship was Dainetris' contribution, and Sietinen had reduced SiNavTech's usage fees for the navigation beacon network. But just like her experience with Karter at Apex twisting DGE's intentions, or Talandis Textiles going rogue with the Baellas shipments, this didn't always go as intended. The decrees filed on the capital planet of Tararia, where the High Dynasties had their seat of power, were often twisted into unrecognizable actions by the time the implementation reached the outer colonies.

"What does TalEx hope to accomplish?" Iza asked the old woman, hoping for a local perspective.

She sniffed. "I shouldn't be telling you anything. You

probably came here to pick up rocks for TalEx and got shot down. Now you're looking for your friends to see if you can still collect, make your money, and leave Hubyria and her problems behind."

Iza didn't disagree with the woman's assessment of the situation.

"My name is Iza Sundari." She gave the older woman a slight bow

The older woman giggled as if she were tickled. Then composed herself. "Just Aeva Brandis, no need to show off here."

"I mean no disrespect, Miss Aeva. What is it your people need? Maybe I can help."

"What we need and what they want are two different things. You can't help, and probably don't know the first thing about being hungry."

"Actually, I do. Grew up on a rock with a lot of hardworking people like this one." She gave Aeva a few moments to let that sink in. "Let's start with what's going on in that building where all the miners rushed in after they grabbed that TSS Agent." Iza kept her eyes intent on the woman as she casually leaned against the edge of the counter.

"Oh, that's Yeaga's place. She's leading the miners in this crazy strike against TalEx. They think they're going to keep everyone's jobs and get more money by making noise and drawing in the TSS. Idiots." Aeva spit on the concrete floor in disgust.

"You disagree with the tactic?"

"I've been around a long time. I've never seen violence solve a problem between an employer and his employees." The woman gave Iza's sidearm under her jacket a significant look of disdain.

She has a right to her opinion and I have a right to mine. Iza

shifted so her jacket hid the bulk of the gun. She needed to
know if there was a chance she could still come out of this
whole thing with the haul and get her money.

"Everyone's working for someone, unless you're High
Dynasty." Iza opened her arms, holding open her empty hands.
"I'm nothing more than someone with a boss, just like
everyone else. If I don't handle my business, I'll end up working
off my debt, which gains interest and more debt each month.
There's a benefit to people like us helping each other."

The woman continued to fuss over cleaning her display
case and straightening her wares. Then, she stopped and
sighed. "Once you get to my age, you'll understand that there's
no way for people like us to get ahead."

"Then forgive my youthful optimism that there's still a
chance for me," Iza said. "My ship went down not too far from
here. I'm supposed to collect my haul and leave, and that's what
I hope to do."

"You're not the only one."

"You mean, there are other ships stranded down here?"

Aeva shrugged with one shoulder. "Anyone who's not a
local has probably gone to the mines to collect whatever the
miners left behind when they halted work and started their
rebellion. Problem is, there are so many mines, it's hard to
know which one has enough stuff to make a worthwhile haul.
Last I heard, there was a ship that crashed to the south of town,
and they've been combing the area looking for the rock they
were supposed to pick up. Though, I don't know what they'd
do with it, since their ship is grounded." Something in the old
woman's tone hinted that the other cargo ship's crew was on a
futile hunt.

"But the mine they're looking for isn't around there, is it?"
Iza asked. *Rocks are rocks. As long as I pick up what the shipping
manifest called for, it doesn't matter which mine they come*

from.

She held her breath and waited while Aeva lifted a basket of jewel-toned rings so she could dust underneath.

"No, it's not." Aeva had a twinkle in her eye.

"Just point me in the right direction," Iza said, wishing she hadn't sounded so eager.

Aeva didn't seem to notice. "Over the third ridge to the west, there's an old cavern where they were mining before they dropped everything to join Yeaga's cause. If you hurry, you'll get there before anyone notices. But better make sure you've got a way out of here or the miners and the other cargo haulers will come after you."

"That's not far from where we crashed. One other thing, what can you tell me about Yeaga?"

Aeva rolled her eyes. "Don't cross her."

"She's holding a friend of mine."

Aeva nodded slowly as if putting the pieces together. "The TSS Agent—I heard them shouting in the streets right before you came in. You're in more trouble then you know. He won't be going anywhere unless Yeaga wants him to."

While not the best news, Iza suspected her passenger wasn't in immediate danger. *These people couldn't possibly hold an Agent if he wanted to break free, but I don't see Jovani fighting his way out if there's another solution.*

Iza nodded to the old shopkeeper. "Thanks for the tips. I hope the people of your town are able to get what they're owed by TalEx." She turned to leave.

Aeva spoke up. "Despite their methods, I do understand what they're trying to do."

"Can I trust Yeaga?"

Aeva gave her a measured look and shook her head as she answered. "No."

—

Iza wasn't sure why, but she trusted the old antiques dealer and made a mental note to remember her when things settled down on Hubyria.

As she exited the shop, she caught a glimpse of Braedon creeping in the shadows between two of the buildings a block down the street. She'd have to grab him before he was snatched up, too.

Sneaking up on Braedon wasn't difficult. When Iza brushed his shoulder with her hand, he let out a sound that could only be tied between a squeak and a snort.

Iza's hand flew to his mouth. "It's me," she whispered in his ear

He relaxed. "Stars! Did you see what happened? I was about to—"

Iza held up her hand to head off what was no doubt going to be a novel-length explanation for why he was skulking around. "Let's get back to the ship and we'll discuss it there."

"What about Jovani? We can't just leave him."

"We're *not* leaving him, but I'm also not rescuing him with only you for backup. No offense."

"None taken."

While Braedon followed her back to the ship, he filled the night silence was nonstop talking. "I told Jovani he looked too much like an active TSS Agent. He needs to listen to me. I'm doing my best to keep him out of trouble, but he's got to meet me halfway. This whole thing was a bad idea. We should've gone back to the ship when I said so."

"If we'd gone back to the ship when you suggested it, then we wouldn't have a lead on where to pick up cargo or a way off of this planet."

"You did all that in the time we were apart?"

"Yes, and what exactly did *you* accomplish?"

Braedon stayed quiet for almost a whole minute.

That's what I thought. Iza continued, "I also found out a bit about the woman that's leading the miner's rebellion. Her name is Yeaga, and if my source is to be believed, she won't like that we're planning to complete the hauling job we were hired to do."

"How are you going to get Jovani back?"

"One thing at a time."

There were lights on when they reached the ship, which they'd left darkened.

Stars, what now? Iza pulled out her pulse gun.

Braedon had been about to say something, but she shook her head for him to stay quiet. He kept behind her as they crept on board the ship. Iza looked around, trying to decide where to search for the intruders first. Both Iza and Braedon jumped as Trix stepped out from behind a partition.

"Welcome back," the android greeted.

Iza smiled at her friend while Braedon caught his breath from the surprise.

"You're working again!" Iza walked around Trix in a quick circle to check her for damage. Her self-repairing skin had already recovered from the bangs sustained during the rough crash.

"Yes, my backup system is designed to compensate for an EMP and—"

"We have bigger issues and I need your help," Iza cut in. "We need to repair the ship as quickly as possible. I've got a lead on where we can pick up materials to complete our haul, and I may be able to get some spare parts together if we're smart about it. How's it going here?"

"The output from the PEM is currently at twenty percent, due to damaged relays; to repair the system, we would need three Y72 capacitors. The front hull of the ship has been damaged but the consoles are intact. We will also need a new intermix regulator for the ion reactor in order to sustain life support. I suggest we return to Beurias for more extensive repairs."

Iza checked off the issues in her head as Trix listed them. With the PEM only operating at a fraction of its capacity, the ship was without its jump drive or subspace communications, even if they could get if off the ground. They could head out sub-light speeds using what power they could draw from the PEM and the backup ion reactor for life support, but it would take forever to make it to Beurias without the jump drive.

"I take it we have no spare parts on board?"

"No, you said we would get stocked for emergencies after we got paid."

That sounds like something I'd say. Even though she already knew the answer, Iza had to ask. "What are the chances we'll be able to jump the ship in its current condition?"

Trix seemed to be doing the actual calculations. "There is a one in nine-hundred-nine-nine billion, nine-hundred-nine-nine million, nine hundred ninety-nine thousand, nine hundred-ninety-four percent chance that we will be able to fly the H3X without the parts needed."

"Why can't you just say one in a trillion?" Iza asked throwing up her hands and letting them fall against her thighs.

"You asked me what were the chances. I'm confused by your frustration."

"Again, I can give her a little more personality, if you'd like." Braedon cracked his knuckles as if preparing to get to work.

Iza waved a hand at him. "Nevermind. If you've done all you can here for now, I need you to haul our cargo back here and secure it in the hold. Braedon and I will get the parts we need for the ship. When that is complete, I'm going to need you to put some explosives together for me."

"I must remind you, we do not have extra components to make anything that will do much damage," Trix replied.

"It doesn't need to. Just make me as many things that go boom as you can with what we've got. There's a cavern beyond the third ridge to the west of the town. There should be a rock shipment prepped and ready inside, which will hopefully be enough to fulfill our hauling contract. Grab as much as you can get back to the ship."

"Yes, Captain," Trix acknowledged.

"Where are we going?" Braedon asked.

"You and I are going to see if we can make some new friends."

14

"HOW FAR IS IT?"

Iza was unable to suppress her eye-roll at Braedon's question this time. "I don't know, and since you've asked me twice in the last thirty minutes, I suggest you stop or you can turn back and I'll go on my own."

The journey south over the rocky hills in the dark was becoming second-nature to Iza, though Braedon was doing his best to get on her nerves. He fell quiet again for just long enough for her to think. How was she supposed to convince the crew of the other cargo ship to give her the parts she needed?

They moved along the southern ridge of foothills where the woman said the other ship's crew had gone in search of the mine. Trix said the capacitors and intermix regulator were relatively universal parts and were fairly unassuming pieces of equipment, despite their critical importance to the engine system. She thanked the stars that at least one of the power distribution cells hadn't blown, which would have left the PEM completely inoperable. While twenty percent output wouldn't allow them to jump, at least the ship would still be able to take off.

The other cargo ship would no doubt view her as the competition, making it unlikely they'd be willing to sell her their spare parts. Iza didn't expect anything from them; that was the best way going into any negotiation situation in which she had no leverage.

Braedon must have been thinking along the same lines when he spoke up, just as the silence was becoming comfortable. "What do we know about these people, anyway?"

"Nothing much. They're a hauling crew Yeaga and her people brought down with their EMP cannon before us. They've been looking around here for the shipment, but according to the person I talked to in town, there's nothing around here. I just sent Trix to get the materials to the west."

"Sounds like they might not be in a good mood."

"Yeah, maybe not, but we don't have the luxury of waiting around for their mood to improve."

Braedon's face drew together with confusion. "Hey, are we anywhere near where you were supposed to land for the pickup you were hired to do?"

"Yeah, the cannon shot us down when we were coming in for the landing. Why?"

"Well, if your contact said there's only one place around here with a shipment ready for pickup—"

Iza's heart skipped a beat. "Either there's a lot of material there, or two ships were hired for the same job," she completed for him." *Stars, why didn't that occur to me before?*

"It's probably nothing to worry about," Braedon said. "A mining colony like this must have freighters in and out of here constantly."

Iza looked up at the empty sky. "I haven't seen any signs of activity since we crashed." Her chest tightened. "I think we may have been set up."

"Telling you, you really need to name your ship. It's bad

luck," Braedon muttered.

She ignored him. "We need to focus on getting the ship running again if we're going to get Jovani out. Unless he rescues himself first, which a former TSS Agent shouldn't have any trouble doing."

"I dunno, there were a lot of people that swooped in to lock him up."

While Iza didn't doubt he *could* free himself, it was unlikely he'd be able to do so alone without it potentially turning into a bloodbath, which she imagined he'd want to avoid. "We'll figure out something."

"Maybe this cargo ship crew would help us get him."

"No," Iza said quickly to shut down the idea. "The last thing we want is for them to know we've already had a run-in with the locals. Least of all that we're carrying a passenger that looks and acts a lot like a TSS Agent."

"He said he was kicked out."

"Is that what he told you?"

"You don't believe him?"

"All I know is he got himself and the rest of us, including Viper, out of Sarduvis in less time than it takes to wink and smile. I don't know what I believe about him just yet."

"Good point."

The scent of campfires and cooked food wafted from beyond the ridge. "We're here," Iza said, though it was unnecessary.

The other cargo ship had apparently crashed in the middle of a small valley, and the freighter's trajectory could probably be seen from orbit. The crew had set up a perimeter, so Iza and Braedon needed to stay out of sight until it was time to meet the captain. They crept along the edge of the camp, keeping out of sight long enough to see what was going on below.

She observed the camp from behind a grouping of

boulders. It was as Iza expected; the cargo ship had landed nose down in the dirt, but the lights were on and there seemed to be a flurry of activity. On the side of the large freighter, she saw the name spelled out in large capital letters: 'IRON DOG'.

"I count at least a dozen crew members," Braedon whispered to Iza.

Iza did a quick calculation of her own, scanning the perimeter. "Could be closer to twenty. There are two more or so walking the perimeter on the opposite side of the ship, plus an unknown number of people on the inside." *This might be a little more difficult than I hoped.*

"What's your plan here?"

"We need parts for our ship. I'm going to ask politely if they'd lend us some."

"And if they refuse?"

"I'm not sure yet, but either way, I'll do the talking. Just stand there with your mouth closed and try to look angry." She glanced at his face and choked. "What is that?"

"That's my angry face," Braedon said still trying to hold the awkward features.

"You look like someone trying to lay an egg, stop it."

Iza stepped boldly out from the protection of the rock face with her handgun on her hip in clear view. Several of the crew stopped to raise their weapons as she approached the ship with her hands splayed out in front of her.

"I'm Captain Iza Sundari, just looking for your captain if they're around."

One of the crew members motioned toward the ship with his head. A woman with a short crop of brown hair sneered at Iza before going inside to get the captain. Iza lowered her hands but kept her face neutral as the remaining crew formed a half-circle around her and Braedon.

"Smells good. What have you got cooking?" Braedon asked

one of the men pointing a weapon at his head.

Iza realized too late that she should have left him behind cover. Braedon talked too much, especially when he was nervous. Iza leaned toward Braedon to remind him to keep his mouth shut, but she wasn't sure he took the hint.

The light coming from inside the ship obscured the view of the captain as he approached. Built like a tank, he meandered down the ramp toward her. The captain, in fact, looked like an old dog himself, with the weathered skin and muscular upper body of someone who'd hauled his whole life, inexplicably paired with narrow hips and short legs that seemed too small to support his upper half. A large, tan hat covered his head and darkened his eyes, disguising the color.

"Well, what's a tall and gorgeous captain like you doing creeping around on this mining rock in the middle of the night?"

Braedon laughed. "I'm sorry, I know you told me not to say anything, but he's being so obvious."

The man's smile faded as he glared at Braedon. Iza raised a hand and gave Braedon a nod to step back. He held up his hands and took a deliberate step backward.

Iza turned to the captain again. "I think you know. My ship was shot down by an EMP cannon, just like yours."

"Yes, the miners' strike. It's a nuisance. Don't get involved with them, whatever you do. Their little protest is only going to lead to more trouble."

"Can we talk?"

He spread his large hands wide and smiled. "Of course. Talk."

She wasn't going to get the courtesy or the treatment of a trusted friend, that was fair. She'd prepared herself for that much. Iza steeled her back. "If I can't get my ship moving, my passengers and I are stuck on this rock. I was hoping you could spare a few parts."

His crew kept quiet, but their heads turned as one toward their captain as he spoke.

"What kind of ship do you have, Captain?"

"An H3X-Z500."

He let out a low whistle. "Nice and shiny too, I bet. Sorry, Captain, you've come all this way for nothing. We don't have any parts that would suit your ship. As you can see, we've got a cargo ship."

He was condescending, but she didn't argue. She had her reasons for choosing her ship. The sight of his bulky cargo freighter only reinforced that she'd made the right choice. It also confirmed they had the intention of taking a lot more of the raw materials than her smaller ship could carry.

"He's lying," Braedon said as he took a step forward. "I may not know much about cargo versus passenger ships, but I gamble, and I know when someone is bluffing. This guy is lying to you, Iz."

Iza didn't like how familiar he was being with her name, but instead of correcting him, she turned back to the captain, trying to see what he saw. "Captain?"

The older man laughed heartily and then nodded. "Okay, what do you need? I'll see if we have the parts on hand, but no promises. We're not running a charity out here. We've got our own problems, too."

"All I need are three Y72 capacitors and an intermix regulator, if you can spare them."

"Three capacitors and an intermix regulator, that's it?" He rubbed the scruff of hair on his chin as he squinted at her, then glanced at Braedon.

"Once we complete our next haul, I can pay you back," Iza said.

"Ship like that… you working for Apex, I take it?"

"Yes."

"Karter's a slimy little weasel. He should have told you that a vessel like that one won't survive hauling from planet to planet out here in the outer colonies. I'll see what we've got. Ben, hit the engine room storage and see if we've got the captain's parts on hand. The rest of you, back to work."

The flurry of activity Iza had witnessed earlier commenced again, leaving the three of them essentially alone.

"I'm Captain Marten Douketis, nice to meet you," he said holding up his hand in greeting.

"Same here. And thank you, Captain Douketis, for considering my request."

"No, call me Marti. We have to stick together out here. Who's your perceptive friend?"

Iza turned to Braedon and waited for him to introduce himself.

"I'm no one of importance."

It wasn't what she would have said but he wasn't wrong, so she shrugged. Since when was he so quiet and tight-lipped?

A black bag was handed to Douketis a minute later by one of the crew members.

"Here you go."

Iza opened the bag to check for the parts she needed and found them all there as Trix described.

"Thanks, Marti, I promise to pay you back. I'll reach out to your crew once I get paid."

He waved a hand at her as if pushing away her words. "I know you're good for it. Listen, a piece of advice," he stepped closer so he could lower his voice. "It's rough out here. Some days things go your way, some days they don't. But either way, we keep hauling."

Iza nodded. It seemed there might be some code among the haulers. It was nice to be a part of it, instead of being on the outside looking in all the time.

"Thanks again," Iza said.

He lifted his hat and sent them on their way.

—

By the time they made it back, Trix was finished loading the raw rock material onto the ship. She noted the small hover carts parked outside.

"You found some transport." Iza couldn't contain her excitement.

"Yes, and materials that we can use to make your bombs," Trix said.

"Good."

"Again, I would advise you against it."

"I know, but we have a rescue mission to perform, and I'm going to need the distraction. I'll be careful I promise."

Trix wasn't convinced. Iza could see her running the calculations even before she opened her mouth to give them.

"The likelihood of effectiveness is—"

"I don't want the odds this time. One of my paying passengers is being held against his will and we're going to help him. For now, I need you to get the ship up and running with the parts we got from Captain Marten Douketis."

"Marti," Braedon corrected with a smirk.

Iza rolled her eyes. "Yes, I remember. See what you can do with these," she said, holding them up.

Trix inspected the parts. "Yes, these should work. I will begin the repairs."

As soon as Trix headed to Engineering, Iza bent over to stretch her back. She was aching from all the climbing and traversing over rock. Braedon came up beside her. He'd gotten dirt all over his clothes again, but he still managed to look better dressed than any of them.

"Do you think your telepathic friend has broken out of custody yet?" she asked him.

Braedon seemed thoughtful. "I'm not sure. He's got the ability to do some damage, but I'm not sure at what level."

A fair level, considering how he softened our ship's crash. Iza frowned.

"Maybe he's still scoping out the situation," Braedon continued. "Recon before action seems to be his approach. I guess it's a TSS thing, you know."

Iza nodded. She needed to get back to work, so she wasn't willing to wait around for him to work at his own pace. For her rescue plan to be effective, she'd have to get close.

She eyed Braedon. "Hey, what was that between you and Captain Douketis?"

"There's this thing that happens when two players sit down at a table and challenge each other. It's not something that can be taught or explained. That man was bluffing, but he had something he was holding back. I'm no telepath, but if Jovani was there he could tell you exactly what he was up to. He was lying to you about more than the parts."

"Braedon, I'm going to need you to stay here and watch my ship while Trix and I go and get Jovani."

"No way. Jovani's my friend. I'm going to get him."

"That's the reason you're not going. Trix is better backup, in any case."

"Don't leave me behind, you know I can be—"

"Resourceful. Yes, I know, and I'm counting on it."

JOE'S FIRST MISTAKE was taking his eyes off Braedon. His second was *not* taking his eyes off of Iza.

He'd sensed the miners coming for him, but with limited time to react, he fell back on his training—observe, plan, react. When dealing with the general public, the TSS was discouraged from using full force. It would be far more effective for him to learn what had caused this disgruntled mob to attack him and bring down their ship using their EMP cannon. Considering their response, it was doubtful they were the first ship to be targeted.

A tickle of anticipation crept up Joe's neck as the group finally dragged him out of a dark storage shed where they'd dumped him after he was snatched—presumably an attempt to soften him up. Many hours had passed, though he hadn't wanted to pull out his handheld to check the exact time and risk alerting them to the device. The fact that they hadn't frisked him showed he was dealing with complete amateurs.

No one in his group of escorts spoke to him directly, except to encourage him to walk faster or make a turn in either direction. He guessed they were now bringing him to speak to someone in charge.

This is it. His entire mission was to gain intel on possible insurgencies in the outer colonies, and a mob like this one fit the description.

As he took in the details of the town and people escorting him, he noted a treasure-trove of information that he'd be able to relay to TSS Command. He imagined himself back at Headquarters within the week, where Agent Mandren and High Commander Wil Sietinen would pat him on the back over drinks in his office. He'd be able to go to his sister's wedding as an accomplished Agent, no longer a disappointment to everyone around him. Maybe Iza would even come as his date.

Don't get ahead of yourself. You're not in the clear yet, Joe reminded himself. He kept his focus on every aspect of his surroundings, not knowing what might be most important.

"Inside." One of the men who'd been escorting Joe gave him a rough prod at his back when they reached the front door of a prefab structure at the edge of town.

Joe stepped into the dimly lit building. It appeared to have once been some kind of restaurant. Its interior furnishings had been dismantled or turned over, leaving standing room only. At one end of the space was a long, rectangular table serving as a desk. A middle-aged woman with a flowing, blonde ponytail sat with a cup of steaming liquid at her side. She glanced up as the mob advanced but seemed more interested in the handheld in front of her.

The mob crowded around her, waiting to see what she'd do.

Joe kept calm, though he wanted to snatch his arm from the grip of the burly man at his side. He'd let things play out for now. The longer the blonde woman waited, the quieter the mob grew.

She picked up her mug and took a lingering sip before

putting it back down, finally turning her attention to Joe. Her blue eyes were steady and calculating.

"You're late." The woman's voice had a strange tone, as if she were pushing her volume above a whisper. The scratchiness of it made Joe want to clear his throat.

"I've been held for hours," he replied. "I suggest you take my tardiness up with your men."

"Don't play with me. This is the part where you tell us what you're going to do about our demands," the woman said. She waved a hand in the air, and someone brought Joe a chair and unceremoniously pushed him down into it.

What is she talking about? He shrugged. "You and your people seem to have mistaken me for someone else."

His words were still echoing through the crowd toward those standing in the back before the middle-aged woman with the rough tone spoke again.

"My name is Yeaga. I'm leading the miners' movement against the exploitation of the corporations. As a TSS Agent, I assume you're familiar with our situation, are you not?"

"I am not."

Yeaga, nor Joe, could get another word out as the crowd burst into more angry shouts. He didn't have to be a telepath to know their intentions. This time, Joe made out the words, 'hang' and 'kill' before Yeaga tilted her head and smiled at him. Though it wasn't a friendly smile, Joe returned it. Yeaga waited for the crowd's angry murmuring to die down before continuing her inquiry.

"Let's start at the beginning. Name and rank?" Yeaga's voice held a militant tone, as if she'd once served, though her age and circumstances said otherwise.

He thought of telling her the truth. He was on a covert mission of another design. He'd never heard of their troubles and he'd go ahead and report it to his superiors as soon as he was within beacon range. Instead, he chose to use the alias, should they decide to look him up, it would corroborate his story. He figured honesty might get him in more trouble at the moment.

"My name is Jovani Saletas, no rank, former TSS Agent now working in private security on the H3X ship you dropped with your EMP cannon this evening."

The crowd was so quiet now, the sound of someone sniffing echoed off the bare walls of the room.

"You're not TSS and you have no idea what's going on here?" Her question was more like a statement, spoken for the rest of the room to hear.

Joe answered it. "I do not, but considering the 'welcome', I'm curious as to what's going on out here."

That seemed to be the right answer because Yeaga laughed. Several others in the crowd joined her, though it was doubtful they understood her humor.

"Bring our guest a drink."

Someone scurried to do her bidding, and again Joe was forced to wonder who this Yeaga woman was and how she'd managed to get all of these people behind her. If it weren't so rude, he probably would have probed her mind for the answer. Instead, he'd try to be patient. At the moment, he was safe and had no reason to use his abilities to hurt anyone.

"Even a former Agent might be of some help to us during this upsetting business."

She waved a hand, dismissing the crowd who grumbled at having been so close to an answer but not receiving one.

"You're probably wondering how I came to be leading this rabble." Jeers of laughter from the dispersing crowd prompted her to pause until they quieted. "In due time, I may tell you. But first to the business at hand. Do you still have contacts in the TSS?"

This was dangerously close to giving up his cover and mission. Joe shook his head. "No, I didn't leave by choice. They threw me out and I never looked back."

"That's too bad. We could use someone with your cool head on the other side of the table. Any other Agent would have probably tried to fire on us and clean up the mess later."

If she only knew. Joe shrugged one shoulder, trying to look noncommittal, while he forced down a wave of anger about the disrespectful characterization of his fellow Agents. "TSS Agents are trained for negotiation. I'm nothing special," he said, keeping his tone level.

Yeaga's head tilted to one side. "That had a note of truth to it. Why did you say you were kicked out of the TSS?"

"I didn't." Joe wasn't a gambler, but he could bluff as well as any con artist. That's why he was there.

Time to get to work. He tilted his head. "So, what exactly is going on here?"

A mug of hot liquid was placed on the table in front of Joe, and he took it. It smelled better than coffee, so he took a sip and his eyes flew open in surprise. There was a sweet taste to it but a kick of something at the end.

"The miners use it to stay awake on long digs. It's a secret recipe, so don't ask."

He nodded, enjoying the brew as it warmed him. He could already feel the stimulating effects.

Yeaga rolled her narrow shoulders and then leaned forward, steepling her hands on the table. "Hubyria is the supplier of thirty-one percent of the tridillium needed to create the ships that Tarans use for transport on the other worlds. We mine some of the strongest, most stubborn rock you'll ever find. It's so hard, it requires extreme levels of heat to melt it down." She took a sip from her mug and placed the cup down again. "My father was a miner, and his father was a miner. My father met my mother on a dig, and they both did backbreaking work until they died far too young to care for their child."

"I'm sorry." Joe couldn't imagine growing up on this planet without parents.

"But, by the time I'd lost them, I was ready to take their place. I became a third-generation miner determined to live and die as my parents had, within the mines. If you haven't noticed, the young and old stick it out together here. This isn't the kind of place you walk away from. It's too important to the families on this planet as well as for the Taran people."

Someone stepped over and whispered something in Yeaga's ear. She nodded then returned her attention to Joe.

"I wish I could say my story was unique, but it's not. Most of us are chips from the same stone. So, when the Taran elite decide they want to have a war, we supply the materials for their ships and their weapons. Our people have been worked to the bone, and now that there are two minutes of peace, they're saying they can't afford to pay or employ all of us."

"There are plenty of other jobs out there. Have you considered getting into something else?"

"Nothing pays like working the mines, and no one can work the mines the way we do. What the local Enforcers and dynastic leaders don't seem to get is we want more than just our jobs. We want security."

"That's sort of what they do." Joe tried to laugh it off, but Yeaga didn't see the humor in it.

She waited for him to take the hint. "You're all alike. It must have been easy for you to just drop your TSS life like it never mattered to you, but it's different for us. We live and breathe the mines until it takes us. We raise our children to love it as much as we do. Taking that away from us means you're taking away our future. Without us, there's no one to mine the caverns rich with the raw materials that make hull plating and cannons that keep you alive when you're fighting for your life against the enemies of yesterday, today, and tomorrow. That's what we've built here."

Joe couldn't wait to contact Headquarters. This was exactly the kind of thing that the High Commander would love to know. The TSS could swoop in and save the day, helping the miners, and getting Joe his life back. He fought to keep his smile in check.

"I wish there was something more I could do."

"About that," Yeaga said.

She nodded to the nearest man with rust-colored hair over his head and face. He waved two other men forward, and the small group created a path where they dragged Iza forward.

"I believe there *is* something you can do."

— — —

Iza took in the scene in front of her as she struggled against the tight handgrip the men had on her arms. There were more than a dozen people gathered around the walls of the room and still more streaming in with the commotion. The place smelled like a mine, probably from rock tracked in from the miners milling around.

At a table in the back of the room, Jovani was seated across from a blonde woman.

That figures. Here Iza was doing her bomaxed best to save Jovani, but he was having tea with the enemy.

The two men holding Iza let her go at a nod from the petite blonde woman at the table. *So this is Yeaga. She doesn't look too tough to me.* From behind, with her long ponytail and small waist, she could be mistaken for a fourteen-year-old. But everyone in the room seemed to obey her every command. She was the one running the show, so Iza kept her eyes on her, ignoring Jovani's shocked expression.

"Sorry I'm interrupting your tea-time," Iza said, scowling down at Yeaga.

To her surprise, Yeaga smiled. Her face transformed, the hard edges softening, and her raspy laugh was probably the most provocative thing Iza had ever heard.

Yeaga stood while her men kept Jovani in his seat by placing a hand on each of his shoulders. "No problem, we were just finishing up. Jovani, here, was just promising to help me, and it seems that offer would extend to you, since it's your ship we'll be needing."

How dare he offer up my ship to help these people start a rebellion against the corporations! Whatever Jovani had agreed to was of no concern to her, and she'd make that clear soon enough. Iza's eyes narrowed. "And you are?"

"You know who I am. My people saw you talking with old lady Brandis. But I haven't gotten your name yet."

"Captain Sundari."

"Well, Captain, as you can see, we're having trouble with the local Enforcers. We were hoping for TSS intervention, but it seems we haven't made enough of a show yet to get their attention."

Iza shrugged one shoulder. "I'm sorry, am I supposed to care about what you're doing here? Just because you have an excuse for kidnapping someone doesn't make it okay."

Yeaga paced behind the table, unconcerned about Iza's lack of sympathy. "Jovani says you arrived on an H3X that needs repairs. We might be able to help you with that. I assume you were also trying to rescue him when we captured you?" Yeaga said. "Being friends with us could be to your benefit."

So smug, it's going to be a pleasure to see that expression change in about two minutes. Iza stood her ground. "That's not entirely true. I allowed your men to capture me."

Yeaga raised an eyebrow and picked up her cup, finishing its contents before nodding. "Well, if that's so, then you're in the middle of a rescue and I'm delaying your progress. Please, continue," she said with a wave of one hand.

"As much as you might like hanging out in this hovel, *I* have other places to be. I hope you don't miss it when it's gone."

Three, two, one. Here comes the first boom.

Nothing.

Iza counted in her head again, going over all of her steps. She'd placed all three makeshift bombs herself. The first should have exploded already. The second was due in another minute.

Yeaga snapped her fingers as if getting an idea. "Oh, you're probably wondering what happened to your explosives. We found them, which is why we were able to catch you so quickly." The satisfied expression on her face only angered Iza more.

Jovani started to speak, but Iza glared at him and Yeaga raised her hand to silence him. He squirmed under the two men holding him down but obeyed.

Yeaga turned back to Iza. "Like, I was saying, we're having some trouble here that a ship like yours could remedy. It's going to require going a little outside the lines."

"You shot my ship out of the sky with your cannon. We're stranded on this backward rock. But even if it wasn't, I would hardly help you."

The crowd around them stirred to life again, murmuring against Iza, and she heard their plans for her if she should choose not to help them.

"May I say something?" Jovani asked.

Yeaga nodded without taking her eyes off of Iza.

"If I may, we have a unique opportunity here. Iza needs work. She's not interested in your cause and, quite frankly, though I'm sympathetic, I'm no use to you without a ship. If you can pay, there might be a way we can help you."

"I'm not helping her," Iza growled. "My ship is still nothing more than a giant chunk of grounded metal." That was no longer true, thanks to the parts they'd procured from Douketis, but there was no need to tip their hand.

Yeaga smiled. "Well, as it happens, that's our specialty. We may be able to get your ship back into the sky, but first, we're going to need some kind of guarantee that you'll help us."

"How much?"

"Just something that tells me you're serious and you're not going to just take off with our money without helping us."

"No, how much do you plan on paying me?"

Yeaga nodded. "If you're willing to help us, we can offer you above and beyond what other employers are paying."

"I doubt a wayward group of out-of-work miners have enough financial backing to afford anything."

"You'd be surprised at the yield our EMP cannon has brought in. All that matters is you need the money and we can pay."

Iza didn't respond so Yeaga continued.

"The supplies we need are fairly easy to get with a ship as maneuverable as yours. However, they're not going to give it up willingly. We have a local contact on Phiris who can get us access to what we need. Everything will be ready for pick up, and you'll be paid when you deliver. If the local Enforcers find out, however, they'll be after you. Though, you don't seem like the kind of woman, Captain, who's unfamiliar with life inside a prison ship."

Iza kept her expression blank, but rage boiled inside her. Had she been gifted with abilities, she imaged her stare would have melted Yeaga's face off.

Yeaga smiled predatorily. "Now, back to my original

proposition. What can you give me in good faith?"

An explosion rocked the foundations of the building, giving Iza time to toss Jovani's mug of hot liquid on the woman and bolt for the exit. As she'd discovered in her reconnaissance earlier, there was a small door in the back room leading to the outside.

A hand on Iza's shoulder had her leaping out of her skin steps before the door.

"It's me," Jovani said when she turned to face him.

"Don't do that!"

She and Jovani raced through the door and out into the black of night.

"Where are we going?" Jovani asked.

"Shut up and run!"

The sound of pulse fire behind them kept her from looking back. A cluster of rocks ahead would protect them if they could make it. The terrain of jagged rock left them completely exposed as they raced toward cover, twisting her ankles and stabbing her feet through the soles of her shoes.

Panting as they climbed around the taller rock, Iza was thrilled to run into Trix.

"You did it," Iza said, embracing the android's neck.

Trix seemed embarrassed at the attention. "It was exactly as you suspected. Someone was coming up behind you to disable the bombs, and all I had to do was wait until they left to initiate their timers again. I apologize for the slight delay; the miners were not efficient or fast."

"How did you fix her so fast?" Jovani asked when he saw Trix.

"Iza did not fix me. I have an independent rechargeable battery source encased in a faraday cage within a polycarbonate shield, impenetrable by EMP. My system appears to shut down while the backup battery continues to collect data and reset all of my systems once the threat is neutralized."

"Nice."

"Yes, it is nice. Also, I am grateful that you were able to activate the manual system and use your telekinesis to land the ship. It was quite ingenious and no doubt saved the crew."

"Does that mean the ship is repaired?" Jovani asked.

"Yes, while you were having tea with the Queen of the Miners, I was trying to find us a way off this planet," Iza said as she continued to traverse the uneven, rocky terrain.

"My evening wasn't all chatty fun," Jovani said. "How'd you get the ship running again?"

"We were able to retrieve the parts we needed from a nearby cargo freighter," Trix replied when Iza didn't offer an explanation.

The group fell silent as they climbed around the rocks through the dark, putting more distance between themselves and the angry miners.

"I think Yeaga was going to help us," Jovani said at last, breaking the quiet.

Iza scoffed. "No, she wasn't. She was going to help herself. Once she had what she wanted, there'd be nothing and no one to stop her from grounding us again, permanently."

Jovani shook his head like he was still waking up from a dream.

Iza stopped and turned to face him. "Look, I don't know what she told you, but she has her people searching the area looking for our ship. She doesn't need any of us to fly it; she can do that all on her own. So, whatever deal she was making with you wasn't legit or even lucrative. Get your head out of the clouds and get back to reality. People aren't just standing around waiting to help you. They always want something from you, and if you refuse to give it to them, they'll just take it."

"Not always," Jovani said, his voice carrying more heat

than she expected from him.

Whatever feelings for him she was pushing down bubbled up again. She countered the sudden emotion with a reminder about who she was talking to. "The sooner you learn about the real ways of the universe, the better off you'll be. I'm not surprised you didn't make it as an Agent." The statement came out more vicious than she'd intended.

"What?" There was a flash of fire in Jovani's eyes she hadn't seen before. "You don't know anything about me."

Now they were nose-to-nose, but Iza wouldn't back down.

"Sure, you look the part, but you believe almost everything you're told. No one is going to give you something for nothing."

"Get over yourself. Not everyone wants something from you."

"No?" She raised an eyebrow in challenge.

"I know enough about people looking out for themselves to recognize the difference between real need and greed. I may not be an Agent anymore, but that doesn't mean I gave up on helping people."

"You want to help people? Help us get out of here so the rest of us can have a warm bed to sleep in."

"What's that supposed to mean?"

"What you do with Yeaga is your business. In the future, just leave me and my ship out of it."

"Don't try to make this about Yeaga. If you gave people half a chance, you might be surprised."

"I gave half the people a chance and look where it got me." Iza didn't like how bitter the words sounded, but it was the truth. Sometimes, a cold slap of reality is what people needed. In her case, it had meant survival. Iza turned away from Jovani; he was too close.

"You're the most stubborn woman I've ever met," he yelled

at her back.

"You're the most gullible."

"Captain?" Trix asked, interrupting their rhythm.

"What?" Iza didn't mean to yell it the first time and repeated her question with more control, "What is it?"

"There is a problem with the ship. From this distance, I should be able to interface with the communications system, and it is not functioning."

Without another look toward Jovani, Iza raced back to the ship.

When they arrived, the ramp door was open and it was as black as the night inside.

That's strange, the auxiliary lighting should be on. Someone could still be on board. Iza pulled out her pulse gun.

—

At the top of the ramp leading into the dark cargo hold, Iza nodded at Jovani to take one side of the ship while she took the other. A signal to Trix instructed her to head straight up to the flight deck. Inside, without moonlight for illumination, she could barely see.

To Iza's distress, aside from her shuttle, the cargo hold was empty. Someone had taken the rock shipment that Trix had diligently loaded. There were only a small number of people who might have taken it, and Iza didn't like any of the possibilities.

Iza crept along the side wall of the cargo area until she tripped over something. It groaned, and she realized it was Braedon.

He curled into a ball at her touch. As her eyes adjusted to the dark, she could just make out bruises forming on the side of his face and forehead. Both his lip and knuckles were bloodied. One eye was already swelling, and he looked like he'd been on the wrong side of a land vehicle collision.

"Braedon, who did this?"

The word was a whisper but it was clear. "Marti."

Jovani rushed over to them from the other side. "Braedon?"

Iza nodded.

He knelt down next to Braedon to examine his injuries. "He put up a fight."

The sight of handheld lights caught their attention, and Iza motioned Jovani to hide behind the bulkhead closest to where Braedon lay hidden.

The intruders stopped a few meters away.

Iza held her breath. *Where is Trix?*

"The cargo?" a man asked. The voice was familiar. Iza squinted into the dark, and she was able to make out Captain Douketis' features.

"It's loaded and ready. Do you want us to grab anything else?" a woman replied.

"This looks like something interesting." The captain tossed a small box up in the air and caught it again in his palm.

The object was unmistakably the mysterious box that Iza had found in the hidden compartment, and the fact that Douketis had it in his hands meant that he'd riffled through Iza's personal items in her cabin. The thought that he'd been in her private space made Iza sick to her stomach. *Oh, he's going to pay.*

She nodded for Jovani to go around behind them while she stepped out in front, her pulse gun raised to their faces.

"Yes, it does look interesting," Iza said. "It also happens to be mine, so I'll take it back if you don't mind." She held out her hand as steady as steel.

"You're outnumbered, Captain." Douketis tilted his hat

back and smiled. The woman next to him with spiked pink hair had her gun directed at Iza.

Jovani emerged from the shadows on cue, putting a pulse gun muzzle to her ear. "Don't turn around." The woman reluctantly held her arms up, and he took her weapon with his free hand.

Just then, the main lights turned back on. Trix was on the flight deck.

Jovani stayed behind the two intruders while Iza waited with her palm open for Captain Douketis to hand over the box.

After a moment, he tossed it to her and raised his hands, but a smirk tugged at his lips. The sound of approaching vehicles meant his crew had returned from transferring the cargo from Iza's ship to theirs.

With a silent look of agreement, Iza and Jovani marched the captain and his companion to the bottom of the ship's ramp.

The captain's crew realized something was wrong the moment they stepped out from their transport vehicles. Though they trained their guns on Iza and Jovani, they held their fire for fear of hitting their own people.

"Sorry, kid," Douketis said. "The minute you left, I remembered who you were. I couldn't let Scrap Rat get the best of me. Your old captain and I used to run together."

Iza dug her gun into his back. "Too bad you're more loyal to him than to being a decent person."

"Decent? You believed that stuff about a code among haulers?" He chuckled. "Sorry to disappoint, but out here in the black, it's every man for himself. I'll tell you what... I promise not to shoot you from the sky when we leave you behind on this rock."

"Aren't you cute. Get off my ship. Trix, start the engines."

The engines roared to life and the ship lifted off the

ground. Jovani casually pushed the woman with the pink hair off the edge of the ramp. Though she yelped, she was caught by her friends below.

"This is for Braedon," Iza said as she lifted the pulse gun to Douketis' back.

"Wait, allow me, Captain." Jovani stepped forward and pulled back his fist, hitting Douketis square in the jaw. The older man stumbled forward, and Iza kicked him from behind, dropping him off the edge.

Iza and Jovani raced up the ramp as it closed, diving to either side to seek shelter behind the bulkheads as Douketis' crew began firing.

"We're in! Time to go, Trix," Iza said as the sounds of gunfire pelted the hull. "And get the shields up!" She beckoned to Jovani. "Let's get Braedon to the infirmary."

Together, they lifted Braedon from where he'd hidden in the cargo hold and dragged him to one of the beds. Iza called Trix down to the infirmary, since she didn't need to be on the flight deck in order to pilot the ship, and then raced through the cabinetry, looking for bandages.

"I think he's coming to," Jovani observed.

Braedon's eyes fluttered open and he caught sight of them. He struggled and flailed his arms as he tried to leap to his feet.

"Easy, not so fast," Jovani said, taking one of his arms and resting it at his side.

Trix entered the infirmary and began checking his vitals. "His heart rate is erratic, but his pupils are dilating. He does not have a concussion. He seems to be functioning normally. I will need to do a scan of his vital organs to determine if there were any severe injuries."

"Do it."

Braedon's internal scans showed up on the holodisplay, and Trix nodded. "He will be fine. There are some signs of dehydration, but water and rest will help him heal."

"Did Douketis and his men take back the parts?" Iza asked.

"No, the ship's functions are returning to normal, though we do not yet have jump capability as the system is still re-initializing."

"Did you happen to save those hover carts?"

Trix gave a single nod. "Yes, stored in one of the cargo lockers."

"Good thinking. Set a course for Beurias."

"Wait, if they took all the rocks, then where does that leave us?" Jovani asked, looking to Iza.

She shrugged. "Screwed."

16

"STATUS?" IZA CALLED out when she reached the flight deck after Trix.

"Plotting a course for Beurias."

"Let's put this planet in our rear viewports. Stay low until we're out of danger from the EMP cannon, then head up to the jump point."

"Yes, Captain."

"What about the miners?" Jovani asked. "Shouldn't we tell someone about what's going on here?"

"Tell who? In case you haven't noticed, the Enforcers don't care about the miners—or hardly anyone, for that matter. And the TSS has bigger things to worry about, don't they? Besides, Yeaga can take care of herself."

"No EMP cannon activity on sensors, Captain," Trix reported. "Ten minutes to jump."

Iza turned back to Jovani. Of course, he was right about needing to tell someone. And she would, if she were anyone else. Not a scrap rat from the streets with everything to lose. Now, the most she could hope for was to keep her ship. Everything else had to wait.

"I had a job to do, and they've ruined that, so what they

need isn't my problem. I need to report this to Karter and get another job, or I won't make enough for the rent, which puts you and Braedon out on the street. So, the question you should be asking is how fast you can help me or get out of my way?"

"I know that what happens to you and this ship affects all of us. What I don't understand is what happened to your sense of duty to your fellow Taran citizens. Shouldn't we try to help each other if it's in our power to do so?"

"Not today." Iza turned away from him, avoiding the intensity of his stare. "Trix, connect me to Karter. Jovani, go see your friend. If he's feeling up to it, let him rest in his own cabin. Who knows how long we'll have it, so might as well enjoy it."

Jovani nodded, but she saw the stiff way he walked away and the tension he carried in his jaw and shoulders. But when he reached the door, he whirled around to face her.

"Don't turn into Captain Douketis. He probably believes he's doing what's best for him and his crew, too." Then, he was gone and she was left staring after him.

Iza could handle his anger, but the disappointment in Jovani's voice made her heart sink. What happened on Hubyria didn't sit right. Those people needed help; she just knew she wasn't in any kind of position to aid them.

With just Trix left on the flight deck, Iza initiated the call she'd been wanting to make since the moment they crashed.

Karter's line went through to Becca. "I'm sorry, Iza, Mr. Hyttinen's in a very important meeting and asked not to be disturbed. May I relay a message for you?" the receptionist asked.

Iza huffed. Keeping her tone curt, she spoke, "Yes, would you mind telling the lowlife snake that his last bomaxed job almost got my ship destroyed and everyone on board killed? Those damages will need to be covered by Apex

Manufacturing Enterprises, since it is quite clear that he sent two haulers to do one job. My passengers were subjected to unnecessary dangers as a result. I would also like it noted that the H3X came under fire by one of his corrupt haulers and crew. The situation on Hubyria among the miners and the corporations is volatile, and any further contact with the colony should be monitored closely. Should he like his money on time, he should arrange for another haul right away."

"I have it, no problem, and I'll let him know as soon as he's free," Becca said, seemingly unfazed. "Is there anything else I can do for you?"

"No."

More irritated than when she began, Iza terminated the call and sat down in a huff.

"What is the probability that Karter sent two different ships to haul the same cargo?" she asked Trix. Though she'd stated it as a certainty on the call, she didn't have much more to go on than a hunch, and it had been gnawing at her since Braedon pointed out the strange circumstances.

"I am sorry, there is not enough information to extrapolate."

"It doesn't matter." Iza waved off the thought.

"We are in range of the nav beacon. Would you like me to initiate the jump?" Trix said, keeping her focus on the stars outside the viewport.

"Yes," Iza stood up to leave. "I'll be in my cabin if anyone is looking for me."

She'd been avoiding the cabin since her run-in with Captain Douketis, knowing he'd rummaged through her private things. The room had already been a mess after the crash landing, but it was worse knowing he'd had his hands on everything.

Straightening up helped ease her mind. She made her bed and set the small table and chair to upright again.

She pulled the small box she'd taken back from Douketis out of her pocket and held it in her hands. There were a few scratches in the wood from when it had fallen off of the shelf, but nothing else. She held it up and rotated it. The mystery box seemed to come alive, humming again just like the first time. *What in the world are you?*

Iza ran her fingernail along the edges for the fifth time, looking for anything that might be a clue as to how to open it. Maybe she was taking too basic a look at the item.

She initiated a visual and signal analysis with the ship's computer. Using her handheld, she scanned the box and waited for the system to tell her if it was some kind of trick item. The assessment was done in under a minute.

"Would you like the result saved to your handheld?" asked the ship's non-sentient AI, CACI.

"Yes."

Iza scrolled through the report. When she saw its origins were unknown, she frowned.

The item had been dated at over a hundred thousand years old by various antiquities dealers and museums. Though it had changed hands many times, none of the records indicated where it may have come from. She lost the trail of its history about seven hundred years back. Even stranger, she felt confident that nothing made out of wood should have survived for millennia outside a proper storage case.

What is it doing here?

She had more questions than answers and not many people who could tell her. Karter would know who the ship previously belonged to, but there was no telling how long the item had been hidden away. With any ambiguity about the proper owner, she wouldn't put it past Karter to claim it as his own.

No, better to keep it a secret.

She addressed CACI again. "Is there any other information about this kind of artifact?"

"No, there are no other records pertaining to this item."

Why won't you open up your secrets to me? Sooner or later you're going to love me.

Iza laughed to herself and put the small box deep inside her nightstand drawer. Leaving her room, she thought about the ship and the day she'd found the box. Maybe there was something else to it. She'd check the hidden location to see if she could find another piece.

Considering the hour and the whirlwind night, she should be resting, but an unsolved mystery was too much stimulus for her brain. As she climbed down the stairs into the cargo hold, she spotted Braedon. He moved out from under the stairs—suspiciously close to where she'd been heading, herself.

Iza narrowed her eyes at him and placed her hands on her hips; the cargo hold was her business alone. "Shouldn't you be in bed?"

Braedon flushed. "I tried to lay down and couldn't get comfortable. I was hoping to make myself tired counting compartments on the ship."

"You shouldn't be down here," Iza said.

Braedon tended to ramble, but at that moment he was as quiet as a trapped bird.

No, there's something else up with you. Iza looked around him toward the stairs; she didn't see anything amiss. *Why would he be looking around down here?* She was tempted to ask him, but the question meant revealing there was something there for him to see.

Braedon had a hard time keeping his eyes on her face. "I get these weird dreams sometimes. I don't like to talk about it that much because, when I say they're weird, I mean they're *really* bizarre. They wake me up, and instead of going back to sleep, I walk around looking for things to count. It's good to have a place to deal with disturbing thoughts, you know? I didn't mean to cross some kind of line."

He was right, of course. She hadn't explicitly told the passengers they couldn't be in the cargo area, but she'd thought it was common sense—especially after the manure run. Perhaps it was time to establish some ship rules.

"In the future, avoid hanging around the cargo hold. Some of the cargo I haul is sensitive and I wouldn't want anyone snooping around to get hurt." Iza hoped her expression made it clear from where the true danger came. "Now, go and get some sleep. You still look like someone recently kicked in the head. Try counting breaths or something instead."

Braedon smiled and snapped his fingers. "That's a great idea. I never thought about something that simple." He stopped and then tilted his head the way Trix did when she was working something out. "Did you need help with something in the meantime? I'm already here."

"No, go rest. You've had a rough day."

"Okay, well, goodnight."

Braedon ambled passed her and Iza waited for him to be out of sight before she moved to the compartments under the stairs. There might be a key or something to open the box that she'd missed. She opened the compartment door with the secret panel. Her hand reached the back again. *Nothing.*

Iza checked every compartment near and around it. All of them empty. There must be some secret method of opening the mystery box; she wasn't going to find a special key lying around. She'd have to figure out another way to open it.

Empty-handed, she returned to her cabin. When she shook the box, she heard the satisfying *thunk* of the object inside. Iza had a distinct feeling there was something valuable in that box. One way or the other she would uncover the treasure.

17

IZA FONDLED HER necklace as she walked the ship. She never felt comfortable until she'd seen every piece of her domain—as if it would fall apart or break while she wasn't looking. It was irrational, and she knew it, but that didn't stop her from making her daily rounds on the ship.

This evening was no exception. She passed through the cargo hold and then doubled back through the galley on her way to the gym. She needed a workout to relieve the stress building up between her shoulder blades. They'd reach Beurias soon, where she was going to confront Karter. Not only had he ignored her calls, but now not even the receptionist answered. Normally, she'd dive into a workout straight away, but she needed fuel first, and that required a stop in the galley.

Loud shouts and laughter greeted her as she entered, but Iza wasn't in the mood for a sit down with the passengers and crew.

There was a clear view of the void out the side viewport while the ship was stopped for a cool-down between legs of the jump. In front of the window, Trix, Braedon, and Jovani were arranged around the dining table. Trix had prepared a small, balanced snack of meat and vegetables, which was now mostly eaten and set to the side in favor of a round of spacefarers' favorite card game, Fastara.

"Fastara!" Braedon threw down the cards from his hands and the others groaned.

"You can't possibly win that many times without cheating." Jovani picked up the colored cards and looked them over.

"Just admit it. I'm a superior player and you two are going to owe me a fortune."

Iza didn't like the sound of Braedon's jeering and put a stop to it immediately. The last thing she wanted on the ship was a reason for them to try and stab each other in the back.

"I don't allow gambling for credits or precious items on this ship, so you'll have to find something else to gamble with while you're on board," she said.

Jovani and Trix both turned to Braedon at the same time.

"Okay, how about chores? You've got my latrine duty," he said pointing to Trix, "and you've got my heavy lifting." He gave a nod to Jovani.

The other two looked between themselves and decided it was certainly better than nothing and worthy of another game.

"You going to join us, Captain?" Jovani asked.

Iza could see the desire pouring off of him. *What was it with him?* Worse, what was it with her? She clamped down on her own desire at the sight of him.

Yes, the gym definitely, now. She grabbed a piece of fruit. "No, I've got something else to take care of. You guys have fun."

— — —

Joe watched Iza head out toward the gym. Maybe she was interested in blowing off some steam. He wanted the same, but sparring with her would be more fun than lifting weights and pulling ropes on his own. Joe put down his hand of Fastara and followed her out.

"Wait, where are you going?" Braedon called out.

"I have something of my own to take care of," Joe said. He heard the tail end of Braedon's snicker before he was racing to catch up to Iza.

He liked Braedon. He was a lot like Emery, and though he missed his friend, Braedon had become like a little brother. Had it started back on Sarduvis? He couldn't remember—it just was, and now they were stuck together.

Iza was a different matter entirely. There was something between them and he wanted to find out what it was.

He caught up to her in the gym, as he'd hoped. She'd already started beating up on a filled bag twice the size of a large man. Kicking at it and punching, she used as much force as she dared while rocking the thing on its hinges.

It was strange that he couldn't read her, but he ignored it considering she couldn't read him, either. No matter how or when he approached her, he couldn't glean even the slightest impression of her thoughts the way he and other Agents could with most people. There was something special about her, and he was determined to find out what. Maybe she had an ability she didn't know about.

"Now, what did he ever do to you?" Joe was attempting to be playful.

Iza glanced up, panting. Her eyes narrowed slightly, but she didn't answer. Instead, she continued beating the life out of the dead bag.

Undeterred, Joe circled the room, looking for something to do that would keep him in sight of her. Then, he realized he'd seen his classmates spar together lots of times. It was a great way to get to know someone on a deeper level. He was sure that's what Emery had said once. At the time, he'd been talking about Shari, a completely off-limits Trion Junior Agent.

"You want to spar?" Joe asked.

Iza shook her head. "Are you asking me to fight or asking me to bed?"

Joe's eyes widened in shock at the question. Was the room buzzing? His tongue felt too heavy in his mouth when he answered.

"Depends on which you'll say 'yes' to," Joe said. He hoped his bravado would make her laugh.

It didn't.

"No," Iza said as she kicked at the bag.

"No to the fighting?" he asked. *Too hopeful?*

Iza used her elbows and knees to pulverize the bag. It was a wonder it still hung there, as a grown man would have long been on his knees after such a beating. After she'd killed her imaginary combatant, she picked up a towel to wipe off the sweat from her face and hands. She threw it over her shoulder and gave Joe a once over from head to toe.

"No, next time ask the question you want the answer to," Iza said leaving him and the gym behind her.

It was worth a try. His handheld signaled and he glanced at the open doorway. Iza had already passed through her cabin door when he answered, his voice low and cautious.

"Yes."

"I received your message. What's going on?" Mandren asked.

"There's trouble on Hubyria."

"What kind of trouble?"

"The kind that ends in ships being targeted with EMP cannons and TSS Agents getting held captive."

Long pause.

"Were you discovered?"

Yes, and I'm still alive. Thanks for asking. "No, they didn't find out who I am, but it was close. I believe there's more than just civil unrest happening there. They have legitimate concerns that should be heard."

"Fine, see to it."

"What?"

"Handle it. You have the credentials to represent us."

"There's a problem. I'm with a hauling crew. When we were attacked, all our access to communications went with it. I would have contacted you sooner, but we barely made it out with our lives. I'm no longer on the planet."

"If the situation is as unstable as you say it is, you should return. You're the closest Agent we have. We need a representative there to monitor the situation. Once you inform your crew of your true identity, they won't mind dropping you off as soon as possible."

"I don't think that's a good idea, sir," Joe said.

There was another long pause before Mandren answered. "No one asked you for good ideas. You were asked to observe and report back. Continue to do so or your mission and position within the TSS will be in jeopardy. Remember how you came to be out there, Agent Anderson."

How can I forget? You'll never let me forget. The use of his real name had driven the point home. Joe could feel the heat rising in his chest and neck as he fought for control of his temper. They didn't listen when he spoke, and they treated him like he was from the most backward planet in the Taran system. He'd seen worse and knew himself to be right.

"The miners have seen my face. I've already given them my alias and I have a ship that will give me access to more than just one population of disgruntled miners. If I tell them the truth now, they won't trust me or the TSS and all of my intel will be for nothing... sir." Joe hoped he didn't notice the pause as he remembered to address his superior officer with some semblance of respect.

Agent Mandren took another long pause. "Standby."

Standby? What does that mean? Joe waited for him to return, listening to silence. It was in that silence he heard something that made him whirl around.

When he turned to the doorway, Trix was standing there. He turned off the handheld before clearing his throat.

Was she standing there the whole time? Did she hear anything about the TSS?

Joe didn't ask her the questions racing through his mind. Instead, he put the handheld in one of his pockets and strode up to her. "Can I help you with something?"

"I have been practicing my culinary skills. I would like to request your presence at dinner this evening in three hours."

Joe wondered at Trix. She was an advanced piece of technology, more advanced than anything he'd ever encountered in his former travels with the TSS, and not remotely in the same league as anything on Earth. What would be the purpose of her learning to cook? She answered as if she heard his questions aloud.

"I learned to prepare food as part of my education. My parents had intended for me to be a domestic caretaker."

Joe knew little of Lynaedans, and what he did know was by reputation more than fact. Their technology was some of the most advanced within the Taran Empire, in part because of their insular ways and singular focus on forward progress. While AI was simply a tool on most other worlds, Lynaedans had created sentient AI, like Trix, which were treated as full people in their society. Joe could see how people might want an android to serve as a nanny—always even-tempered, strong, capable of learning any skill. The fact that Trix had gone from household duties to being the engineer on a spaceship wasn't a career path he'd anticipated.

"Really? I had no idea. Someday, you'll have to tell me how you ended up touring the stars with Iza instead."

Trix evaluated him. "If your work is complete, I hope you will consider joining the rest of us in the galley."

Maybe she did overhear my conversation. His handheld pinged in his pocket and he fought not to look down at it. *Bomaxed Mandren, you're going to get me killed.*

"What are we having?"

Trix seemed to hesitate. Was deception possible for an android?

"It's a surprise."

Joe swallowed and watched her turn to leave. He called out after her with more enthusiasm than he felt. "I'll be there."

Stars! I'm toast.

— — —

Rolling her shoulders wasn't releasing the stress Iza had building up inside her. Eating dinner hadn't helped, instead making her sluggish. Before that, the gym had only made her frustrated, especially when Jovani had shown up and all she wanted to do was let him kiss her. Maybe then she'd get clear of the fog that was blocking her from seeing a way out of losing her ship.

They were scheduled to reach Beurias the next afternoon, and Iza had nothing. No cargo to deliver, no credits, and her rent due in one day. She hadn't thought through the timing of the payment when she'd signed the lease papers, somehow having it in her head that she'd have a full month before the first payment was due. Instead, it'd been less than a week, and she was already at risk of losing the ship.

She decided on a lukewarm shower. The four showerheads

beat against her skin as she turned in a slow circle. Then, she cranked up the temperature, letting the heat release some of the tension in her sore muscles. Iza moisturized her wet curls until she could run her fingers through them and then braided her hair into one large plait to keep it from tangling in the night. She didn't wait for the dryer setting to dry her hair, since it always took too long. Instead, she stepped out and slipped into a tank top and underwear before she leaned over and opened her bedside table.

As she reached inside to pick up the box, someone signaled at the door. Trix was supposed to be monitoring the flight deck and everyone else should be asleep. If Braedon had come to blabber about how he couldn't sleep again, she would put him to sleep with a swift kick to the—

Iza moved to the door, bracing herself. When the door slid open Jovani was standing there. Bare feet, bare chest, wearing a pair of shorts and nothing else.

Did he walk through the ship like that? Impressive. Iza was about to ask the question when he stepped inside her cabin. The shortened distance between them electrified as she stumbled backward.

The door automatically closed behind him. "Were you expecting someone?"

"What are you doing here?" Iza tried to step back, but the wall was closer than she'd estimated and her heel hit the edge. She bit her lip instead of wincing hoping that Jovani wouldn't notice.

Jovani glanced at the door then back at her. Then he sighed. "I can't stop thinking about you. There's something here. I'm guessing you feel it, too."

Iza was about to shake her head in denial but instead found herself staring into his eyes. They were the most striking sky-blue she'd ever seen, glowing with a soft bioluminescence.

Her hand lifted to his face without thinking. "What happened to your eyes?"

"The contacts bother me. They make other people more comfortable, but they drive me nuts."

Oh. Her mouth formed the word but no sound came out. She tried unsuccessfully to pull her gaze away.

He stepped closer. He was a breath from touching her and yet it felt like they were already touching—the 'something' between them burned inside her.

"I think it's time we explore this thing and find out what it is."

Iza's mouth had gone dry or she'd have said something, she was sure of it.

Jovani smiled as if he could read her thoughts. Actually, he probably could and it made her stiffen.

"What happened there? You changed for just a second."

Iza found her tongue at last, "I don't want you reading my mind."

Jovani's head tilted to one side. "You're kidding, right? I haven't been able to glean the slightest things from you since the day we met. You seem almost resistant to telepathy. I thought you were actively blocking me this whole time. If you weren't, that leads to more questions, but nothing I need the answer to at the moment. There's only one question I want you to answer and then I'm off to bed."

"What?"

"Do I have your permission to kiss you?" He inched forward and her chest brushed against him, but he kept his hands at his sides.

"What if I say 'no'?"

"Then I'll leave, but I think we'll both regret it."

Iza's head made a circle instead of whatever it was she meant to say.

"Yes."

Then it was as if the only thing in the universe were his eyes and mouth and they were both on fire.

Iza was so close to the life she wanted. Getting involved with the first or second guy who came on board wasn't her thing.

She pulled back. "I'm sorry, I can't." Her face was only a breath away from Jovani's.

He brushed the back of his fingers along the edge of her face. "I respect that you don't want to go any further tonight, but I don't want to leave. Can I stay?"

Iza nodded, unable to trust herself to speak, and led him over to the bed. Jovani lay down and pulled her back to him. He kissed her temple.

They stayed together like that in silence for some time, quietly enjoying each other's presence with little between them. She felt safe and comfortable in a way she rarely had throughout her life, and she wondered at how it was possible with this man she barely knew.

In time, they started talking. It was natural and easy, as if she was catching up with an old friend. He told her about growing up on Earth in a city called Minneapolis. He spoke about his sister and how they struggled to connect, even when both of them were recruited into the TSS and left their former lives behind. Iza told him how she couldn't even remember her father's face anymore. Fighting back the tears of painful memories she never discussed, she revealed how her early years on her own had been the hardest of her life, and how without Trix she'd never have survived it.

Iza didn't remember when they stopped talking or when she fell asleep. When the next morning arrived and Jovani slipped out of her bed. Immediately, she missed his warmth curled around her.

Before he departed, his kiss caressed the top of her forehead. He looked back as he closed the door, the smile on his face mirroring her own.

TRIX WAS STANDING at the helm monitoring the ship's systems when Iza walked onto the flight deck.

"Good morning!" Iza greeted.

"Good morning. Your endorphin levels are elevated, as is your heart rate, and yet you seem well-rested."

"I am."

"Did you have sweet dreams?"

"Sweet dreams?"

"It is an Earth phrase I learned from Jovani," Trix explained. "It is when you sleep well and dream of good things."

"Then yes, I did have sweet dreams."

"Were you alone?"

"No, as a matter of fact, I was with Jovani," Iza said, still beaming.

Trix seemed surprised. "I see."

Iza caught something in her tone that made her look more closely at her friend as her smile faded. "Yes. Is there a problem with that?"

"I did not realize you knew him well enough to share your bed with him."

The simple words were effective. Trix was right. Though Iza hadn't slept with him, she'd let her guard down with him in a way she never had with anyone else. What did any of them know about Jovani? His story about being ex-TSS turned Braedon's private security was hardly the truth. Everyone knew it. But could he fake the connection between them? No, she doubted he could fool her in that way. *The truth couldn't be that bad, could it?*

Iza huffed, collapsing into the captain's chair. She didn't want to talk about it anymore; her night with Jovani was starting to take on a bitter taste. "Let's talk about something else."

"Are you prepared to meet with Karter Hyttinen today?"

What a lovely transition, Trix. Iza sank deeper into her seat. "What does the contract say about being late?"

"Page seven, paragraph eight: 'If the purchaser is unable to make their scheduled payment on the date and at the time previously determined, the purchaser is in default and will incur the total cost of the vehicle immediately. If such is unattainable, then the purchaser is in breach of contract and can be prosecuted to the full extent of the law and the vehicle and all rights to ownership will be returned to Apex Manufacturing Enterprises.'"

"Is there anything about, negotiation, or renegotiation?"

"Yes."

"What does it say?"

"'The terms of this contract are non-negotiable.'"

Iza sighed. That didn't leave a lot of wiggle room for her to work with Karter. He wasn't likely to give her a break, but considering the circumstances, she had to try.

—

They landed the H3X near Apex Manufacturing Enterprises. The moment they touched down, Iza noticed the *Iron Dog* docked nearby. It could only mean one thing: Marten Douketis also worked for Karter. It *hadn't* been a coincidence that they'd been grounded on the same planet. Karter had played her after all, and Douketis had been in on it—probably from the beginning.

Jovani seemed to sense her anger and came to stand at her side. "Are you sure you want to go in alone?"

No, she wasn't sure. Karter was one thing, but knowing that Douketis was there added another layer that she wasn't sure if she could handle without rearranging his nose on his face.

"Yes, I have to do this alone." Iza rolled her shoulders and then smiled at Jovani and touched his arm. She had him to thank for how good she'd been feeling until only moments ago. "But thanks, it means a lot that you want to back me. However, it might be better to keep an eye on your employer." She glanced toward Braedon, who was rubbing his hands in anticipation for his own business. He'd requested an hour off the ship and she'd granted it since they wouldn't be around for much longer than that. Though, when she suggested it, Jovani seemed annoyed. "Problem?"

"No, you're right," Jovani agreed. "I have work to do. Just ping me if you need backup."

"I will," she said, but it was a lie and they both knew it.

—

Captain Marten Douketis was directing his people when Iza arrived, but he turned when he saw Iza leave her ship and head toward him. He came to meet her midway with a pleased grin on his face, then stopped to place his hands on his hips as he called out to her.

"Stars! Has anyone ever told you that you're gorgeous when you're angry? Lose your friends?"

Iza didn't stop walking. Instead, she pulled back her fist and let it fly.

She felt the joints in her knuckles crack, but it was worth it to see the shock on his smug face. Jovani's punch had likely been more painful to the man, but this was certainly more humiliating. Later she'd lament the pain in her hand, but for now it was satisfying.

Two of Douketis' crew members standing behind him moved forward to defend him, but he held up a hand to stop them from advancing.

He was still working his jaw as he smiled. "What's the matter, Captain? I only did what any hauler would do. I got the job done. Had you been more experienced, you would've seen that, too."

"You lied to me, stole the cargo off my ship, and tried to steal from me."

"We both know I would have had that cargo and been long gone before you ever arrived, had the miners not shot us down. Let's agree to let the past die." He held out a hand.

She sneered at it. *The nerve.*

Instead of giving him any more of her time, she walked on.

"If you lose your ship, you're welcome to join my crew. I could use a scrapper like you."

Iza continued toward the showroom building, the sound of Marten Douketis' boisterous laughter trailing her.

She'd lost her last shipment and six whole days. There was nothing to be done for it with only one day left. Twenty-five hours wasn't enough time to get the credits they needed for this month's rent. Fury didn't cover the flood of emotions she felt at seeing Douketis, but there were plenty more for Karter.

The showroom floor was buzzing with activity when Iza arrived, as if it were some kind of sale happening. She didn't stop at the main floor. She didn't even stop at reception. She came barreling through the door of Karter's office before the receptionist had time to catch her. Inside the door, however, there was no one inside. The office was empty.

Becca entered in behind her, smoothing out the bottom of her skirt.

"Mr. Hyttinen is not in today," she said, keeping her tone even.

"Where is he?" Iza demanded, whirling on her.

"He's not obliged to inform me of his whereabouts at all times, nor am I permitted to share it with you if I knew."

Becca kept her eyes on Iza, but she was careful not to change her expression in any way that might be confused with temper. She was worth whatever Karter was paying her.

Instead of yelling at the receptionist, Iza took a deep breath to steady herself. Becca had already gathered herself and straightened her brown shirt and matching skirt over her bare legs.

"Of course, you can wait outside in the lobby, but I don't have any information on when he'll be coming in or *if* he's coming in at all today."

Iza nodded and let the woman escort her out of Karter's office. She only had one day left, and her plan to berate Karter and then beg for more time was now off the table. She had no choice but to leave and take her people with her. If she stayed without another job, she'd be breaking her contract and Karter would take the ship. She needed to find another job, and fast. Something close and that would pay emergency prices.

"Shall I let Mr. Hyttinen know you were here?"

"No. Don't." Her smartest move now was to get to work before he figured out she was going to be short on funds for the month. "I'll be in touch when I have his credits." Iza was about to leave when another question occurred to her. "How long has Marten Douketis been working with Karter?"

The receptionist looked down at her handheld and after a few taps, she read off the display.

"Douketis has been an employee of Mr. Hyttinen for the last ten years."

"How long has he owned his ship?"

"I don't have that information here. May I ask why you have an interest in Captain Douketis?"

"No."

Iza whirled on her heel and headed back to her ship.

The *Iron Dog* was already gone when she reached the docking area and she was glad of it. She still had to wait for Braedon and Jovani to return, and the last thing she needed was another confrontation with Douketis. She'd run out of steam when she discovered Karter wasn't around.

On the flight deck, Trix was waiting for her. "How did it go?"

"Not well. Karter isn't here, which doesn't change anything. Our time is almost up and I need options. Are there any jobs in the sector less than a half-day from here?"

"There are one hundred thirty-six jobs available."

"Of those, how many of them end near this system?"

"Sixty-five of them need delivery completed in this vicinity."

"How many of them pay at least ten thousand credits?"

"None."

Iza swore. That meant, no matter what she did she'd be stuck owing Karter credits tomorrow. Was it worth the risk to recoup some of the credits if not all of them? He might be more lenient if he had most of his money. She considered that for a moment. No, chance. He'd been nothing but a stickler for the rules. He'd also made sure that the last job was incomplete by sending another larger freighter.

"Any jobs that pay close to that amount?"

"Yes, one. It is a farming colony that has an overdue shipment of crates due today. They are willing to pay seven thousand credits, negotiable."

"Negotiable?" Iza wondered if she could get a few more credits out of the deal.

If she hurried, she might get this one done and have time for a second. She had to try.

"I HAVE SOME good news and even better news," Braedon said as he stood in the galley with the others. As soon as he and Jovani returned, he'd summoned everyone to the impromptu meeting.

Iza gave Jovani a quick sidelong glance; they'd already agreed not to discuss their undefined something with the rest of the crew. She'd held up her end. An evaluative look from Braedon had her wondering if Jovani had done the same.

"Iz, you're glowing," Braedon commented.

Iza tried to regain command of the uncontrollable smile on her face. "Don't call me that."

"Wait, I haven't seen Jovani frown all morning, and he's usually angry by 08:00. Are you two...?" Braedon made an obnoxious shape with his two hands pressed together.

"Mind your own business," Iza said.

"Grow up," Jovani said at the same time.

"Come on, just a juicy tidbit."

Jovani punched him hard in the arm, causing Braedon to let out a yelp. "Get on with your news."

Braedon massaged his arm. "See, I used up most of Jovani's money to earn a lot more money and wound up in Sarduvis for my troubles. He paid for our down-payment and I was supposed to have the rest back by now. As it happens, I don't, but that's a story for another time."

"You told me you were robbed," Iza said, her voice rising an octave.

"I was. I won the VR tournament fair and square, but when the Guard raided the place, I was swept up in the crowd and all the credits I earned were confiscated."

"You gambled away all your money?"

"Not mine, really; that was Jovani's." Braedon looked at Jovani, who shook his head, and then back to Iza, shamefaced. "I may have a small gambling problem."

"How come you didn't tell me any of this before?" Iza turned her attention to Jovani.

"Well, at the time," Braedon continued before Jovani could speak, "it didn't seem relevant, as we'd pre-paid for three months' rent. However, when we were on Beurias a week ago, I set up a deal that would earn us our money back in a big way. Except, instead of paying me, they accused me of cheating. I guess that's no surprise, considering how they seem to handle business around here."

"What exactly are you trying to say?" Iza asked.

"I went back there to try to strong-arm my money back, but they came with reinforcements. Long story short, I didn't get what they owed me."

Iza moved so she was on the same side of the table as him. "Are you some kind of idiot or something? What did you promise them in exchange for this great return that you now don't have?"

Braedon scuffed the toe of his boot along the floor. "Just some collateral—a shuttle. Specifically, your shuttle."

Iza wanted to punch something, and the closest target was, appropriately, Braedon's face. She was tightening her fist to swing when Jovani spoke up.

"Tell her your bright idea, before she flattens you."

"Right! I'm getting to the good news part. I found us a way to clear my debt, pay Jovani back, and have a bit leftover to pay you for the trouble—all in one go."

"I don't see why this is my problem. I still physically have the shuttle, so its credit-value as collateral is on you, not me."

Braedon took a step back. "About that… Remember how I said I'm good at hacking? I may have altered the registry details a little bit."

Jovani had to hold Iza back from attacking Braedon. "How dare you!"

"It was guaranteed ROI! They cheated me!" he insisted. "If they hadn't been scammers, you never would have known, and I'd change it back. I just needed it as a placeholder. They weren't supposed to ever have legal precedent to seize the shuttle… until things went sideways, of course."

Iza stared at him with disbelief. "Trix, is that even possible?"

Trix tilted her head. "I have confirmed that the registry details have, indeed, been altered to Braedon's name and there is a flag on its registry," she confirmed, to Iza's horror. "I had not interfaced directly with the shuttle since we acquired the H3X, so I did not notice these alterations. I'm sorry, Iza."

"You have nothing to apologize for, Trix." Iza glared at Braedon before rounding on Jovani. "Were you in on this?"

"I didn't know the details, I promise you. I never would have accompanied him if I'd known what was really going on."

Iza's head swam. *Am I going to lose the H3X and my shuttle, too?*

"I have a way to get out of this," Braedon continued, still making a point to keep his distance from Iza, even though Jovani was standing between them.

"More gambling?" Iza fumed.

Braedon's face lit up with excitement. "No, that's the thing. There's no gambling involved."

"Right now, I'm short about ten thousand credits. If you think I'm going to put my fate in your incapable hands, you're sorely mistaken."

Jovani made the error of reaching out to comfortingly touch her arm before she turned away. Then, as if remembering, he recoiled and raised his hands in the air.

"Hear him out," Jovani said. "If he's wrong, neither of us will have to worry about him being a nuisance anymore."

"True. Though I wish you'd said that last part with a little less enthusiasm," Braedon said. "This job is close, and it's quick, and it will rake in approximately fifty thousand credits, give or take. I'll split the profits with you."

Iza scoffed. "That's impossible. We just ran a scan for jobs in the sector, and there's nothing in the area that pays that much."

"This isn't your typical hauling job," Braedon explained.

I can't believe this is happening. Iza wasn't sure whether to laugh or cry, she was so angry. "Trix, what are our options?"

"To retain both your shuttle and the H3X, you require funds that you presently do not possess. This job would supply the necessary credits within the required timeframe, if it pays what Braedon suggests." Trix paused. "To put it bluntly, there are no other options."

The android's assessment confirmed Iza's fears. "What, exactly, would we have to do?"

Braedon perked up. "A few weeks ago, I didn't realize it, but I'd run into some folks who needed credits almost as bad as we do now. Turns out they were from Hubyria's mining colony. At the time, they were still trying to get the money together to begin their own shipping business. They want to break away from the dynastic Corporations and support their own people. I thought it was a valid idea, but I didn't have anything to offer at the time. Now we do."

"My ship," Iza said under her breath. "The one you *haven't* gambled away yet."

He brushed off her verbal jab. "They've got a job for us, but it's through another broker. We wouldn't have any direct contact with Yeaga and her people. I double-checked on it today. I know how you feel about her, but we'd be getting paid through someone who doesn't need to wait on the miners to pay before they pay us. We'd be paid as soon as the job is complete."

"This stinks like week-old fish. We should be getting at least half of the money upfront, then we don't have to worry about Karter taking the ship before this job is done."

"We asked about that," Jovani said. "Of course, they declined. Tell her the rest."

Iza raised an eyebrow. "There's more?"

"The job isn't exactly by the books... or on the books," Braedon confessed. "The miners need food that's being diverted to other colonies—colonies that aren't in need, just stocking storehouses because the Corporations refuse to provide for the miners while they look for ways to create their own shipping business."

"What you're talking about is stealing from one colony to give to another."

"It's not a colony. The goods come from a central planet with more than enough to give. We're just *reapportioning* the goods from one location to another that needs the help."

It was risky business getting into illegal hauling this early in her career, especially with a couple of guys who were technically passengers and not crew. Sarduvis was like a foul breath on the back of Iza's neck that never went away. She'd be locked up for real and for good if she were caught, and Desirae would be laughing her down the corridor to her permanent cell. Iza swallowed hard at the thought and let the rest go.

"Where do you stand on all of this?" Iza asked Jovani.

"I'm against it. I told him you'd never agree to it. It's not worth risking our lives if we get caught."

Not to mention, she could still lose the ship; the H3X meant everything to her now that she had it. She'd do anything to keep it and although she'd tried to do most things on her own, she knew her solution wouldn't get the job done. Neither plan got her the money she needed on time, so she could risk being late and having the money all at once or she could come up short but be on time with most of it. Iza thought of Karter and wondered where he was. His decision would be her undoing, so she'd have to contact him first.

Iza nodded. "Start coming up with an approach and I'll contact Karter before we leave."

Braedon let out a whoop before he left the galley and headed toward the flight deck with Trix.

"Wait, what?" Jovani asked, turning to her. "You can't be serious."

"I need to do whatever it takes to hang on to my ships," she said as she started pacing.

"There are other ways, don't go down this path." Jovani stepped in front of her and held up his hands.

"In case you haven't noticed, I was already down this path when you met me."

Jovani took a step back. His disappointment was obvious as he pursed his lips. "You're making a mistake," he said, his voice rising. "Once you take this step, there's no turning back."

"Then it's my mistake to make. I'm not begging you to come along." Iza placed her hands on her hips in challenge.

Jovani balled his hands into fists but he backed down.

Iza sighed. "It won't matter one way or the other if Karter's not willing to accept my late payment. The sooner I know which way he's leaning, the sooner I can make a decision on this."

Jovani stayed still when Iza moved to signal the flight deck from the comm panel.

"Trix get us in orbit."

"Where are we going?" Jovani asked.

"I think you already know. We're done here on Beurias and I want to be ready to head to our next location as soon as we're ready."

She moved to pass him, but he stepped in her path.

"I can't be okay with this," Jovani said lowering his eyes and then meeting hers.

"Why are you still trying to live up to the TSS? They already said they don't want you."

Jovani's eyes widened in surprise, then he seemed to understand and shook his head. "This isn't about the TSS, it's about doing what's right."

"What's right depends on the person you ask."

"Stealing food isn't right."

"It is if your family is hungry and you've got credits to pay for it but the people with too much aren't willing to even sell it to you."

"There are other ways."

"Not today, not for me. I don't have time to appease your sensibilities, so do what you need to do."

Jovani put a light hand on her shoulder. She bristled at first, then relaxed into it; she was getting used to him already. The way their lips and hands fit together, it was like they were made for each other. It was going to hurt when he left. She pushed the thought aside.

"I better go. I need to call Karter before we jump."

"Is he likely to give you an extension?"

"Not for free. It's going to cost me, I'm just not sure how much yet."

Iza walked away from him, holding her necklace between two fingers and fighting the desire to run. Nothing was better than having her own ship and her own life, but running was an entirely different kind of life. She wouldn't subject the others to it. She was the only person obligated to stay with the ship; the others were free to go their own way and live without looking behind them.

In her heart, she knew she'd miss the good-natured bickering and their quirky ways, but it wasn't their fight. It was hers. Jovani she'd miss more than anything, but she wouldn't ask him to stay. Either way, it was time to find out what it would cost her to delay her payment to Karter.

20

WHEN HIS PRIVATE line rang, Karter knew who it was. He'd been expecting the call since the night before.

After Iza had come charging into his empty office, he was surprised she'd left so soon. She must have thought she had a chance of getting another job completed in time. He'd scrambled to ensure there were none. It was underhanded, but it would get him the only two things he needed: the H3X and Iza.

As a man, he found her intriguing. A woman of such spirit was hardly the type he'd imagined settling down to live out the rest of his days. However, she could serve a purpose. The demands on his time meant too much to him, but his mother had threatened him for the last time. She'd started to work her hoodoo on his global and galactic interests, and soon there would be no one left who would do business with him.

Regardless of his personal feelings, he needed someone to fill the role as a partner, at least in the meantime. There was only one woman whom trouble always seemed to follow, and her immediate needs coincided with his own.

"Hello, Iza, what can I do for you this morning?"

Karter was careful to sound pleasant but not chipper.

There was only one reason she'd be contacting him over a subspace comm link instead of coming to see him personally.

Using his handheld, he sent a message to Desirae: >>The H3X captained by Iza Sundari is in default of payment. Apex Manufacturing Enterprises will be pressing charges against the accused. Please collect Apex rep and proceed to property at once - KH<<

Desirae would leap at the chance to arrest Iza. His cousin's obsession with Iza was legendary and would play well to what Karter had in mind. He hoped it would do more than get him out of the circumstance he found himself in.

He'd been lured by the appearance of freedom, but in the end, he'd been made to slave for the Corporations in a way he hadn't planned. His mother didn't see it; she only worried after her own welfare. But things were falling into place.

"I'm calling because I won't have your money today as required," Iza said over the audio-only comm link. "Although, I suspect you knew that would happen, since you made sure that the job you sent me on was doomed from the start."

"Why would I injure myself in such a way? I want to be paid. Hurting you would only keep me from getting what I want."

"Really? That's strange. Since the moment that Captain Marten Douketis stole my cargo, he returned right here to you. Despite your underhanded motivations, I have a way of getting all the money I owe you for this month by tomorrow. Will that be satisfactory?" Karter could hear her ask the question through clenched teeth.

It had been sloppy of him to use Captain Douketis in that way, but he couldn't go back now. He'd already put everything in motion.

"It won't do. I apologize if I gave you any indication that a breach in the contract would be overlooked. This is an infraction that cannot be rectified in the manner in which you are suggesting," Karter kept his tone neutral and his wording legal as he was recording the conversation for future use.

"You've put me at a disadvantage. Why did you agree to lease the H3X to me in the first place?"

"I only gave you the ship you chose. Had I insisted on a different one, you could perhaps blame me, but in this case, it is only yourself you can blame."

Karter turned off the recording.

"However, there is one way in which we can resolve this matter and avoid any further infractions. Won't you at least consider it?"

"You already know the answer," Iza said. There was a long pause on the other end of the line. "What you're asking, I can't do."

"I understand. However, you'll have to accept the consequences of that decision and that means the immediate confiscation of your ship."

"You wouldn't."

"It's already done. It's my sincerest hope that someday you'll change your mind about me. However, for now, I think we must accept things for what they are. Perhaps some time on Sarduvis will change your mind."

—

Becca waited to be acknowledged at the door of his office until after Karter terminated the call.

"Yes, Becca?"

She held out a cup of his favorite brew with a smile on her face.

"Thank you," he said.

"Sir, the information you were looking for has come in." She held out a tablet for him to examine.

"What information?" He was annoyed that he'd had to ask. She was being far too vague for his taste. Then, his gaze landed on the name of the file.

"I thought you'd want to see it right away," she said.

"You were correct. Thank you. Now, let's see what trouble Iza's crew has been getting up to," Karter muttered to himself. He was three pages into her report when he raised both eyebrows in surprise.

Becca was having far too much fun baiting him that she didn't tell him right away. Instead, she pulled out her handheld and showed him a picture.

"Who's the woman?"

"Someone's not-so-dead mother."

"Who, one of the passengers?"

"No, the woman—Iza Sundari."

"Well, that was unexpected." Karter gave Becca a look and she nodded in confirmation.

"I thought that might be of interest to you."

"Where was this image taken?"

"Tararia. She was just walking around minding her own business, it seems. However, I don't think her daughter realizes that she's still alive."

"That does make for an interesting turn of events."

"There's more," Becca said leaning forward. Karter's eyebrows rose at that. She'd gone above and beyond again; maybe she was gunning for another raise. He already paid her too much as it was.

"The young man traveling with her, the TSS Agent."

"Former Agent."

Becca shook her head.

"More like undercover. He's still an Agent for the TSS, Sacon class, and his real name is Joseph Anderson. He's from Earth, of all places."

That did get his attention.

"What's an undercover Agent doing on Iza's ship?"

"I don't know, but I thought it might have something to do with whatever that man is looking for on the ship."

Karter took another sip and put the cup down. "I doubt that very much. Even so, it's my problem to deal with. I appreciate the information you were able to gather. Instead of asking how you got it, we'll slide past it. I would like you to keep this little investigation between us. I'm happy to compensate you handsomely in return."

Becca lifted a manicured hand as if to wave away the compliment. Her handheld signaled and she looked down and then back to Karter.

"Investigator Hyttinen has arrived, sir."

Karter grabbed his overnight bag from the case behind him and held it in one hand. "I'll be away for a bit on business."

Becca nodded. She was new to the position, but her ingenuity should be rewarded. Despite multiple dead ends, she'd gotten him exactly the information on Iza's crew he'd been looking to obtain.

"Thank you. Please see that everything here is as it should be in my absence. I won't be long."

As she left the office, Karter turned to stare down at the corporate legacy he was trying to save. The ships on the showroom floor gleamed in their quiet glory. Quiet. Strange, the floor was empty. Not one customer or employee roamed around. It was still two hours before the official end of the day, and most of his employees liked to impress him with their dedication to work.

"Becca? Where is everyone?"

"They've been given the rest of the day off," said Mr. Arvonen as he entered with two large personal guards, one on either side of him. The left had let scars form on his face to further intimidate, and the other on the right had a look far too handsome for someone with hands the size of a man's head.

Mr. Arvonen moved to sit down in front of his desk while his guards remained at the door. He brushed his white hair back from his high forehead. The signs of a full and rich life were reflected in his tightly-fitted waist coat, which he adjusted as he settled on the guest chair.

The old man's full features turned down as he fixed his gaze on Karter. "My ship is still not here. I should have known not to send a boy to do the work of a man."

Karter was getting tired of Arvonen's constant berating. Even so, instead of frowning at the insult, Karter smiled as if he'd been complimented. It was one of the tactics he used while negotiating with difficult clients—make them believe that they're telling you you're the sun if it gets them to stop and think.

"Where is it?" the old man asked between his teeth.

Karter glanced up and caught sight again of the man's guards. They were tensed and ready to move, though their expressions were blank. Karter wondered if his own security would come charging to his rescue or if they'd been dismissed along with the salespeople. So, instead of wrapping his hands around the man's neck and squeezing until his eyes bulged, he answered.

"The ship is safe and still under my jurisdiction. If you tell me what you want from it, I'll see that you receive it."

"You double-crossing bomaxed idiot! I don't have to tell you anything."

Arvonen visually had to calm himself and thrummed his fingertips on the edge of the seat. The design and material should have made the sound inconsequential, however it was loud and irritating. Karter smiled as if it didn't bother him.

"If this fails—"

"It won't fail, sir," Karter assured him. "Everything is going according to plan, and you'll have your ship in a matter of days.

When are you going to tell me what this is all about?"

"I'm not. Once I have access to the ship, I'll tell you only what you need to know and nothing more."

"About your son—"

"Don't ever mention my son," Arvonen roared.

Karter took another deep and calming breath. "I only meant we would make a better team if you trusted me with your vision," he said, unable to mask his annoyance.

"That's where you've forgotten your place. We're not a team. Nor are we equals. Please remember that in the future. I'll deal with my house you deal with yours."

"Yes, sir." Karter kept his expression neutral, though his pulse was racing. The large statue on his desk beckoned him to pick it up and throw it, but he fought the impulse. "As soon as I have the ship's coordinates, I'll send them to you."

"I don't need you anymore to get my ship. I'll handle things my own way."

The older man picked off an invisible piece of lint and tossed it aside as he stood up to leave. He carried a cane that was not used for walking, crafted from glossed wood with a sharp end and a curved head made of metal. It was a fierce-looking accessory, and Karter wondered who'd be feeling the brunt of it today.

Karter didn't see the pulse gun until it was aimed at his chest. The single hit on full charge instantly dropped him—not a shock meant to stun, but kill. The old man stepped over him and walked through the doors, followed by two others. As the life seeped out of Karter, he wondered what would become of Iza now that she was free of him.

—

When Karter woke up, Becca was at his side calling out

commands. There was a vague sense of feet running to do her bidding.

She reminded him of the captain of a ship as she directed others. He'd been smart to promote her to replace his former assistant. In such a role, he needed someone more than an assistant. Someone he could trust. Who'd always be there when he needed help. Now, as he lay on the floor of his office dying, he couldn't think of a better time for someone to demonstrate their loyalty.

Becca gave him a nanotech booster and he felt the inside of his body making the needed repairs so he could take a full breath again.

"What happened?" he croaked.

"That old man shot you. I knew he was trouble when he made us all leave. I came back with a few members of the staff as soon as we saw his shuttle depart. You're going to be all right, just hang in there."

Becca's blue eyes were red, as if she'd been crying. How come he hadn't noticed how pretty her eyes were before? Karter's vision blurred as he again struggled to focus on her face. He made a mental note to give her a raise, regardless of her already inflated salary.

"Where did he go?" she asked.

"I don't know."

21

"How long until we can jump, Trix?" Iza asked.

"Ten minutes."

"What happened?" Jovani questioned.

He and the others were sitting around the galley table, waiting for her to tell them the next move.

"Karter," Iza said trying to push down the betrayal. "He isn't going to give us an extension."

Jovani gave her a look like he was ready to fight, but Braedon had wisely positioned himself on the other side of the table from both of them.

Iza could hardly blame Jovani; he'd been caught up in Braedon's destructive orbit as much as her. The frustration about their current situation was palpable.

"What are we going to do?" Braedon asked.

The question hung in the air around them as the others waited for her to respond to his question. She had no idea what the others should do, but she knew what she had to do.

"You need to get off this ship as soon as possible. I can drop you off on Demarsa. There are plenty of cities where you could lay low."

Jovani stiffened and she rushed on before he could protest.

"It's not safe here anymore. I know you pre-paid for three months, but Karter isn't going to give me an extension and he's sent the Enforcers after me. I've already given you back your credits so that you can have something to board another ship."

"I have no intention of leaving," Trix said in her monotone style.

"Yeah, I know," Iza rolled her eyes. "I've already tried to get rid of you before." As Trix walked out, Iza turned to Braedon and Jovani. "You both need to be prepared to leave."

"We're not leaving you here," Jovani said. He moved to stand beside her, as if physically he could protect her.

That's one of the things she liked about him. As strong as she was, she appreciated he wanted to look out for her in any way he could. Though she appreciated the sentiment, there was no helping her, and staying would only get him in trouble.

Jovani looked at Braedon, but his head was down. "This has to be the worst idea I've ever heard," Jovani muttered.

"I'm looking at two impounded ships and who knows how long on Sarduvis if they catch up to me," Iza continued. *When they catch up to me—no 'if' about it.* "The pleasure cruise is over. You need to think of yourselves." Iza looked from one to the other.

"I didn't mean for this to happen," Braedon murmured.

"It's not all on you," she said. She couldn't deny that she was bitter about Braedon's part in the trouble, but she'd have still been in a bind with the H3X even without him bartering her shuttle. If anything, taking away the option of retreating to the smaller craft as a fallback plan was the nudge she'd needed to face her troubles head-on.

I couldn't go back to that life barely scraping by on the shuttle. The H3X is the only future I wanted. In spite of herself, her gaze drifted to Jovani. *Well, maybe not everything.*

"There's another way, we just need to figure out what it is,"

Jovani said, his fists closed tight.

I already miss those bomaxed blue eyes. "There isn't. Even if I had the money, Karter won't take it. But as it stands, nothing I do is going to make matters any worse. So, I'm going to pull that miner job on Phiris. The rest of you need to get out of here while you can." It was unfair to ask them to sacrifice themselves for her ship.

"I set up that job! I need the credits," Braedon said.

"And I'll get you your half if I succeed in pulling it off, but I don't want to risk you getting arrested along with me if I don't," she told him. "Like it or not, you're leaving the ship so be ready to go. We'll reach Demarsa in a couple of hours. Meet me down in the cargo hold with your things and we'll part in peace."

Braedon turned to head for the flight deck.

"Where are you going?" Iza questioned.

"To input the codes you'll need to get through the security net on Phiris. That way, you won't have any trouble getting in and out with the crates."

"Thank you," she said.

"It's the least I can do. Again, I'm really sorry." Braedon ran back and hugged her, then rushed out to hide the emotion on his face.

When they were alone, Jovani grabbed her by the hand and she didn't resist. Though his mouth moved, no words came out.

She looked into his eyes. The next part was harder to say, but she needed to say it. *Just like I rehearsed it.* "It was fun, you and I, but it was never meant to be. Let's just leave it at that."

"Don't," was all Jovani said.

"Don't what? You have already expressed your opinions on the morality of what I plan to do. I'm officially an outlaw. You can't live that way; this is no longer the place for you."

"No, I–"

Iza sighed before he could finish. "Please, leave. We both know there was no other way for this to go. I can't keep you from what's to come if they catch up to me." *And they will catch me.*

—

Iza was lying on the bed in her cabin with the lights off, thinking about her next move, when she got the signal from Trix.

"Captain, we have arrived."

Iza's heart sank. The thought of losing Jovani physically hurt, which shouldn't be possible in so short a time. He was special, and every time they were together it was harder and harder to be apart again. She gripped her necklace, wondering if he'd leave and find someone else. It didn't sit well but, if she were being completely honest, she only had herself to blame for her situation. Karter didn't force her into the H3X; she'd volunteered. The rest of the trouble was minor by comparison.

Karter and Desirae would try to catch up to her as soon as possible. She might have to hide the H3X and come back for it. The best move was to consider making a run toward the outer colonies on the other side of the Empire, further from Tararia and the influence of the authorities, with the hope she could find a place to blend in. She'd take only off-the-book jobs, and she and Trix would keep a low profile. Demarsa would be their last chance to pick up supplies before they were on the run, so she'd make the most of it.

"Trix, meet me down in the cargo hold. We've got work to do."

Iza walked to the hold and was surprised that no one else was there yet. Trix was the next to arrive.

"Where is everyone?"

"Braedon and Jovani have already left the ship."

"What?"

"Is there a problem?"

"Not exactly, I sort of thought the jerks would let me say goodbye." Iza shook off the familiar regret. "Let's go."

The cities of Demarsa were full of tall buildings in exquisite curving shapes, their elegant glass and gleaming metal surfaces reflecting the afternoon sun. The scene when Iza stepped off the ship with Trix was striking, and for a moment, Iza found herself being one of the gawking tourists she'd often bemoaned on the middle Taran worlds, like Kinterin. Though shy of the grandeur found on the elite central planets, such worlds were wealthy and sophisticated compared to the outer colonies. In recent contrast to Hubyria, she was reminded just how inequitable life could be throughout the Empire. She quickly gathered herself and returned her attention to the task at hand.

That's when she saw Braedon and Jovani, standing there with satisfied expressions on their faces.

"What do you think you're doing?" Iza asked them, even though her heart skipped a beat at the sight.

"We're staying," Jovani said, crossing his arms over his toned chest.

Braedon nodded. "We agreed that we're better off sticking together."

"I'm pretty sure I made it clear that it was, in fact, not better. There might be a way to hide the H3X until things cool down, but Karter Hyttinen has a long reach, and his cousin Desirae in the Guard, won't stop looking for me. She and I have a history."

"Desirae is a jealous little imp and a bomaxed fool," Trix said imitating the tone Iza had used when she'd said it the first time.

"True, she'd love nothing more than to drag me back to Sarduvis."

"You're not getting rid of us that easily," Jovani said.

Iza had to choke back the emotion. When had anyone ever chosen to stay with her? She couldn't remember, and it was making her tear up. Iza looked each of the young men in their eyes, seeing that they agreed. They were going to stay, despite the circumstances. She let go of the ball of pain she was holding in her gut and rolled her shoulders.

Braedon cleared his throat and started filling the awkward silence with anxious rambling. "So, while you were preparing to say your goodbyes, we were thinking of what to do next. If you're okay with it, we can run down the plan we've come up with so far."

"I'm open to ideas." Iza looked over at Jovani. Something was bothering him, but she didn't know what or if he'd share it with her. They hadn't exactly defined their relationship, and she'd been ready to throw it out the window at the first sign of trouble. He might not be ready to trust her with his feelings just yet.

"You're okay with this?" Iza asked him.

Jovani looked at her levelly. "I'm in."

A simple, no nonsense response, giving nothing away. He could be so infuriating. Iza nodded, satisfied that everyone was on board.

"My original plan will still work," Braedon said. "After we deliver the goods, they might even agree to provide cover for a time."

"You have a serious savior complex, but that aside, you're not wrong," Jovani said. Then he turned to Iza.

"I, personally, like the idea of helping people who need it," Iza replied, "but do you think your mediator on Hubyria will come through?"

"I do," Braedon said. "The deal is solid."

Iza considered the proposition. The idea of working for Yeaga grated on her nerves. She wasn't sure if it was because the others were so eager to or if it had something to do with their last encounter. They'd get more than enough for the ship lease payment, should Karter change his mind. If he didn't, they'd have enough credits to make a run for it.

"Alright, I'm listening."

—

The four of them sat around the galley table for the next two hours planning for the job until they were sure everyone knew their parts backward and forward. Braedon circled the table, giving out directions like a conductor with a musical orchestra. She'd never seen him so comfortable taking control.

"Iza and Jovani, you'll get the crates from within the warehouse. Trix will wait at the entrance as look-out and help get the crates to the shuttle while I set up the distraction," Braedon said as he summed up everything. "Are we all clear?"

"Yes," they said in unison.

"Good, be ready to head out in one hour."

When the meeting adjourned, Jovani moved to stand beside Iza. He spoke low so the others wouldn't overhear him. "There's no coming back from this, you know."

"Yeah, I know." Iza shrugged. "I've done it before."

"Stolen?"

"Survived."

"Is it the same thing?"

"Sometimes."

Iza thought back over her youth, remembering times when she'd done a lot worse. Taking on a ship of her own, she'd hoped never to have to face those kinds of choices again. Now, she was staring down a man whom she was starting to trust and making a choice that would affect them both.

"When are you going to get used to the fact that we like being here with you?" Jovani asked softly.

"We?"

"Me."

Iza swallowed the lump in her throat. "I'm not sure I ever will, but I can't say I don't like it. I've just never had people stick around. Not even my parents. It's something I've learned to question."

"You don't ever have to question my devotion."

The sincerity in his eyes made her knees weak. She wondered when she'd get to see his real blue eyes again.

"We all knew what a risk this job was," Jovani continued, "and we're willing to see it through. When all of this is over, we'll go someplace quiet where we can sleep all day and party all night, with or without clothes."

"Without clothes, definitely," Iza said with as much mischievousness as she could manage. Then, still feeling honest she added, "I'm used to looking out for myself. Having people and crew is hard."

"Yes, it is."

Iza was already getting used to having Jovani around and that scared her. What would she do if Karter or Desirae threatened him or any of the others? Braedon was just a kid. The fact that he went out of his way to help other people put him on her good side, even though some of his plans had landed them in more trouble. Trix would be loyal even if they took her apart piece-by-piece.

If they succeeded, they'd be supporting the thousands of people on Hubyria to help them secure a better quality of life. It didn't seem like a bad thing to be helping others while at the same time helping herself. It had an honorable quality. This was the best option for keeping them alive and out of prison. She so badly wanted it to work.

"The question is, do you think it's worth it?" she asked.

Jovani placed one hand on either side of Iza's face; the warmth made her want to sigh. He pressed his lips down softly on hers. It started sweet and undemanding, then it deepened. The hunger in it made her want to give and give until there was nothing left. She felt his hands on her back and then lower, pressing her against him. When they pulled apart, they were both breathless. Jovani looked her in the eyes and whatever he saw there made him smile.

"You tell me," he said.

She was on fire as she watched him walk casually away.

22

THE MYSTERY BOX Iza had found on the ship filled her dreams and mind with impossibilities. She knew it was the box because nothing had ever felt so real to her before. The hum of music lingered in her mind after she woke up. There was some kind of connection between her and it.

Is this thing only affecting me? Is it dangerous? The last thought kept her from sharing her discovery with anyone else. Jovani and Trix would want to throw it out the airlock, but something made her keep it a secret. She wanted to protect it, for now.

Iza was still staring at it when time elongated for a moment and the background mechanical hum of the engine faded. *We shouldn't have completed the jump yet.* Before she could make it to her cabin's viewport to confirm if they had dropped out of subspace, overlapping warning klaxons sounded throughout the ship.

Iza quickly stashed the box in the safety of her side table drawer before dashing into the corridor.

The alarm systems on the H3X continued blaring as she raced toward the flight deck. Jovani was just ahead of her.

"Looks like the jump drive deactivated," he said, waiting

for her to catch up.

"EMP cannon again?" she speculated.

"Fired in subspace? No way. Plus, that would have taken out all of the systems. The lights and life support are still active, so we at least have the backup ion reactor."

They found Trix, also still functioning, standing in the middle of the flight deck with her head tilted to one side. She spoke before they could ask the question.

"The connection to the ship's PEM has been severed, and the pion drive is disabled. There is some kind of inhibitor. It appears to be a product of Apex Manufacturing Enterprises."

Iza swore. Of course, Karter would think to put on a boot to prevent the ship's function. Why hadn't she thought of checking for it earlier?

"Was there any indication it was there before?" Iza asked, hoping she wasn't the only one who overlooked it.

"No. It was buried within the subsystems of the ship's main processor. It is designed to go into effect once triggered remotely with the lockdown codes. The command was transmitted via our connection to one of the navigation beacons five minutes and thirty-five seconds ago. It has locked out all propulsion controls. We're drifting on inertia between star systems."

Iza pinched the bridge of her nose. She had to give Karter credit for knowing how to cripple a ship. Taking out access to the PEM would prevent them from jumping or calling for help over subspace communications, and taking out the pion drive meant no sub-light propulsion.

"Is there a key code?" Jovani asked as he sat at the helm, his hands moving over the controls.

A prompt screen appeared as a holographic overlay in front of the forward viewport.

"Yes, however, there are infinite numbers of

combinations," Trix stated.

"We only need one." Jovani activated the ship's internal comm.

"Braedon, get to the flight deck." He closed the comm. "That kid can crack just about anything. Maybe he can help."

As soon as Braedon arrived, Jovani stood up and made room for him.

"I've got a code for you to crack."

"Seriously?" Braedon's face went from confusion to anticipatory in seconds. He pushed up the sleeves of his shirt and put his hands over the console. "Who created the code?"

"Karter," Iza said with confidence. "He'd hardly leave it to the likes of Becca or one of his other assistants."

"This is going to be fun," Braedon laughed. "There was this one time—"

The proximity alarm sounded, and they all stared at the stars out in front of them. Braedon's next words hung in the air unfinished and forgotten. The small specs of light moving toward them were barely discernible from their distance.

"It is an Enforcer fleet of three ships, headed straight for us," Trix said in answer to their unasked question.

"We're screwed." Iza ran a hand over her hair. She gripped the co-pilot seat as Braedon continued to tap away at the keys.

"I need more time," Braedon said without looking up.

"Why aren't they shooting at us?" Iza asked.

"They are scanning our ship for weapons," Trix said.

Jovani leaped into the seat in front of Iza.

"Weapons are down. Only basic environmental systems are functioning at the moment. I'm not even sure these buttons I'm touching are doing anything."

The panic of escape was rising in her chest as Iza looked at her frantic crew and then back at the screen.

"Trix, I need options."

"You can surrender. The entire crew will be arrested and detained on Sarduvis to await trial. I will be dismantled and my processors recycled into new systems."

"No, I want *viable* options."

Trix turned to look at her as if she were speaking in a foreign tongue.

"Stall them!" Braedon called out.

"Karter is on that ship," Jovani called out.

"What?"

"He's there, I can sense him on board the lead ship."

"Can you get the code from him?" Braedon asked.

Jovani looked at Iza and nodded. She knew it went against everything in his code as a TSS Agent to search someone's mind like that, and yet he was willing to do it for her.

"The likelihood of Braedon deciphering the correct sequence code is one in three-point-seven million," Trix continued. "The lead Enforcer ship is hailing us. It is Investigator Hyttinen."

Could it get any worse? Karter and Desirae on the same ship ready to bring her in—it was like something out of a nightmare. No doubt, the minute the H3X came up delinquent, she'd been called. Karter would want to be here personally to take the ship and rub Iza's nose in it.

Then, something about the moment reminded Iza of a dream she'd had recently. In it, she'd stood on the flight deck alone. The ship was stopped and she'd done something. *Why can't I remember what I was doing?*

"Do we have communications?" Iza asked.

"Yes, local ship-to-ship," Jovani said. "But just a second. I'm going to dampen the signal. It will keep the communications garbled."

"Thanks," Iza said squaring her shoulders. "Open the channel."

"This is the Enforcer B652. I am Investigator Desirae Hyttinen. H3X-Z500, prepare to be boarded. You are in breach of contract. Your ship will be impounded, and your passengers will be detained for questioning in the recent robbery in which this ship was identified."

At Jovani's signal, Iza began speaking. "I'm sorry, could you repeat that? The transmission was all garbled."

"This is Enforcer B652. I'm Investigator Desir—"

"This is really embarrassing. We're having trouble reading you over here. Could you please repeat your message?"

Jovani muted the open comm link with the Enforcer ship. "I've got it!" he said, turning to Braedon. "1ZA-5UN0-AR1."

"I should have known." Braedon shook his head. "Iza Sundari."

Iza's brow knitted. "What?"

"I knew he had a thing for you, but bomax if he didn't put your name as the code to the ship."

Even though the code had been input, the front console was still red with warnings about the jump drive being inoperable while going through its startup sequence; however, full control had been returned to the sub-light antimatter pion drive.

"Ten minutes fifty-five seconds before the jump drive is reinitialized," Trix stated. "And, even with the element of surprise, we will not be able to outrun three Enforcer ships at sub-light speeds."

"No, we can't," Iza said.

Jovani and Braedon turned in their seats to face her in unison.

"Unmute the channel," Iza ordered.

Jovani stood up and moved to her side, his eyes pleading. "What are you doing? We can still try to make a run for it."

Iza shook her head. It wasn't worth the risk. If she turned

herself in, the others could potentially go free. If they ran, they'd all be liable for her crimes.

The red warnings on the front console suddenly turned to blue.

Iza came to attention. "What's going on?"

"Jump drive primed, course plotted, engage?" Trix asked.

"Yes!" Iza said as the others chimed in at the same time.

The hum of the jump drive vibrated the deck. In a swirl of blue-green light, the ship slipped into subspace. It would take the Enforcers more than a while to figure out their course.

"How did that happen, exactly?" Iza asked.

Braedon put his hands behind his neck. "I don't like prison, so I bypassed the initialization sequence. I figured it was unlikely we'd actually blow up."

"You did trick the systems into believing the drive was ready, but it taxed the distribution cells," Trix said. "It could have burned them out."

"Yes, but it didn't. Good work Braedon," Iza said. "We should drop out of subspace and plot a new course in case they are able to access our original beacon sequence. Let's hide our trail."

Trix nodded. "I will see to it."

Iza allowed herself to smile. "We've got a job to do, so let's go get our haul. Let me know the moment we reach Phiris."

"Yes, Captain."

She turned to leave and felt Jovani follow. He may be a former TSS Agent, but he still acted like one. If every time she broke the law she had to defend herself, they should part ways sooner rather than later.

Once she'd reached a private section of the corridor, she addressed him. "If you're into perfect women, you're going to be disappointed with me." She tried to continue down the corridor, but Jovani used his body to block her and she wound up bumping into him.

"I could never be disappointed with you," he said leaning down and placing a light kiss on her cheek.

He was infuriatingly handsome. It was strange how he could disarm her with desire in his eyes or a half-whisper. Even now, pressed up against the bulkhead of the ship and with Braedon and Trix just out of view, she couldn't resist his touch and found herself giving in, the pressures of the day dissolving. All she wanted to do was melt into him.

"Promise me when this is all over, we'll get some time together. I can't stand being away from you," he said.

Iza wasn't sure she could form a coherent sentence so she nodded. Then, she wrapped her hands around his neck as his mouth crashed in hers. There were no thoughts of anyone else and hardly any thought at all. Pressed together, there was nothing between them but flesh and bone.

When they parted, they were both gasping. Jovani seemed as shocked as she was by the burst of passion. For Iza, it was as if her feet had left the ground and only now did she notice the hard surface of the ship under and behind her. Jovani was the first to find his footing and staggered away with a satisfied grin on his face. Iza was left struggling to control her breathing.

She straightened her clothes and ran two hands over her curls. She turned toward the flight deck before she remembered she was heading for her cabin.

What in the world am I getting myself into?

— — —

Joe had ignored the last twelve messages from his superiors, but when the latest one came in from the High Commander himself, it wasn't one he could disregard. Wil Sietinen didn't get involved in the everyday goings-on of

Agents and certainly didn't make administrative calls. If he was making time to contact Joe, he'd better respond.

Joe took a deep breath before making the return call. He'd already checked the area for anyone listening, and this time in his cabin was the closest to privacy he was going to get.

"Hi, thanks for getting back to me." When the High Commander answered like he was taking a call from an old friend, it took Joe off his guard.

"Um yes, sir, this is Agent Joseph Anderson reporting." *Was that formal enough or too much?*

"Wil is fine. It's Joe, right?"

Too much. "Yes, Joe."

"So, it seems things have cooled down for the time being in your sector. I wish I could say the same for elsewhere, but there's too much going on and never enough Agents."

Why is he telling me this? Thankful that he couldn't be reached telepathically at this distance and that the call was voice-only, Joe took another deep breath and made his request.

"As I mentioned in my formal report, by keeping my cover and maintaining relations with the miners through the crew I'm currently serving with, I was able to diffuse the situation for now. The miners are far from happy, but with a little independence they might be willing to listen when the time comes."

"Agreed. Despite Ian's opinion to the contrary, I think you did the right thing by remaining where you are."

Joe didn't know whether to be happy or upset by that bit of news. Being near to Iza was all he ever wanted most days, but he'd be lying if he said he didn't miss Headquarters and his pitiful excuse of a life there.

"I just wanted to let you know personally how much I appreciate what you're doing for the TSS and thank you for your sacrifice. It's not an easy assignment, but you've made it your own, and that's the kind of dedication we need in the Taran worlds right now."

There was something of sorrow in his words and Joe wondered what he meant by it. Could there be something bigger brewing? It seemed so, but he had his own troubles, and one of them was dealing with the local Enforcers.

He explained the situation to Wil, hoping the High Commander could pull a few strings to help him along, either through military channels or his family connections with the High Dynasties. Wil listened as he spoke without interrupting, and when Joe was finished, there was silence.

"Sir?"

"Yes. I understand the dilemma, but I'm afraid I can't help you out of this one."

"Without your assistance, we could lose the ship, the crew, and we'd all be put in jail."

"That's the risk you take when you skirt the law. I appreciate your creativity and willingness to get your hands dirty, but in this case, there'd be no way to bail you out without it turning into a political nightmare. Not only would any outside intervention draw unwanted attention to your crew, but it could also leave you open to further action by the local Enforcers, which would defeat the purpose. I need you to maintain your cover and complete the mission."

"For how long?" Joe regretted the question immediately and wished he could swallow the words back down his throat, but it was too late.

Wil didn't seem to notice. "For as long as it takes. I promise you, when you're needed back here, we will call you. But for now, you're doing great work. Despite the circumstances that put you there, I couldn't imagine a better person for the job."

"Thank you," Joe mumbled.

Joe's heart sank. With those complimentary words, Joe

knew he'd be in the outer colonies for some time. Thankfully, he had Iza and the others to keep him company. Thinking back over the last few weeks, he'd been worse off before with no ship and no friends. This was a leap forward in comparison, but it would all be for nothing if Iza lost the ship and the crew got arrested.

"I look forward to your report, Agent," Wil said, preparing to sign off.

Then, an idea came to Joe. "One more thing, sir—Wil. I realize you can't help me with the local Enforcers in any direct way, but perhaps you'd consider getting me a piece of equipment."

"What do you have in mind?"

"Might it be possible for you to arrange some upgrades to the ship—to make it so the Enforcers would have difficulty tracking us?" Joe knew it was a longshot, but he had to try.

Wil didn't reply at first. "You mean, an independent jump drive?"

"Yes." Joe held his breath.

"I never wanted that technology to find its way into civilian hands," Wil said.

"I know it can be dangerous, but the ability to maintain a semblance of stealth is the only way this mission will be able to succeed."

"It would certainly give you an edge, but it's just too dangerous for an untrained navigator, I'm sorry."

"What about a Lynaedan android?" Joe asked.

"Yes, one would have the computational capacity to operate the independent jump drive navigation with a reasonable measure of safety. Why, is there one on the ship's crew?"

"There is. Trix. She's always spouting off awkward stats about our current biological state."

"Yeah, they like to do that." Wil was silent for a few moments. "Admittedly, it would be helpful to have an Agent with access to an undercover ship with that kind of maneuverability. I'll authorize the upgrade."

Joe breathed a sigh of relief. "Thank you."

"There is, however, the matter of how to complete the installation of the new nav console and reactor. How do you intend to get the ship into a spacedock without blowing your cover?"

"Leave that to me."

"All right. I'll locate an appropriate facility in your vicinity and send the details."

"I really appreciate it. This will make all the difference."

"I hope so," Wil said. "Don't abuse it."

"Never, sir."

"Good luck out there." Wil ended the connection.

Joe felt lighter. He couldn't get used to calling the High Commander by his first name, but the man had a way of making him okay with it in the moment.

While the TSS couldn't intervene to get the Enforcers off Joe's tail, at least they could make it so his ship could never be caught.

"CACI," Joe addressed the ship's computer, "where is Trix?"

"Trix is currently in Engineering."

Couldn't be more perfect if I'd planned it. Joe headed for the belly of the ship.

When he arrived in Engineering, Trix was alone, as Joe had hoped and expected. She was in the middle of what looked like a diagnostic of the power distribution cells, which she'd feared were damaged in Braedon's reckless, but necessary, quick-start of the system.

"Jovani, why are you here?" Trix asked when he entered,

without looking up from her work.

"I wanted to talk about something with you. Privately."

"Is this about your sexual relationship with Iza?"

Joe flushed. "No, we haven't—" He shook his head. "Nevermind. Have you... been listening to my private conversations?"

"They are not private when conducted in a common area of the ship."

"What have you heard?"

She turned to face him. "You mean about you being an undercover active TSS Agent?"

He braced. "And what if I am?"

"Then I am grateful to you for using your influence to free us from Sarduvis." She turned back to the diagnostic.

"That's it? No 'how dare you mislead us'?"

"Do you intend to harm the ship or its crew?"

"No. Quite the opposite, in fact."

"Then your profession and personal relationships are none of my concern."

"You won't tell Iza?"

Trix paused again but didn't turn. "I would advise you to tell Iza yourself, but relaying such information about passengers would betray the privacy I promised to maintain."

Joe stepped closer. "Trix, I may have a way to keep Iza and everyone else on this ship safer, but I'd need your help to pull it off."

"What action do you propose?"

"I want to upgrade the ship with an independent jump drive."

Trix wheeled around to face him, her face showing as much shock as he'd ever seen her display. "How did you gain access to such a drive?"

"Friends in high places. But we'd need to get into a dock,

and I don't want Iza to know I had anything to do with it. As far as she's concerned, I want the ship to be going in for... hull repairs, or whatever."

"We do, in fact, require structural repairs to microfractures sustained during our crash on Hubyria."

"Great, does that mean you'll help?"

Trix tilted her head. "Yes, I will assist in facilitating these upgrades."

"Thank you, Trix. You won't regret it."

23

IZA HADN'T BEEN thrilled about the unexpected detour to the Aerendale Shipyard near Phiris when they should have been picking up supplies, but Trix insisted that the structural repairs were required before they made any more jumps. If the android said the half-day detour was necessary, Iza wasn't about to complain—not after her prior objections to repairs had resulted in them nearly being stranded in the void. Now, with the Enforcers on their tail, they couldn't afford any mechanical issues.

Once the repairs were complete, and the ship was purring even happier than when Iza had gotten it, they had jumped the rest of the way to Phiris. While the ship remained in automated high orbit, the four had taken the smaller shuttle down to get a closer look at their target.

Iza ached from laying on her belly in the dirt, where she'd been surveying the storehouses from the top of a nearby hill. They were planning to make their move that evening, and the timing had to be accurate. The planet's arid climate was ideal for doing the job at night. The days, however, were hot and Iza had peeled off her layers earlier to combat the extreme heat. Now, the air had grown cooler, and in combination with her wet skin, she shivered.

Jovani returned from the shuttle with her jacket. She handed him the binoculars so he could watch the storehouse security while she slipped her arms into the warm sleeves.

"Thank you," she said as she wrapped her arms around herself.

"You're welcome. Any change in their intervals?"

"No, they're still on two-minute rounds, two guards per storehouse, and two guards on the front gate."

Jovani frowned as he turned to face her. "Did you notice they were carrying plasma rifles?"

"Yes, is that a problem?"

"Doesn't it seem odd to you that a standard food storage facility would have rotating security carrying high-grade weaponry behind a force field with randomized code entry access?"

"When you say it like that..." Iza said. Then she went back to watching the guards. "What else do you think they're storing down there?"

"I don't know, but I'm sure it's something more than food chips," he said turning to face her again.

"The hardest part is going to be unlocking the warehouse door without being seen."

"Braedon says he can do it. He got us through their border security completely undetected."

"He'll also need to remotely hack that perimeter shield. If anything goes wrong."

"Despite the rotating codes, he seemed sure of himself," Iza said.

"Yeah, because he's so resourceful."

They shared a knowing look before turning their attention back to the storehouses.

"Any crates shipping out?" Jovani asked.

"No, but another truckload arrived and the crates were unloaded to the fifth warehouse half an hour ago. It seems they haven't reached capacity yet."

"Why won't they sell some of their surplus to Hubyria? It's not like they can't spare it." Jovani had more disdain in his voice than Iza would have expected from someone who'd been a part of 'the system' for the first part of his career. Then again, he was *former* TSS for a reason.

"When laborers are in conflict with their corporate overlords, the fastest way to affect them is to cut off their food and supplies." Iza thought back to what Aeva had told her and the difference between what they needed and what they wanted. The Corporations would make them suffer on both ends.

"I thought the changes in leadership on Tararia had made life better for people out here in the remote colonies?"

Iza shrugged. "People in their castles on Tararia think a lot of things."

"I don't think they live in castles, exactly."

She rolled her eyes. "It doesn't matter. Yeah, it *has* gotten better in some ways since the leadership change, but there's still a long way to go, and nothing gets better if you don't speak up."

"I suppose so." Jovani fell silent as he watched the activity below.

The Hubyrian miners and their families were a nuisance, which meant the easiest course of action was to withhold goods and services—essentially, starve them out. Braedon's mysterious contact on Hubyria wanted a mere two crates of dehydrated nutrient chip emergency rations to allow the miners to weather the strike. She still suspected that Yeaga was behind the job. Each crate held five thousand bags, each containing two hundred round chips. With a little water, the chips would rehydrate to feed thousands of people. Yeaga and her group of miners would be able to hold out against the Corporations for more leverage—the longer the strike, the more lost profits. Eventually, the heads of TalEx and its subsidiaries would have to listen.

The particular grouping of warehouses they were going to hit had five large buildings filled with goods. The grouping had small foothills on one side and desert on the opposite, which would make escape difficult since the only options were running away uphill or in a straight line with no cover. However, the same challenges would affect the security in pursuit.

Should the worst happen, Iza had an escape plan. They wouldn't make it over either landscape with the crates. If they were discovered, the shuttle would be sitting on the other side of the foothills, well within reach, and could be maneuvered by Trix to pick them up in a hurry.

The first of the warehouse buildings sat on the left edge of the property from their viewpoint and had the most activity, even at night. It was nearest the entrance and held the everyday food shipments, such as grains, protein, and other supplements. The facility was surrounded by a three-meter-tall force-field fencing system, with only the one entrance. That front entrance was secured by an electrified fence, which had to be manually disengaged to allow the supply trucks to pass. The three middle buildings had an overlap of guards walking in pairs so there was never a gap between shifts. Only the warehouse on the far end was a viable target. Even though it was in front of the steepest drop from the foothills, the warehouse's entrance faced outward toward them, making it a straight shot to the door. It also housed the largest supply of the emergency nutrient rations they were after. Their main obstacle was the perimeter fence. They had nothing that could manually get them all through, but they had Jovani with his telekinetic ability. If they timed it right, they could get over the fence without a sound.

Iza lifted the binoculars to her eyes and the dark landscape became distinct with the augmented night-vision. The movement of the warehouse security was the clear, predictable pattern that they'd anticipated. The guards kept to opposite sides of the building in two teams of two. She stood up and turned toward the shuttle.

"It's getting close to the end of shift. Braedon are you ready?"

"Yes, I'm ready. Of course, now I wish I had grabbed something to drink before I sat down. The tension is already making me sweat. When this job is finished, I suggest we find a nice lake and spend a few days enjoying the water. There's this really nice place with a retractable dock that sits in the middle of—"

"That's enough," Iza said cutting him off.

"The guards are up to seven-minute increments. We need to move," Jovani insisted.

"Jovani and I will go in as planned. Trix, you follow us and be ready to get the first crate back here. If anything goes sideways, you know what to do. Braedon, that leaves you to get us through the warehouse door."

"You've got it," the young man acknowledged.

"Have you got the disruptor ring?" Iza asked Trix.

"Yes," the android confirmed as she reached for the loose loop she'd attached to the belt of her pants.

"Remember, it's your last resort since it will set off all the alarms in the place. But, in a pinch, it will get you out of there in a hurry."

"Understood."

"It never hurts to have a back-up plan." Iza checked over her items to confirm she had everything she needed. She gave one final nod to Braedon. "Be ready to send me the code."

"I was born ready." He grinned.

"See you soon." Iza pocketed the binoculars in her pack and then started down the side of the hill toward the warehouse.

Jovani cast a telekinetic shield over them to hopefully diffuse their heat and other energy signatures enough to prevent detection. Still, without stealth suits, they needed to avoid being seen.

Iza was careful to navigate around the large searchlight beams sweeping over the landscape while moving as quickly as she could. They had to hurry to get through the perimeter and to the door before the guards passing between the buildings caught sight of them. They watched as the two remaining guards passed between buildings one and two toward the back before they made their move. Trix was already out of view, and she would stay hidden until Jovani returned with the first crate while Braedon waited back at the shuttle.

At the base of the hill, Jovani quickly levitated Iza over the fence. Her skin tingled as the air seemingly congealed around her. She fought the impulse to squirm as he picked her up and set her gently on the inside of the fence. She'd never seen—let alone felt—telekinesis up close like that, and it thrilled her.

Then, Jovani seemingly leaped into the air, higher than any person should be able, and gently dropped down next to Iza. After the display—using only a fraction of his abilities—Iza had no question why most people didn't get in the way of TSS Agents.

—   —   —

Joe restored the shield masking their signatures and ran behind Iza to Warehouse Five. That's where Braedon's key card came in. It had come from his contact and he'd assured them it would work once he'd uploaded the current code. He watched as Iza stared at the card reader then made her first attempt to use it to open the door. Nothing happened. She ran it again.

"Braedon," Iza hissed into her handheld.

"Hold on, the code just changed. Updating the keycard now."

"Hurry up, or we'll be seen."

"Scan it again it should work now."

He saw Iza brush the card over the panel for the third time. There was a loud click as the locks disengaged from the heavy metal door. They slipped inside before the guards saw them. Once inside, Iza was able to use her handheld to serve as a flashlight for them to get a better look at the warehouse. Crates of dehydrated chips the size of a small car, and nearly as heavy, filled the warehouse from floor to ceiling in neat rows. The sight of the surplus made it easier to justify their actions. Two crates out of hundreds wouldn't be missed but could do a lot of good on Hubyria.

"I saw a couple of crates on the floor. Let's check to make sure they're full," Joe said, running ahead of her.

She caught up with Joe a moment later leaning over his right shoulder to look as he opened the first crate, lifting the lid clear of the box. Inside, the food chips—transparent and black pieces—glistened against the light from their handhelds.

"All your daily vitamins and nutrients in one little chip," Joe said in his best announcer voice.

Iza giggled and he loved the way the sound tickled his belly.

As soon as they closed the lid of the first crate, Joe froze; two guards were making casual conversation as they made their way around the warehouse. Iza switched off her light and they waited. The guards' conversation made no mention of a theft in progress, so all was as it should be. Joe gave her a nod of reassurance.

Together, without the light, they balanced the crate between them and shuffled it across the warehouse floor. Joe found the physical labor prevented further strain on his abilities, allowing him to focus on maintaining the stealth shield.

As soon as the guards had cleared the opposite side of the warehouse and were out of view, Iza opened the warehouse door. Joe levitated the crate through the opening and over the perimeter fence, where Trix was waiting to receive it.

Iza was standing next to the second crate when he returned. It was easier to carry it the second time, even in the dark. They were two meters from the exterior door when the alarm sounded.

They both let go of the box and looked up. Iza stared at him, eyes wide.

Joe shook his head. "The alert didn't originate inside here. Do you think they spotted Trix?"

Iza frowned. "I don't know."

"Guards are headed right for us," Joe whispered. "Hide!"

Iza dove to the right behind a row of crates. Joe scrambled behind a lower set of crates on the left.

The guards raced inside and spotted the crate, which had obviously been moved.

"Sound another alarm. We've got thieves in this warehouse, too," the first guard instructed.

"If they're here, how come the alarm sounded in Warehouse Three?" asked his companion.

"An organized effort. They might have already made off with a few crates. We'll have to check the inventory."

"That'll take forever," the companion complained.

"It's our jobs if we don't. Let's start by clearing all areas. If any of the criminals are left behind, we need to take care of them."

The silence must have been agreement because they sorted out which rows of crates they were going to search. Iza was flush against the crates behind her, but she wouldn't stay hidden for long. Joe mentally tried to calculate her odds if she stayed where she was or if he moved to cover her position. He watched Iza as she squinted her eyes closed, bracing for a plasma rifle hit to the chest. She'd never make it.

A stack of crates clattered to the ground before he could take a step. It came from the far corner of the warehouse, and both security guards ran to investigate. After a short scuffle, there were two thumps as if two people had fallen to the ground. Joe could only sense one person left and his mind was relaxed and familiar.

"You can come out now, Scrap Rat," Captain Douketis called.

Iza stepped out to face him while Joe approached from behind, keeping his weapon trained on the older man without flinching. "What in the bomaxed business are you doing here?"

Douketis tipped his hat to her. "Doing a job, same as you."

"What's in Warehouse Three?"

Douketis waved a hand. "A little of this and that." He glanced around and caught sight of the crates. "Not food chips. Something with a little higher market value."

"Weapons," Joe said.

"Your boy here is smart. I say keep him."

"Your people triggered the alarm, you idiot," Iza said between her clenched teeth.

Joe watched Iza's hands clench into fists at her sides as if preparing to strike. He wondered if Douketis knew how close he was to being pummeled. Trix was nowhere to be seen— presumably, she'd gone to hide when the alarm sounded.

Iza looked down at the crate they had been carrying as if trying to decide if it was worth it. Joe did his own calculations. He could levitate it over the fence, but it was too cumbersome for him to use telekinesis to get back to the shuttle in one trip while maintaining any sort of cover shield for them. Their lives were far more important than the food chips.

"Let's get out of here," Joe said. "Forget the crate."

"We need two crates," Iza hissed.

"Well, it looks like we might be able to help each other," Douketis cut in. "I'll help get you another crate in exchange for safe passage off of this planet since my people will have pulled out already."

Iza squared her shoulders and started for the door.

They didn't have time to discuss a deal with him even if they wanted to, which Joe didn't. He grabbed Iza by the hand, pulling her along after him. There were more guards coming; they had to hurry. They needed the shuttle, but Trix was the only one who could remotely pilot it over.

He reached the door at the same time as the guards.

They're just doing their job. That's what he told himself as he used telekinesis to throw the first guard into the row of crates on the right.

The second guard fired on them. Joe had anticipated the shot and tossed him to the left. The wayward shot from the guard's gun made a hole in the warehouse roof and they ran outside to avoid the falling melting metal. Exposed and out in the open, he barely had time to deflect a third guard knocking him hard to the ground on his back before a fourth had his plasma weapon trained on them.

Iza raised her pulse gun, but the guard was already firing as he yelled the warning.

"Stop!"

Joe didn't think as he leaped.

— — —

Iza watched as the plasma rifle fired. It was aimed at her, and at this close range, death was a real possibility.

Well, this is going to hurt.

But instead of being hit by the concentrated plasma blast, she was thrown to the ground by Jovani. He was hit in his right arm, and the burning flesh made her retch. It must have knocked him out because his dead weight had her pinned under him.

Douketis dropped the guard with a pulse blast before he could change targets. Iza didn't realize she was just sitting there until Douketis pulled Jovani off of her, rolling him to one side, and lifted her to her feet, pulling her forward.

"Leave him. He's going to get us both killed."

Iza dug in her heels. "I'm not leaving him."

The engines of her old AS-255 roared and appeared just in front of them. It dropped to the ground.

She moved to cover Jovani's face from the dust as the door opened smoothly. Trix bolted out, taking in the scene. Her eyes lingered on Douketis. "The *Iron Dog* shuttle has left orbit."

"Trix, Jovani," was all Iza could get out.

Without hesitation, Trix lifted Jovani, careful of his injured arm, and ran up the ramp.

"What about your crate, are you just going to leave it?" Douketis complained.

Iza ignored him as she followed Trix on board.

Braedon moved from the console to help settle Jovani on board. Then, he looked up and caught sight of Douketis. "What happened out there, and what's he doing here?"

Iza tore her eyes away from Jovani's horrific injury to glare at Douketis.

"Kid, take me with you," Douketis pleaded with one foot on the shuttle ramp.

"Why should I? You wouldn't do the same for us," Iza spat, baring her teeth.

"That's probably true, but you're better than me, and we both know it."

Iza growled, pulling him inside and closing the hatch behind him just as more guards rounded the corner and started firing.

Douketis dropped to the floor to help wrap Jovani's nearly-severed limb. She kept replaying the moment in her head. It happened so fast. Jovani was moving to block the shot before she even knew what was happening. He took the hit for her in the arm as he pushed her to one side and they both went down.

Gunfire continued to pepper the hull as they lifted off the ground and raced back to the H3X.

"What happened?" Braedon asked as he whirled away from the console.

Iza's stomach churned at the sight of bloody bandages around Jovani's arm. The burn smell was bad. She pushed down her nausea to answer Braedon.

"Douketis and his crew triggered the alarm and we all got caught in the crossfire."

Iza grabbed the medkit while Braedon brought over the spare blanket and pillow she kept on board. She moved to support Jovani's head with a pillow while Braedon tucked a blanket around him to help with the shivering from shock. Iza focused on Jovani's ashen face while Douketis finished wrapping his arm and shoulder.

Jovani's eyes fluttered open, unfocused as he looked up at her.

She leaned in and stroked his face. "You're safe now."

But the lie stuck in her throat. No one was safe with her. It was her problems that had gotten them into this situation in the first place. Maybe that had been her problem all along. People around her died or got hurt. She hung her head.

"He's bleeding out faster than the nanites can repair the damage. Do you have a surgeon on board the H3X?" Douketis asked.

"No," Iza said her lips tight. *What have I done?* She looked around the bare shuttle with only one crate of food chips and then down at the small medkit.

"He's going to lose his arm, if not his life," Douketis said.

"I know."

24

"THIS WASN'T YOUR fault, kid. He dove in front of you. I saw it with my own eyes," Douketis said to Iza.

They were seated on the shuttle bench Iza used as a bed, looking down at Jovani, who lay ashen and unmoving. He was probably trying to make her feel better, but it only made her feel worse. Trix insisted that they refrain from moving him and causing any more damage.

Once they'd docked with the H3X, Trix helped rush Jovani to the infirmary. While the facility was much better equipped than the small medkit in the shuttle, it didn't have an automated surgical unit that could handle anything nearly as complex as reattaching and filling in the missing pieces of an arm.

Such a severe injury was also beyond Trix's capabilities in the time they had available to act. The android rewrapped Jovani's arm, but they all knew it wasn't a solution.

"He has already lost too much blood and his heart and respiratory rates are elevated. His arm will not last long in this condition. It needs to be removed and regenerated,"

Regenerated. Iza's thoughts were going a kilometer a minute. How was she going to get him a new arm? At the moment, they were running from Karter and the Enforcers. The minute they showed up at a hospital, they'd all be caught.

"You're going to need a doctor who won't report this to the Enforcers," Captain Douketis said.

"Doctors are required to report certain things, but Healers aren't under the same rules," Braedon said worrying his bottom lip. "I know of someone in the area who would help him."

"Well, let's get in touch. We don't have a lot of time here. Are you sure a Healer can fix this?" Iza asked.

"She's amazing. There's nothing she can't fix. Besides that, she's gorgeous. There was this one time—"

"Spare me the bedtime story," Iza cut in. "Just give Trix the coordinates so we can get help sometime in the next year."

Braedon moved to the console on the side wall of the infirmary to input the coordinates for Trix.

"We are being hailed," Trix said, getting a faraway look in her eyes as she processed the communication.

"Who is it?" Iza asked. She protectively moved closer to Jovani.

Douketis grunted. "Probably my people. I knew they'd come for their captain eventually."

"Yes, it is the *Iron Dog* freighter. How would you like to respond?" Trix asked.

"We only got half of what we needed," Iza muttered.

"My deal is still on the table," Douketis told her. "We could still both walk away from this with credits if we play it smart."

"That business can wait. Tell them we have another pressing matter. Jovani needs help now."

"My people aren't going to take orders from you," Douketis blustered.

"Trix, plot a course to Braedon's coordinates," Iza instructed.

Trix nodded her understanding and jogged from the infirmary.

"You're making a mistake," Douketis grumbled.

Iza glared at the other captain. "I suggest your people wait here for us. They will or they won't. But either way, it doesn't matter to me."

———

After the short jump to the small settlement where Braedon assured them the Healer was located, Braedon seemed more than a little nervous.

"Is there a problem?" Iza asked him.

"No, she's, like, the nicest person I know. She'd never hurt anyone, especially me. We go way back."

Iza doubted the length and depth of their relationship, given Braedon's young age, but she wasn't in a position to argue. "We'll be back as soon as we can be," she told Trix. "Let the *Iron Dog* know we'll be returning with their captain shortly."

They took the shuttle down to the planet's surface. On the approach, Iza wondered at the beautiful landscape, more lush and green than any place she'd had ever been. They landed the shuttle in a small clearing, but there didn't seem to be a path through the dense tree line and brush to reach the Healer's house Braedon had pointed out from the air.

Iza followed Braedon down the exit ramp. She'd lost sight of the squat, one-story residence surrounded by wildflowers that they'd seen from the shuttle on top the nearest hill. It reminded Iza of something she'd seen in an old vid.

Braedon let her clear the path ahead. She was hit and scraped repeatedly with twigs and branches overgrowing around them until they plowed through to the other side and in front of the house. The gardens surrounding the home were breathtaking, filled with a variety of bright flowers and vegetation. There were no orderly rows or design, just wild beauty left to devour the landscape and the house, as it too was covered in the lush fauna.

A young woman with olive skin and curly brown hair came running out from the house waving her hands, her long light pastel robes fluttering in the breeze.

"No, you can't be here. Your shuttle is crushing my plants. Get that beast out of here!" She flashed angry green eyes at them as she spoke, which narrowed to catlike slits when her gaze settled on Braedon. "What are *you* doing here?"

Before he could speak, she was already shaking her head. "No, you've got to go. I don't want anything more to do with you."

"We need your help," Iza said when it was clear the young woman wasn't going to listen to Braedon.

The woman turned on her angrily. "I don't know what he's told you, but he can't be trusted."

"Our friend he's badly injured," Braedon explained. "He was shot in the arm—almost took it clean off. Come on, Q, we need you."

"Don't call me that," the woman snarled. "If his arm is coming off, I suggest you apply to have a new one grown. I don't do that."

Braedon raised his hands in surrender. The situation was disintegrating faster than a burning star.

Iza took a step forward, her own hands raised in the air.

"I don't know how you two know each other, but please hear me out. My name is Iza Sundari, and we have a friend who is hurt and could die in addition to losing his arm. If we could go to a regular hospital, we'd be there. Braedon swears you're the best Healer in the sector and that you wouldn't turn us away. If he's done something to change either of those things, I will see that he makes it right." She gave Braedon a look and he nodded.

"He means a lot to you, the injured man," the woman said.

Iza wasn't sure how to answer that, so she told the truth. "Yes." Her gaze dropped to the ground and then back up to the woman's face. "You'll be compensated for any assistance you can give us."

"I don't need the money, but I'll help you. Just keep that idiot away from me." She waved dismissively at Braedon.

"Done."

The woman turned on her heel to re-enter her home. She returned minutes later with a satchel strapped across her body but still no shoes on her feet.

"Where is your friend?"

"He's back on my starship." Iza looked down at her bare feet in question, but Braedon shook his head as if to say, 'don't ask'. "Is that going to be a problem?"

"I was raised on a starship among the Aesir, and it's not something I'd wish on my worst enemy. This garden and this soil I toiled with my own two hands. Someday, I hope my children will continue this natural home away from the stars. But, if your friend is as bad as you say, I better come with you."

They trekked back through the foliage to the shuttle. The woman followed in silence as they boarded and initiated the takeoff sequence.

When Iza glanced down at the ground as the shuttle lifted off, she noticed three people leave the safety of the trees to go to the place where the shuttle had been. They appeared to be lifting the grass.

"They're repairing the damage your shuttle caused. You should be thankful," the woman said from the seat behind Braedon. Iza wasn't sure what kind of nonsense that was, but she'd worry about it after Jovani was better.

Braedon was quiet the whole way back to the ship, which was unnerving. Iza kept glancing over at him to make sure he was still breathing.

Unable to endure another minute of the intense silence Iza spoke. "I didn't catch your name, Doctor…"

"Cierra Quetzali, reformed Healer."

"So you were never a doctor?" Iza turned to glare at Braedon.

"It means I've abandoned the traditional constraints of being a Taran doctor and have embraced the principles of healing."

"I see." She didn't, but Iza didn't have another option.

Captain Douketis was waiting when they reached the docking bay on the H3X. He started to speak, but Iza waved him away. "Wait for me in the galley."

Braedon started talking like a faucet stuck in the 'on' position the minute they reached the corridor.

"Jovani is in the infirmary. The captain will show you to him. We patched him up the best we could, but he's just hanging on. Perhaps you could help him with the pain. We don't have the supplies to do that, it's probably what's keeping him unconscious. He's a good guy, Jovani. He's supposed to be my security, but he's no good to me with one arm, you know?"

His last statement made Cierra Quetzali stop and turn to face him.

"No good to you?" She took a step forward as Braedon took a wary step back.

"That's not what I meant. He's part of the team and my friend. I don't want him to wake up and think he's got no chance, you know?" Braedon stammered under the intensity of her gaze.

Whatever happened between the two of them, Cierra

wasn't over it. The more he talked, the more Braedon buried himself. Iza was about to step in when Trix met them in the corridor outside of the infirmary.

"It is too late. He is dead."

Cierra leaped into action. Before any of them could get back into the room, she was at Jovani's side working with hands and mind to get him back. The long tone coming from the medical monitors indicating his heart had stopped cut off as she disconnected the leads, letting them fall to the floor with a metal *tink*.

Jovani's ashen face stayed inanimate as she pumped her palms against his chest to restart his heart. Trix held out the handheld heart defibrillator to her. Cierra ignored it. Iza and the others each slid a meter backward, as if pushed by an invisible wave. Iza sensed the same electrical prickle on her skin that she'd felt when Jovani lifted her over the fence.

So that's what was meant by Healer. She's Gifted... Iza hadn't expected Cierra to have telepathic or telekinetic abilities. Such gifts were rare—more than rare most places in the outer colonies. Iza had heard of the Aesir being a rogue sect of Tarans, but she hadn't realized there were Gifted among them; for that matter, though, she didn't know *anything* about the group.

Jovani's eyes remained closed as Cierra started to hum. It wasn't so much a tune as a set of tones. There was a change in the tone with each breath and she hovered over him as if to guide Jovani to breathing.

Iza found her breath matching the calm and steady pace that Cierra encouraged. At the same time, she waited for Jovani to gasp for breath or sit up, but it seemed that only happened in the vids. Instead, there was a pale pinking of his cheeks as Jovani took his first breaths. His eyes remained closed and his body still, but Cierra smiled. Iza didn't risk speaking until

Cierra moved on to redressing his severed arm.

"Is he alive?" Iza asked unable to believe her eyes.

"Yes, for now. I can't promise he'll stay that way. If you have the means to regenerate his arm, that would be the fastest way to health. However, a proper hospital will keep him alive if you can manage it."

Iza shook her head and pressed her lips into a firm line.

"I've already redirected the ship back to where we came from. We need to finish the job or we won't have the credits to get him the arm. I need everyone on the flight deck."

"I told you she could do it," Braedon whispered as he left.

When they were alone, Iza let her eyes fill with the tears she'd been holding back. When she could finally speak, she turned to Cierra.

"Thank you."

"I promise to do what I can, but I can't stress enough how little time we may have to get him more extensive treatment," Cierra said.

"Keep him breathing let me worry about getting him a new arm." Iza stole a glance over her shoulder at Jovani, and her thoughts torn between staying at his side until he opened his eyes and going to work. Again, she wished she could communicate with him telepathically. She wiped hard at her face. *Don't you dare go anywhere.*

Iza made her way to the galley where Douketis was pacing like a caged animal short his one meal for the day. Thoughts of Jovani circled but she pushed them to the back of her mind so she could focus on the job in front of her. She took several deep breaths to calm herself then squared her shoulders to deal with him.

"I've been a patient man," he began.

"No, you haven't, but we'll have you back to your people shortly. We're returning to Phiris now."

"I won't be left down here in the kitchen like some kind of grunt."

"You're right, follow me to the flight deck."

Whatever he was expecting, it wasn't that. He blustered for two seconds before he realized she wasn't slowing down and he should follow her.

Iza waited until her crew and passengers were gathered on the flight deck. "She's good," she said once they were all together.

Braedon lit up. "She's amazing, but she's ticked at me. I guess I shouldn't be surprised. There was a bit of a misunderstanding at the end there."

"For now, Jovani's going to be okay. I need everyone to focus on getting the job done."

"Wait, what job?" Braedon asked.

"We only retrieved one crate, so we're going back to get the other one."

Braedon crossed his arms. "For the record, can I state that this is a bad idea?"

Iza eyed them. "There's no record of this conversation, and you only need to focus on your part of the plan."

"Do you understand how hard it was for me to get the codes the first time.? I'm not sure I could get in the back door like I did the first time. The coding has probably been updated and who knows what kind of safeguards they've added since our first time in," Braedon said.

"This time, we're going in with help." Iza turned to look at Captain Douketis.

He nodded. "Yes, we'll help you get your haul."

"Wait, we're trusting *him* now?" Braedon complained.

"It's a point of personal pride. It's his team that triggered the alarm. This is their chance to get in and get out undetected."

Douketis gave her a confirming nod. "I'll just need to communicate with my team first."

"No, they'll take their orders from me. That way there won't be any chance of misunderstandings. Everyone will get their commands from me at the same time."

Douketis shook his head but Iza held up a hand.

"Look, I appreciate the help, but we can do this job without you. It's up to you. Like you said, we could both come out ahead. Both our crews need to eat, right?"

"True. Okay, I'll agree to it, but we'll want to grab our own haul."

"We won't prevent you from grabbing what you want."

"Captain?" Trix began.

Iza held up her hand to silence the android before she stated her objection to the plan. "Look, I know things have gone backward and sideways, but it won't be for nothing if we get the job done. Are we agreed?"

Douketis nodded. "Get my people on the holodisplay."

"Trix, call the *Iron Dog*."

As soon as his second-in-command, the woman with the spiked pink hair, was on screen, she seemed pleased to see her captain on the flight deck. "Is everything okay, Captain?"

"Yes, we're going to help Captain Sundari get her haul and then get a piece of our own while we're there. Get our people prepped and ready to return with a shuttle to the surface."

To her credit she didn't even flinch, however, another burly man with bright orange hair on his head and bare arms moved to her side as if to confirm it was Douketis speaking.

"Yes, Captain," she said with a curt nod that her companion imitated.

Iza was impressed with the way his crew responded to his odd demands. They had to be wondering what would make him work with them, but they were smart enough not to ask.

"How are we going in?" the pink-haired woman asked.

"Captain Sundari will brief you on the surface. Just be ready for anything."

"Yes, sir."

"Douketis out," he said.

Trix cut the communications.

"Is everybody ready?" Iza asked.

"The likelihood of success is less than five percent," Trix said.

Iza ignored her and turned to Braedon. "Do you think your old friend will help us?"

Braedon worried his lip in concentration, then shook his head. "I doubt it, but I can ask."

"Nevermind," Iza said. "Better she stays with the ship and Jovani at this point, anyway." Then she turned to Trix. "I've got something special for you to do for me."

"I would be happy to help the crew," the android said, rubbing her hands together in anticipation. Though the movement was stiff, it conveyed the point.

"Are you sure you want to trust the haul with the android?" Douketis asked in a whispered voice.

Iza nodded and kept her voice loud enough for everyone to hear. "Trix has a very neat trick you haven't seen. She'll be fine. Just make sure that she's the one carrying the haul."

25

BEFORE THEY BOARDED the shuttle bound for the surface, Iza went to see Jovani one more time. Cierra had dimmed the lights in the infirmary and something was burning in the corner. A pungent woodsy, sharp scent filled the room, making her cough. She held a hand over her face as she questioned the Healer.

"What have you done to my infirmary?"

"I've turned it into a place of healing instead of illness."

Iza would have argued, but the sight of Jovani lying there with a peaceful expression on his face held her back. She'd done something to slow the bleeding where his right arm used to be. The bandages still needed to be dressed often, but he wasn't feverish with infection which meant the nanotech and Cierra's touch was still doing its job.

Iza couldn't argue with the young woman's methods. She'd changed into another one of her flowing pants outfits. This one was the yellow of an aged sun with a white embroidered edge. The material was something that whispered when she walked and showed off her figure in some light. On her bare feet, her toenails were colored with dark red paint and she wore delicate jewelry on her ankles that tinkled when she walked across the floor. When Iza caught sight of Cierra's bare feet again, she spoke up.

"Do you need a pair of shoes? I'm sure we can scrounge up a pair."

"No, I prefer to keep my body connected with the surface on which I walk."

"It's not very hygienic or safe. You could hurt your foot on something here. I have an extra pair of boots that will do until we get you back home."

"Let me worry about my feet. I believe you have more pressing concerns."

It was true. Iza knew she should be on the shuttle with the others, but she wanted to remind herself of why she was doing this. She'd left some of her courage in the corridor on her way to say what she wanted to say to him.

Cierra made herself busy in another part of the infirmary, giving Iza some semblance of privacy. Iza still dawdled over the task, knowing Cierra could hear every word whispered in the room.

She focused on Jovani's face and saw the color had returned. He looked so much more alive than he had when he'd been bleeding out in her hands.

Iza leaned over the left side of his bed, noting the presence of another scent in the air just above his skin. Another ointment had been applied since her last visit. She'd been too shocked to cry then. Now, though, she had to fight the tears as they welled up in her at the thought of almost losing him.

What was it between them, would they survive it? One minute he was kissing her senseless and the next he was diving in front of plasma rifles to save her life. It was all too confusing to figure out in a few minutes.

Iza took his warm, calloused left hand into hers. "You're going to be as good as new. Fight with everything you have.

Remember, you owe me another night without your contacts."

She sniffed at the burning in her nose and lifted his good hand to her cheek, placing a light kiss on his inner wrist.

"No matter what happens to us, take care of him," she told the Healer.

Cierra bowed low without answering. If Jovani were awake, he'd approve of her sparse use of spoken language. It was clear that she and Braedon had been a thing once. Maybe it was true what they said about opposites attracting, but Iza had never seen it up close before.

—

After jumping back to Phiris, the shuttle trip down to the surface was quick and efficient. Braedon was quiet, and even Captain Douketis kept his mouth shut. Iza was left alone with her thoughts to think about what was coming. Their first attempt to get the crates had been thwarted by one of Douketis' people; he'd admitted that much. This time, nothing was going to stop them from getting what they'd come for and they'd brought help.

When they reached the rendezvous location, Douketis' people were already waiting for them. They landed their shuttle facing theirs and disembarked.

So prompt, she thought to herself with more than a little anxiety about teaming up with her recent adversaries. She turned to address the group of five associates. "This time, we won't run into any trouble because we're teaming up. We have to get this right."

"Getting one crate shouldn't be too difficult," Braedon said.

"We're leaving with two crates."

Both Douketis and Braedon paused to gawk at her.

"What?"

"I'm sure you heard me the first time."

"No, I think you need to say it again," Braedon said. "Why would you want to get two crates when we already have one?"

"The extra crate will go to Captain Douketis. His crew is risking their necks so we can complete our haul, but we're not going to send them on their way with nothing."

Douketis' people murmured their agreement.

"We leave with a crate each," Iza continued. "There's enough for them to have food chips for years if they're conservative. Does that sit well with you?" Iza asked, turning to Douketis who was staring at her in disbelief.

"Um, yeah. We'd be very appreciative," he managed.

"Good. Now that we know what the goal is, it's time to fill in the gaps in the details. Captain Douketis, I'm assuming you have a way around their perimeter fencing."

"I do," he said.

"I want you to take a couple of your guys and go after a crate while Trix and Braedon secure a crate for us. Because Trix doesn't have a problem carrying, she can do most of the lifting on her own."

"I will be fine, I do not need assistance," Trix said, sounding wounded.

"Of course you don't, but if something goes wrong, I want someone to have your back. Braedon will have a pulse gun to keep any of the guards off of you."

Trix blinked and then looked at Braedon. "I do not think that Braedon is capable of shooting a guard at any real distance."

Captain Douketis coughed into his hand to cover up the laugh he was stifling. Before the others could join in the laughter, Braedon spoke up.

"Who's going to distract the guards?"

"I can get more guys on that, if you'd like," Captain

Douketis offered.

Iza was pleased to see how eagerly he jumped at the chance to have more manpower on the ground but she shook her head.

"Why send a man when a woman can do the job with half the fuss?" Iza smiled and looked at the woman in pink with the spiked hair. "What's your name?"

"Reis."

"Is that your first name or last name?"

"Yes."

"Okay," Iza said her eyebrows raised. "You and I have a part to play, and we're about the same size, so I brought something for you to change into," Iza said. "Once this begins there's no turning back. If anyone has any reservations about the plan, then speak now."

The others, including Douketis, nodded in agreement.

"I'll help you get your haul and then we're square," he said. "Besides, I'm still sore from the last time you hit me. I have complete confidence in your abilities."

That's all I need to hear.

—

Iza slipped into a short blue dress with sparkling details on the edges. She handed the pink one to Reis; it went perfectly with her hair.

The dress barely reached mid-thigh on either of them. They wore their boots instead of changing shoes, and Iza could only hope they were pulling it off. She had pulled her hair out of the braid and left it loose and wild. She used water she had stored on the shuttle and wet Reis' hair, then combed it flat and made it sweep around the crown of her head instead of standing up all over. It immediately softened her features.

"We'll have to play dumb and lost."

"It won't be a stretch for you," Reis said, glaring at her.

"Just do as you're told and we'll be in and out."

"You don't give me orders." Anger flashed in Reis eyes' as she took a warning step toward Iza.

Iza wasn't one to back down and proved it by stepping forward until they were almost touching.

"For this mission, just follow my lead and you'll be back to kissing Douketis' boots within the hour."

The other woman looked like she was on the verge of decking Iza but thought better of it at the last second. With another eye-dagger glare, she nodded and prepared to step off the shuttle to get back to the others.

While Iza had prepared herself for the reactions from the crew once she'd changed into the provocative outfit, Reis didn't have long to get her bearings. When they stepped out of the shuttle, it was as if they'd been transformed. Instead of waiting for the jeering to stop, Reis stalked up to the loudest man and kneed him in the groin. He dropped to the ground in pain. The others sobered. More composed, Reis turned to Iza with a nod. Neither of them was comfortable with the unwanted attention, but Iza had to admit she liked the way Reis dealt with it.

"All right guys, that's enough fun," Iza said. "Give us ten minutes and then move. You've got exactly twenty minutes to get in and out with the crates, we'll meet back here when the job's done."

—

The guards were more than thrilled to be of assistance when Iza and Reis stumbled up to the gate.

"We're lost," Iza said in the most innocent voice she could muster. "We were supposed to meet up for a party, but this is so far from anything. They dropped us off and I'm pretty sure it's a prank because this doesn't look like an underground club to me."

The first two guards were amenable but on high alert. It was going to take both of them to get them to call their friends over. When they offered them something to drink, Iza snuck a glare at Reis and silent, 'Say something.'

Reis shrugged and replied a silent, 'I don't know what to say.'

Iza rolled her eyes. Of all the women to be doing this with, she was stiffer than Trix.

"Hey, guys, do you have any friends out here that could help us out?" Iza continued. "I don't want you to get in trouble for leaving your post."

"No, it's no trouble. The other guys would just be jealous, anyway, with us getting to help fine ladies such as yourselves."

Iza let the laugh bubble up and out loudly, drawing as much attention as she could. Reis did the same, laughing and stumbling forward against the other guard.

"Oh no, my shoe," Reis said doing her best to sound disappointed. It was more like a child's whine but it seemed to work.

A minute later, another guard appeared from the nearest warehouse. He looked displeased to be the uninvited guest, but Iza did her best to make him feel comfortable, practically falling into his arms as soon as it seemed appropriate.

"I have an idea. We don't need the club at all! Do you have any music?" Iza asked.

"Yes, music!" Reis exclaimed, clapping her hands loudly as the next guard showed up. It was the signal the others would be listening for. With four guards around them, the warehouse nearest would be temporarily unattended.

Iza felt a little bad so blatantly manipulating them, but she didn't blame them for being bored. Knowing the Corporations, none of the guards were paid well enough to put up with their sub-optimal working conditions. She hoped they wouldn't be punished for taking the bait of her diversion from what must be a work life of endless tedium.

"Music's not a good idea," the first guard said, but with a mischievous glint in his eyes. "However, we've got some talent right here."

"Really?" Iza forced her eyes wide with excitement.

"He's down watching Warehouse Four. I'll have my guys go and get him."

Reis leaped up and screamed as if something bit her.

"No way, we've got talent right here," Iza said. "Reis here can sing."

Reis shook her head and bared her teeth like she was going to come over and pull Iza's hair from the roots, but the guys around them suddenly got very attentive.

"The thing is, she's really shy. She's going to need some encouragement," Iza said with a knowing smile at her partner.

She could see the whites of Reis' eyes and what might be real fear.

"Come on, Reis, don't make them beg."

That was exactly what she hoped she would do, but for now, the biggest risk was Reis turning and running screaming back to the shuttle.

Against the odds, though, Reis did open her mouth to sing. That's when everything went crazy.

26

AN ALARM SOUNDED. This time, Iza wasn't surprised; she'd been waiting for it, but she tried to play it off in front of Reis. The guards scattered to their posts, leaving the two women standing on their own.

"I wonder what's gone wrong this time," Reis mused.

Iza shrugged. "I don't know."

They raced to the rendezvous as planned, but Reis had a determined look on her face and Iza kept a close eye on her hands in case she was planning to stun her.

"By the way, can you actually sing?" Iza asked.

Reis gave her a cool look. "You'll never know."

When they returned to the two shuttles, Captain Douketis' crew was taking her crate of nutrient chips onto his shuttle. They had pulse guns pointed at Iza's people. Braedon had his hands up, shifting with nervous energy from one foot to the other. Trix looked over at Iza and blinked twice.

"Sorry, Captain, this isn't going to go as you planned," Douketis said, grinning.

"You're double-crossing me *again*?" Iza's tone was bitter.

"Yeah, I'm surprised at how naive you still are. It's sad, really. But don't worry—we'll make sure the haul gets delivered to the right place."

"You're taking our crate," she said.

"Yes. You see, now that we have two, we can make the delivery ourselves. I'm sorry you won't be getting paid, but at least you'll have enough nutrient chips so you and your crew don't starve while you're broke." Douketis tipped his hat at an angle and then winked at her.

Iza glared at him until he boarded the shuttle with the rest of his team. They were in the sky before she started moving.

"Everybody on the shuttle, now!"

"But we didn't get the haul," Braedon whined.

"Move!"

Trix had the shuttle in the air seconds after Douketis.

Iza sat beside Trix at the helm, almost giddy with relief. "Did you do it?"

"Yes, exactly as planned."

"Good."

"Wait, what?" Braedon asked, realizing that Iza wasn't as upset as she should be.

"I knew he was going to betray us, so I had a plan within a plan."

"Why didn't you tell me?"

"You're not as good an actor as you think you are. I didn't want to tip them off."

He frowned. "What did you do?"

"You'll see," Iza said. She laughed.

"But we still only got one crate." Braedon still looked confused.

"Go look under the sheet over by the bench back there."

He got up to investigate. With a sharp inhale of surprise, he turned back to Iza. "You got them! But how?"

She smirked. "We brought a crate filled with dirt with us. Trix carried the full crate back and swapped it out for the other.

While they were busy setting off the alarms and running their distraction for the main plan, Trix dumped the food chips out of their crate and into our bags and hid them here."

"That's not all," Trix said, sounding rather proud of herself.

Almost on cue, Douketis' shuttle speeding ahead of them suddenly veered to the side and began spiraling back down to the surface of the planet.

"Stars…" Braedon breathed.

Iza smiled in satisfaction. "You didn't notice a delay in heading to the warehouse?"

"Yeah, I did. Trix said she had to go back for something," Braedon replied.

"That's when she went back to disable the other shuttle— enough to down them, but they should survive. They'll have to answer some serious questions about what they were doing down here when the guards find the crash site."

Braedon sat back down in his seat and crossed his arms with a huff. "I could have helped."

"I didn't need your assistance," Trix said. "I am a valued member of the crew; you are a passenger."

"Don't worry, we got both crates and they got nothing," Iza said.

"Wait, so you knew he was going to betray you, so that extra crate is for us?" Braedon finally seemed to have processed the turn of events.

"Yes, they're not as good as real food, but when times are lean we'll have something to survive on."

He didn't seem thrilled about the potential menu item, but he nodded. "What about the *Iron Dog*? Won't they be mad we grounded their captain?"

"Stars, yes! Which is why we need to jump before they figure out their double-cross backfired."

They were nearing the upper atmosphere, and it wasn't long before their ship was coming into view. Iza still loved the sight of it—her very own ship, even if everyone was trying to take it from her.

Just as the shuttle was pulling into the hold, Trix tilted her head to one side. "The *Iron Dog* is preparing to fire on us."

"Jump us out of here!"

From within the shuttle, they felt the slight shift of the larger ship around them and time elongated for a moment.

"There wasn't time to plot a course to Hubyria, but I jumped us out of the system to remove us from immediate danger," Trix said.

"Good thinking." Iza patted her on the shoulder as she rose from her seat.

"That was close." Braedon let out a long breath.

Iza shrugged. "Not really. If they'd been smart, they would have fired on us the minute we returned with their captain." She waved for him to follow her. "I need you on the flight deck. Once we finish this hop, reach out to your contact on Hubyria and let them know we're on our way with their haul. We don't have a lot of time. Jovani is going to need a new arm, and soon."

"Do you have any idea how you're going to get it?"

Iza winced. "Yes. He's not going to like it, but at least he'll have two hands."

—

The H3X arrived on Hubyria at sun-up. They followed the landing instructions that Braedon's contact had provided, which not only ensured they'd meet them to collect the cargo and make payment but also that their ship wouldn't be shot out of the sky with the EMP cannon for a second time.

Braedon had assured Iza that the contact would be waiting

for them when they arrived, but the person was nowhere to be found.

"Are you sure about this?" Iza asked Braedon for the fifth time. They'd been pacing the valley outside of the settlement for close to an hour, and her patience had worn thin.

"Yes, they'll be here. Just relax."

"Me? If you don't stop that incessant toe-tapping, I'm going to hit you in your throat."

"They're here," Braedon said as he covered his throat with two hands as a precaution.

This time, however, he wasn't wrong. Iza spotted a woman coming over the ridge with four young men; the oldest of them couldn't be out of his teens. Iza relaxed when she recognized the woman.

Aeva smiled as they approached. She was using a large staff to help her walk, and that would explain what had taken them so long to trek to the remote meetup location over the rocky terrain.

"It is good to see you again."

Iza returned her smile. "And you. I had no idea you were Braedon's contact."

"Yes, well, as I said before, Yeaga and her people are making it hard for all of us. Though I understand their fight, we need essentials like food and medicine. She's only concerned with her revolt."

"Trix get the crates. I'm sorry to rush you, but we don't have a lot of time."

Aeva waved her hand. "It's quite alright. I'm sure you want to be on your way before Yeaga and her people discover what we've done."

"Are you going to be okay on your own? I can take the shuttle and drop off the crates someplace easier to get to."

"No, that won't be necessary. This is the kind of out-of-the-way place where the others won't look. We'll hide the crates and do what we can to help without getting ourselves or our people killed."

"It's not always easy."

The old woman gave a sage nod. "No, but nothing worth having is."

Iza held out her hand to shake but Aeva stepped forward and embraced her. It was so quick and sudden, Iza barely had time to pat the old woman on the back before she'd pulled away and had turned around to leave. The young boys hefted the crates between them and began making their way slowly back over the terrain.

"Don't forget your payment." Aeva pulled out her handheld to transfer the credits.

Iza raised an eyebrow.

"That's a lot of credits. Are you going to tell me how you came by them?"

"I wasn't always alone. My husband was a miner for a time but he had a very different kind of life before we met. I never had a reason to spend the money until now."

"Why did you stay? I mean, you had enough credits to live comfortably on a central planet instead of…" Iza waved at the barren land around them.

"Instead of working in a jewelry shop?" Aeva sighed then continued. "Like I said, it's not always about what you want but what you need."

Iza didn't quite understand her meaning but nodded anyway. She didn't have time to get into a philosophical conversation.

"Take care," Aeva said, with a wave before she turned to go.

Iza watched her leave then turned to Braedon.

"Let's get out of here before we run into—"

Iza was about to finish her sentence when two small transports pulled up on the opposite side of the ship, carrying Yeaga and three of her men.

She glanced over her shoulder and saw that, fortunately, Aeva and her boys were already out of sight.

"Well, look who's returned," Yeaga said, dismounting the transport. She looked over at the shuttle and then Iza.

"What do you want, Yeaga?"

The other woman raised a blonde eyebrow. "I want to know what you're doing here."

"To be honest, we were just leaving." Iza turned to go, but Yeaga and the others pulled out their pulse guns.

"Not so fast. If you're hauling rock off of Hubyria, you'll answer to me."

"I'm not. See for yourself," Iza said as she held out a hand in the direction of the shuttle.

To her credit, Yeaga did look. She even checked a few of the compartments to see if they'd hidden anything. When she came up empty, she frowned.

"What are you *really* doing here?"

"Not a thing. We've got injured back on our ship, though, and we need to go."

It was then that Yeaga took note of Iza's people and realized who was missing. "Jovani Saletas, is he...?" Her eyes were wide with panic.

"He's alive but seriously injured. We need to get him medical attention." Iza was surprised at the woman's concern but didn't have time to process it.

"Fine, be on your way. But don't come back here."

Iza nodded with a smile. That she could do.

"By the way, there's a quiet little hospital on Galminus that's miner friendly and they won't ask too many questions or report you to the Enforcers."

"Thanks, I owe you one."

Yeaga shrugged then smiled.

"Regardless, *he's* welcome back here. You're not."

Iza had no reason to argue. Hubyria was another place she never wanted to see again.

27

"WHAT'S GOING ON I thought we were on our way to the Galminus hospital?" Cierra asked Iza as she came onto the flight deck.

"We are under attack by an unknown vessel," Trix said.

They'd been on one of their scheduled cool-down stops for the jump drive when the other craft had dropped out from subspace. The ship rocked again as the shields absorbed another volley of pulse fire. A third shot struck the ship, knocking Iza off of her feet. She scrambled back into the captain's chair.

"What kind of ship is it? Enforcer?"

"Can't be. We're only hours out from Hubyria. They would have shown up on our sensors if they were just hanging out here waiting for us to pass by."

"No, it is not registered under any known corporation, TSS, or Tararian Guard entity," Trix said.

"I hope I don't need to remind you that we have a very injured patient in the infirmary. He can't take much more of this," Cierra said.

"What are our options?" Braedon asked.

"We can either stand our ground or make a run for it.

Either way, I'd like to know who's on that ship. Trix, get a closer look at their hull," Iza instructed. "What's that written on the side?"

"It says 'Arvonen One'," Trix reported.

Iza's brow knitted. "Isn't that the same ship we—"

"Yes."

Braedon stared out the viewport. "Bomax, how did he find me?"

Iza rounded on him. "What's going on, Braedon?"

He only stared at the screen then swore under his breath.

"Incoming communication request," Trix said. "Should I accept?"

"Yes," Iza said.

"No," Braedon said at the same time. He looked ready to run, but it was too late. The holo image resolved in front of the main viewport before he could hide.

The color in Braedon's cheeks drained as he stared back at the old man. The vague familiarity of his features should have been Iza's first clue, but she didn't have to wait long for a confirmation.

"Devyn, this has gone on long enough," the older man said.

"Hello, Father," Braedon said.

Iza stood there looking between father and son, not sure how to proceed any more than the rest of them. This seemed to be a private matter and no one wanted to interrupt. Cierra took a step toward Braedon, her hand rising before she seemed to think better of it letting her hand drop back to her side.

"What are you doing on board my ship?" the older man asked Iza.

"Excuse me?" Iza raised a hand and stepped forward behind Braedon. "This vessel is registered to me, Captain Iza Sundari. Could I have the pleasure of your name?"

He stared at her as if she were speaking another language.

Then, his frown deepened as if he was annoyed to have to speak with her.

"I'm Victor Arvonen, Head of the Arvonen Dynasty. You have my son and my ship, and I want them both returned to me at once."

"I'll never join you," Braedon shot back.

The older man smiled at his son as if he'd caught him with his hand in a plate of dessert. "I doubt your shipmates have been made fully aware of your exploits. But that aside, do you have it?"

Braedon squared his shoulders.

"What's he talking about?" Iza hissed.

"It doesn't belong to you!" Braedon yelled back.

"I will have that ship and everything on it. If that means destroying you all in the process, so be it."

"What is the likelihood that he'll destroy this ship?" Iza asked Trix off to the side.

"Based on current evidence, the chances are sixty point three-three percent that he'll destroy us," Trix said.

"I didn't really want to confirm that."

Victor surveyed H3X's flight deck over the holoconference. "My son betrayed me a long time ago, and I've mourned him. Now, I want what's mine."

"Well, this ship belongs to me now and I have the paperwork to prove it," Iza said, focusing the old man's attention on her.

"That weasel Karter Hyttinen of Apex owes me. He should never have sold you that ship in the first place."

Braedon pushed forward so he was face-to-face with Iza. "Don't listen to him. I brought Karter that ship and it was supposed to be on loan, but he screwed me over in the fine print."

Iza's mouth fell open. No doubt she was as surprised as the

rest of them to learn the ship had been in Braedon's hands before hers. *What were the chances?*

"I'm not going to warn you again. Either you turn the ship over to me, the rightful owner, or I'll disable every system you have and take it."

With her hand on her necklace, Iza thought about her options. She gave the man a nod. "Fine."

"What? No, you can't!" Braedon was pleading with her.

"It may not be the wisest choice," Cierra agreed.

"Trix, end transmission," Iza said.

The screen went back to the view of distant stars and the other ship nose-to-nose with them.

"Prepare to jump to Galminus," Iza ordered.

"They will be aware of our move before we make it. They will have time to fire on us."

"I'm counting on it. On my mark," Iza said.

"There is another incoming communication," Trix said.

"What does he want now?"

"It is an Enforcer cruiser ship along with patrol ships. It is Investigator Hyttinen."

Iza swore. "Put it on the viewport holodisplay."

"What?" Braedon yelped just before the comm link connected.

"This is Investigator Desirae Hyttinen of the Enforcer B652. H3X-Z500, you are in breach of contract. Your ship will be impounded, and your passengers will be detained for questioning in the recent robbery in which this ship was identified."

Persistent, isn't she? The script hadn't changed, but somehow Iza's situation had gotten even worse. "Sorry, Investigator, we're in a little bit of a jam here. Do you mind coming back later?"

"Don't ignore the warning again or you're going to wish

you hadn't run. Prepare to be boarded."

"Yes, Investigator." Iza signaled for Trix to end the connection.

"What are we going to do?" Cierra asked when the screen deactivated.

"Let them tether and board. Arvonen won't fire on three Enforcers no matter what they want—right, Braedon?"

"You're right, he won't. But if they catch us, won't they arrest us and take the ship?" he asked he bit his lip nervously.

"Can you think of a better way to keep the ship out of the hands of your father?"

Braedon shook his head. "Has anyone ever told you you're crazy?"

"Jovani's life will probably be spared if we turn ourselves in. The Enforcers are obligated to Taran citizens to do all they can to save one of their own," Iza continued.

"I can get us out of Sarduvis," Braedon said. "There's a guy I know who can get out of anywhere."

"Cierra, you should be fine. Say you were held against your will to save Jovani," Iza said. "It's mostly true."

Iza looked at Trix. It was entirely possible that she and the android would not be spared, regardless of what happened to the others. She could convince them that the others were just passengers.

"I'm going to tell them I did everything alone," Iza continued. "All you have to do is play dumb tourists and you'll never see the inside of Sarduvis prison. Open the channel."

Her voice was firm now that she'd made up her mind. "This is Captain Iza Sundari. We are prepared to receive you, Investigator Hyttinen."

There was grumbling on the other end.

"Trix, send them the codes to the door."

—

The first face Iza expected to see boarding her ship was Desirae's. Instead, it was Karter's, and he was looking more pleased with himself than ever.

The pompous bird.

He strolled through the bay, dressed in a long black trench coat and large black boots, as if prepared to do bodily damage to someone. His arms outstretched toward Iza and his mouth turned down in disappointment as he shook his head at her. "My dear, I'm so sorry it has come to this. I swear I did everything I could do short of a breach of contract. You do understand, I have people to answer to, and this isn't something I do lightly."

Iza felt the stir among her people, but she motioned for them to stay calm. She raised a hand to stop Karter from stepping any closer when it looked like he was ready to embrace her.

"Save me the speech. We both know this is exactly what you wanted from the moment I signed the contract with you."

Desirae boarded next with her team, looking put out that she was upstaged by Karter. She'd pulled her black, straight hair away from her face and displayed her Investigator's rank on her left breast with pride. She wore nothing over her face, but her Enforcers all wore their protective equipment and helmets—probably more for show than expecting Iza and her crew to put up a significant fight.

"You have ten minutes, Karter," Desirae said. "This is highly irregular, and considering the charges, I'm surprised you'd renegotiate at this stage."

Iza couldn't hide her shock. *Renegotiate?*

"Of course. May we speak someplace more private, Iza?" Karter looked around not bothering to hide his distaste for the prospect of being stuck in the cargo hold. When Iza nodded her agreement, he held out a hand for her to lead him away.

Iza paused at the door to her cabin before she thought better of it. The last thing she wanted was him scoping out her personal space; she'd rather keep him as far away as possible from where she slept. So, she turned in the opposite direction toward the galley.

Iza leaned against the counter. He stood on the opposite wall, showing no interest in sitting down. He began pacing while she stood with her arms crossed. For the first time, she imagined him a caged animal on display seeking exercise and a means of escape.

"You've put me in a very sticky position." Karter paused long enough to scowl. "I should have you all dragged in. From the state of the ship, I may be making a mistake by even considering this."

"I still don't know what you're talking about. Why don't you start from the beginning so we can all understand?"

"You didn't fulfill our arrangement."

Too frustrated to remain silent, Iza shouted at him, "That's not true! I have your credits now. I even have more, if you're willing to take it and put this matter behind us."

"I'm not."

That stopped her dead in her tracks. "Why *are* you here, then?"

"I'm not willing to deal in stolen credits. Besides, you've got bigger problems than me."

Iza frowned. *What did he mean by that?*

He continued before she could ask. "I'm here to give you my final offer. From what I understand, one of your crew members—or passengers—is injured, no?"

Iza's lips tightened but she managed to speak through them. "Yes, he needs a new arm."

Karter winced. "Ouch!" Then he shook his head. "I'm sorry for it. Of course, I'll be happy to take care of that for you. We have doctors standing by who can attend to your friend and prepare him to receive his new limb."

Iza couldn't believe what he was saying. Did he want to save Jovani? "Are you serious? Why would you do that?"

"I'm not heartless. I have the means to help your friend, and I want to help."

"Not out of the goodness of your heart. You want my ship in exchange," she corrected him.

"Not quite. That's exactly why I'm sure you'll want to hear the rest of what I came to say."

Iza crossed her arms, daring him to say something that would make her want to listen.

"It's true, I'm not entirely altruistic, but my proposal—as literal as it is—has a few strings attached, and I was hoping I could get on your good side first."

"What kind of strings?" Iza's stomach twisted into a knot.

Karter's expression remained unchanged as he turned to her. "First, let me apprise you on my current situation. As a dynastic heir, things aren't as ideal as most people believe. I have less freedom than you do at the moment, for example."

Iza scoffed. At present, she was facing the death of a friend, the loss of her ship and crew, and life in prison in one of the most inescapable facilities ever constructed—all because she didn't have the money he was born to.

Her doubt must have been obvious as he continued with two hands raised in surrender. "It's true. My mother, for example, is insistent that I marry."

"Marriage isn't the same as being sent to prison."

"You say that now, but if you were in my place and the only thing women saw in you was your potential bank account, you might have a different opinion."

"What about your cousin? I'm sure she'd be happy to oblige. Besides, I don't see what this has to do with me."

"The problem is that I could never be with someone like Desirae, and until I find the person I want to spend my future life with, I'd like to find someone more palatable and one who understands the meaning of a contract."

Iza felt her mouth go dry. She went through every scenario in her mind, grateful Karter had no abilities with which to read her. Though, if Jovani was right, her mind was entirely unreadable. Despite his reassurances, something about that knowledge made her just as uneasy, as if her mind were open.

"You want to marry *me*?"

"No, not at all. We'd hardly be a good match for anything long-term."

Iza bristled. "Then what are you proposing?"

"My hope is that you'll agree to keep up the appearance of being my fiancée while I find a suitable replacement for you."

'Replacement'. Wow, he really knows how to woo a lady. "What, we just start telling people we're engaged?"

"Yes, you'll have to play the part to the full in public. However, in private, I will not make any claim on you. But, everyone must believe that we are together. No one can know the truth. You and I may not be telepathic, but many among us are; if they learned the truth, the whole thing will be for nothing." He fixed his gaze on her. "Do we have a deal?"

Iza could hardly believe she was considering it. But, she dared to ask the question. "What would I get out of this deal?"

"Besides my undying devotion, you mean?" He had the gall to snicker when he said that. "You'll get all the privileges that come from being in a Lower Dynasty. There are many. I'll also be in your debt. This, of all things, could be the best possible outcome for you."

"I want the H3X, free and clear."

"What?!" He choked.

"Dynastic life, blah, blah, blah. I want my ship, and I don't want to make another payment."

"Seriously?"

"Yes."

Karter laughed. "It's so funny how strange mothers can be sometimes. Mine, for example, is making me do something I would do anyway in my own time. Then there's yours."

"What do you mean? Mine Left."

"Yes, that was always the story, wasn't it? What if I told you she's very much alive?"

Iza felt her world suddenly flip upside down and she wanted to choke down the fear welling up inside her like an ocean wave. "I'd say you're lying."

"I thought you might accuse me of that."

It can't be true.

He must have read the doubt on her face. "It *is* true. I knew you wouldn't believe me, so I pulled the footage. It's taken from a month ago, as the timestamp can prove. Your mother was seen on Tararia walking through the market." He pulled out his handheld and began playing the video.

Iza's brain was racing to try and figure out how Karter could doctor the footage and why he'd go to the trouble. Instead, she watched with her eyes wide and glued to the screen as her mother strolled through a market in a small town on Tararia. She was unaware that she was being recorded. The edges of her hair were silver, the only indication she'd aged at all. Her lithe form seemed to glide through the market as she smiled and waved at people whom she knew.

The floor dropped out from under her and Iza had to fight to control her breathing.

If Karter had wanted to break her, he couldn't have done a better job. *It can't be, she wouldn't abandon me to start a new life. She'd given up on living. She...* Nothing about the sight of her mother casually walking down the street a month ago—years after Leaving–made sense. The entire point of the practice was to be an *end* on a person's own terms, not a fresh start.

When Iza didn't say anything else for a full minute, Karter cleared his throat.

It snapped her out of her daze. Iza swallowed the disbelief, pain, and betrayal to force her attention back to Karter. "Regardless of what you think you've found, you're still going to give me the H3X."

"With my resources, it will take no time at all to track down your mother."

"That woman is not my mother. My mother Left when I was ten years old and never looked back. I've been doing just fine without her. The past can die in the past. Right now, I'm thinking of my future and my ship."

Karter smiled as if she'd said something he was expecting. He nodded. "Yes, fine, but you'll have to continue to make the payments as if you don't own it. I can't have people asking too many questions."

"Why don't you just make it *look* like I'm making payments?"

"No, that won't do. I need real credits in a real account. I'll set it aside for you, of course."

"Of course. You want to hold my money in an account of your choosing?" Iza shook her head. "No, way. I earn the money and I'll pay on time but I want access to the credits just in case this entire thing blows up in your face."

Iza was from the street but she wasn't dumb. You keep a close eye on a snake hole and your credits where thieves can't reach. She knew all about what happened to credits you let someone else hold for you.

"Fine. We'll create a joint account so that the credits are

accessible to both of us, should there be any trouble." He flipped through his handheld and tapped out a few commands. Then, he held it out in front of her. "The contract, if you please."

"You want me to sign a contract?"

"This isn't the kind of thing you make a verbal-only agreement to do. My future inheritance is at stake as well as all my current business transactions. I need this as much as you. If you do anything to convince others that we're not actually together, we're both going to lose everything."

"What if I choose not to do this?"

"You and your people will fall into the hands of Investigator Hyttinen and I go home with my ship."

"What about Braedon's father? I mean, Mr. Arvonen seems pretty keen on taking this ship back."

"Let me deal with Arvonen. What do you say?"

Iza began reading over the document carefully. She was interrupted by Enforcers twice. Both times, Karter reassured the Enforcers that he was almost done with Iza and they'd soon be on their way. There were so many clauses and backups in the contract that Iza was sure she wasn't getting all she should out of the deal, but it would have to do. Trix couldn't be in on the deal any more than anyone else, as much as Iza wished she could read over the text on her behalf. Of course, the android could lie, but if dismantled her secrets could pour out like water through her hands.

"What happens if you find someone else to marry you?" Iza questioned.

"I *will* find someone else to marry. At such time that such an arrangement can be confirmed, our contract will be dissolved and you will receive your ship and all credits you acquired during the time of the contract. You, however, won't have that luxury to severing the arrangement at your whim; the lie must stand until *I* find a suitable partner or until my assets can be secured in some other manner."

Iza stared down at the contract in her hands and thought of Jovani. He would be devastated. A sharp pain hit her in the chest at the thought of breaking things off with him. *Is this what real love feels like as it dies?*

A small dot flashed at the section where she was to place her thumbprint signature.

She hesitated. "What happens to the original H3X contract?"

"It's dissolved the moment you accept this one. We don't have much time, Iza. I need to instruct the Enforcers on what to do about the *Arvonen One*. What's your answer?"

Iza stared at the signature line, thinking of her mother. Where would she be if her mother had chosen to stay? Would she have ever met Jovani? Maybe not. Cursing her mother in her thoughts, Iza took her last free breath.

28

JOE SPENT HIS last day in the hospital lifting weights under the supervision of his two doctors. The orthopedic surgeon and neurologist seemed pleased at his progress. They commented on how impressed they were with the rapid regrowth of his right arm and his dedication to improving muscle tone.

"That's all for today, Jovani. You've done well," said the neurologist. "We're going to clear you for discharge."

"Thank you, Doctor." He shook hands with both specialists using his new hand and then went to his room to pack up his things. They'd given him some things to take with him to continue his therapy while in space, since artificial gravity didn't offer the same resistance as planetside conditions.

He sensed someone come into his room. Without turning around, he knew who it was.

"I see my credits went to good use." The man's voice set Joe on edge.

He whirled around to see Karter strolling in as if they were old friends.

"How are you feeling Mr. Saletas?" Karter asked when Joe said nothing.

"I'm well. To what do I owe the honor of your visit, Mr. Hyttinen?"

"I have something to give you, which I'm hoping you'll pass on to Iza for me. It's a gift."

Joe bristled at the use of her first name. He didn't like the familiar way he spoke of her at all. He consciously released the clenched clothing in his hands and finished gathering the few items he had accumulated while in treatment. "I'll be sure to deliver it."

"I know you will," Karter said, then sat down on the edge of the bed.

"Are you well? You seem a little off, yourself."

"I'm quite well." Karter straightened a pant leg. "You know, when Iza reached out to me, I knew something with her had changed. She fought to make sure you got that arm in a way I'd never seen from her before. Being the soft-hearted man that I am, I couldn't deny her anything."

Joe clenched his jaw but remained silent. Let the man think that anything he said was believed. Even he knew better than to think Iza would beg Karter Hyttinen for anything. It made him smile to realize he understood her better than this man.

"I haven't told her the truth about you."

Joe stood still. He glanced at Karter's face to read his features, if not his thoughts.

"The thing about you being an undercover TSS Agent. I haven't told her... Joe."

Joe could see into his thoughts enough to know he was telling the truth, beyond just knowing his preferred nickname. "What's the cost of keeping that secret?"

"She does talk to you about me. That sounds exactly like something Iza would say." Karter laughed at himself.

Joe finished closing his new duffle bag and flung it over his shoulder with impatience.

"The price is that in the future, I may need you. You'll come when I call and you'll do as I say, no questions asked."

The smile from Karter's face was gone and it was replaced with a sneer. When Joe didn't respond, he pushed the large box for Iza toward him.

"Do we understand each other?"

Joe stared at him a solid minute, looking for any sign of deceit and finding nothing. He did know the truth and he would use it against him if he didn't do as he was told. "Yes."

"Good. I'd hate for Iza to be unhappy with you, Joe. She does have a passionate temper."

Karter eased off the edge of the bed and saw himself out. Joe was left standing there looking down at the box, seething. He'd wanted to punch the man in his face but he kept cool long enough to remember what would happen to Iza if he crossed Karter. It wasn't worth it, but someday he'd get a chance and he wouldn't hesitate to take it.

He'd left him with the easy-to-open box on purpose, hoping he'd look inside. Light but bulky, it could be anything from exotic flowers to chocolates. Either way, Joe wasn't going to break another confidence by looking inside. Besides, Joe knew whatever was inside wouldn't make her smile like he could.

Just the thought of it made him feel lighter. He was going to be back on the ship with her and she was safe. That was all that mattered to him. He should probably make time to call his superiors, but he wanted to see Iza first. His report could wait until he'd wrapped his arms around her and been welcomed back.

— — —

It had been three weeks since Jovani had been taken to a

hospital, and Iza was anxious to have him on board again and to get as far away from Beurias as she could get. The last thing she wanted was to run into Karter again. Though she was grateful for what he'd done for Jovani, she'd had to pay, and the sight of him calling her his fiancée was enough to turn her stomach.

The minute Iza caught sight of Jovani, the rest of the cargo hold faded away. His striking blue eyes were staring at her with an intensity and hunger she craved more than breath.

Braedon seemed to be catching him up on all the things he'd missed. He seemed oblivious to the large box Jovani was awkwardly trying to handle. His long-suffering smile faded away when he caught sight of her looking on.

"Our ships were nose-to-nose. I mean, you wouldn't believe it. Here's Iza standing on the flight deck like nothing. This one time— Oh," Braedon cut off when he saw Jovani was no longer listening.

"Your arm appears to be five centimeters smaller in circumference than your left. Does it bother you?" Trix asked.

"No. Here take this," Jovani said passing the box he was holding into her hands without taking his eyes off of Iza.

The others parted to let him through as he raced forward. He threw his arms around Iza, lifting her off of her feet and twirling her around until she giggled. When they were out of breath from joyous laughter, he put her down.

"Good to see you up and about again," Iza said still breathless.

"Thanks." He pulled her in for a hug and whispered in her ear. "I want time alone with you."

He's going to ruin my life.

He didn't know anything about her engagement and she couldn't tell him the truth.

She pulled herself out of his arms and caught the open-mouthed stare he gave Cierra as she joined them in the docking bay, her bare feet silent on the floor. The silk robes whispered as she moved. Iza was getting used to the sound.

"Cierra Quetzali is the one who saved your life."

Cierra and Jovani stared at each other for another long awkward moment while Braedon obnoxiously cleared his throat.

"If you're sick, Braedon, you might want to get something for your throat," Iza said. "Are you two done introducing yourselves telepathically or would you like to say something out loud?"

"Yeah, we're done," Jovani said, giving Cierra a nod then turning to Trix. "Here, let me take that. It's for Iza."

The large, square box was lighter than it looked but awkwardly large, making it hard to hold. It had the Hyttinen seal on the top and Iza's heart sank. Whatever was inside was her 'engagement gift'.

"I'll go put this away. It's good to see you, Jovani. Go ahead and get settled." His eyes never left her face and she had to look away from the intensity.

"Trix, we're done here, so let's get on our way. I believe Cierra said after she saw the improvement of her former patient she wanted to go home. Put in the coordinates for Leveckis."

Iza was about to turn to leave when Cierra spoke up.

"Actually, no," she said in a quiet tone. "I believe I'll stay."

"What?" Iza heard herself say along with Braedon. "You two have been at each other's throats for the last three weeks. You've hindered every job we've taken with your philosophies on life and nature, and now you want to stay?"

"Braedon and I have come to an understanding. Besides, considering your line of work, I believe you may need me again."

Iza looked at Jovani and Braedon, wondering what had just happened. Jovani shrugged as if to answer her unasked question. Braedon stood looking on with his hands balled into fists without saying a word. This was a drama in the making.

"All passengers have to pay rent to remain on board. Are you interested in paying to be a passenger or working as a member of the crew? Before you answer, Healing is not one of the job offers on board. We need people to lift, haul, and take care of the ship's maintenance."

"Actually, we don—" Trix began but Iza raised a hand to silence her.

"Give it some thought. Trix, get us out of here. Either way we're going to Cierra's home so input the coordinates. If she's not getting off, she'll want to pick up a few things."

Iza turned to go; she wasn't going to worry about the rest.

"Incoming transmission message for you, Iza," said Trix. "It is marked 'for your eyes only'. Would you like to take it in your cabin?"

"Yes, carry out my orders as soon as the transmission has ended."

"Yes, Captain."

When Karter's face came up on the viewscreen in her cabin, she wasn't entirely surprised. Iza knew she wasn't going to get away from Beurias fast enough to avoid any contact with him. She was thankful he'd at least opted to speak to her in private. She didn't know when he was going to make their engagement public, but she hoped it wouldn't be on the flight deck of her ship with everyone standing around.

There was something strange about the way he was sitting at his desk, but she couldn't figure out what before he dove into the reason for his call.

"I wanted to let you know that we'll have to delay the public announcement of our engagement for the time being. There's been some trouble here that I need to see to before we share our happy news." He gave her a significant look.

"I've seen many arranged marriages. I wouldn't be the first to look disappointed in the pictures."

"It would help if you could pretend to be excited."

"No, it wouldn't. First off, no one is going to believe we're in love, so you can't sell it that way. If you want to run this kind of con, you have to go with your strengths. I don't play false, so the only way this is going to work is if I can be myself."

Karter raised an eyebrow and gave her a nod. "We'll try it your way, but don't let me remind you of what's at stake if we fail."

"We both have a vested interest in the story. I appreciate what you did for Jovani; it was more than I expected. Though he didn't say so, I know he's pleased."

Karter smiled.

"I'm glad. You'll be taking off as soon as you can, I'm sure. Let me give you one last warning. There's a very powerful man after your ship."

Iza looked away. "Yeah, I remember Victor Arvonen."

"He won't rest until he has his hands on that ship and his son. It seems he's left something behind. Have you found anything on board that he could possibly want?"

"No," Iza said. The lie was quick and easy. *So that's where it came from...* She had no intention of telling anyone about the mysterious box, since she hadn't been able to open it, there seemed no point.

Karter squinted at her as if he didn't believe her, but she held her neutral expression.

"You really shouldn't get between him and his son. The old man is lethal. He won't give up easily."

"I can handle my own." Iza analyzed her choice of words. She'd claimed all of her people as her own. They'd all helped to preserve the ship and her life in some way, and she could admit to herself that she wanted to take care of all of them.

Karter didn't seem to notice. "You think you know them, but you don't."

"What are you saying?"

Karter shook his head as if he didn't want to say. Iza crossed her arms and waited for the dramatics to end so he could tell her what he was obviously dying to share.

"You have a tendency to get attached to people who aren't who you think they are."

"You don't know anything about me." Iza prepared to end the communication.

"Fine. There are four weeks before the announcement. Make good use of it, but don't stray too far. The announcement will be made with you at my side. Don't make me send Investigator Hyttinen to find you."

It wasn't an empty threat. Desirae had the uncanny ability to track anything like a hound. Victor Arvonen was another person Iza had to look over her shoulder to avoid. The one bit of good news was that she no longer needed to fear her ship's propulsion being locked unexpectedly, thanks to some additional handiwork courtesy of Braedon to permanently disable the remote engine shutoff.

Iza nodded. "Just send word. I'll be ready."

"I sent over an engagement present with Jovani," he said.

She looked at the box she'd abandoned on the floor. "That's not—"

"It is necessary."

"I was going to say not appropriate."

"You'll soon see how appropriate it is." Karter adjusted himself in his seat and peered at her from his desk. "Any progress on your mother?"

"No, I've had a few things to worry about lately, and she's

not on my list of priorities."

"She should be. I'm surprised at you; I would have thought you'd want to know everything you could about why she wanted people to believe she Left to die. It seems a strange thing to do with a child at home."

"Thanks for your unwarranted concern, but I'll handle my own business in my own time. If that's all we'll be on our way."

"Yes, of course. I'll see you soon."

Karter ended the transmission and Iza collapsed on her bed.

She wanted to retch. What reason could her mother possibly have for abandoning her as a ten-year-old? Iza couldn't think of one. It was cruel to orphan a small child— especially by stepping away from a life and starting anew elsewhere. It would have been easier to stomach if her mother just opted to die, the way she'd believed.

Under other circumstances, she may have dismissed this news about her mother and not given it another thought. She'd learned to live with her betrayal a long time ago. But, it was the *way* the news had been broken by Karter, delivered as a swift kick to her spirit when she'd already been beaten down by a string of misfortunes, only to then be capped off with the vile fake engagement. Karter had slashed at her potential future with Jovani, ripping open the wound from her past in the process.

The tears were welling up and she couldn't stop them. One minute she felt fine, and the next she wanted to curl into a ball at the thought of what she was doing to keep her ship and crew intact. She knew what the others would say if they knew about Karter. Her mother's reappearance was a whole other matter.

Karter had given her the footage of her mother, and she pulled it up now to look for any signs of remorse. Did her daughter ever cross her mind? If she found her, would the woman even acknowledge her now? Did she know anything about Iza's time on Sarduvis or the streets? Did she care? Could a woman abandon a child and never look back? She'd heard it was impossible, but she was looking at evidence to the contrary. There were too many unanswered questions and the smiling woman going about her business held the answers.

A hot tear fell on Iza's wrist and she didn't bother to wipe it away. She didn't want to cry, but the pain of seeing her was too much to bear. She'd struggled on her own for so long, and all this time her mother was alive. She let the tears fall until she had nothing left.

With the emotional release, her thoughts turned to the end table and the box inside. Whatever it was, Mr. Arvonen wanted to get his hands on it. She lifted the small, wooden box and it slipped a bit in her wet hands. The humming was louder than usual and she had to wipe her eyes again to see through the lingering blur of her tears. The box shifted in her hands, opening with a slight pop. Inside was a small metal sphere.

What in the world?

The etched metal sphere had markings like she'd never seen—deep grooves that traveled over its surface in strange trails. There was one mark that looked familiar. It was shaped like the 'V' of her necklace.

It can't be the same. She held up her necklace to the sphere's surface. To her surprise, a bluish glow of light traveled from one side of the sphere to the other. *What is this thing?*

The sound of the buzzer at her cabin door startled her. It was probably Jovani; he'd seemed intent on visiting her—not that she had any complaints. She scrambled to hide the metal sphere and box in the nearest drawer before she leaped from the bed to answer the door.

However, it was Trix standing in the corridor.

"What is it?" Iza asked, caught off-guard.

"There were some anomalous readings coming from this part of the ship. Are you finished with your call?"

"I am," Iza said with a look at the android. *Maybe the sphere is dangerous.*

Trix tilted her head to one side and the ship's jump drive rumbled. A moment later, time elongated for a moment as the ship transitioned to subspace.

"Is there something else?" Iza prompted.

"Do you want to investigate the readings?"

"Not at the moment. What's our ETA?"

Trix stared at her as if reading her features and taking her body readings. "We'll arrive in a few hours."

"You're no longer giving time in exact increments?"

"No one seems to appreciate when I provide the time in that manner. I have adapted to better suit others."

"Thanks," Iza said still eyeing the android. She'd behaved strangely at times before, but this was new. "When was the last time you ran a self-diagnostic and charged up?"

"I am fully charged and I have a scheduled diagnostic this evening."

Not a moment too soon. "Good."

"And are you well? Your heart rate is accelerated and your eyes are red."

"I'm fine, just got something in my eye."

Trix probably wouldn't believe it, but she wasn't about to explain the reappearance of her mother to anyone.

"What was in your box?" Trix asked, referring to the large box she'd tossed on the floor.

"I don't know yet, I was just about to open it. Give me a few minutes and I'll meet you on the flight deck."

"As you wish."

Trix turned without another word and left. Iza let the door close between them before lifting the box from the floor and tossing it on the bed. She peeled it open and found a handwritten note: 'Just a little something for you to wear during the announcement. Don't be late. – KH'

Underneath the note was an elaborate red dress like she'd never seen. Everything about the design was luxurious, from the detailed edging to the fit. It was probably worth as much as the ship itself. She'd never worn anything so extravagant and had certainly never had such an occasion to be in a place where people would wear such finery. Iza looked through the box there was nothing else inside.

What am I supposed to do, go barefoot?

29

THERE WAS SOMETHING wrong with Iza, Joe was certain. She should have been ecstatic.

They were heading back for Cierra's things. They were going to have a Healer on board. They got to keep the H3X, which meant there were no Enforcers to be concerned about. He had an arm and he was back with his new crew. So, why was the woman he liked most in the world walking around with her face turned down? She fiddled with her necklace whenever she was worried about something, like now.

The others didn't seem to notice, although Trix did appear distracted by Iza in a way that might be the android version of worried.

"Is there anything else?" Trix asked Iza in her way, as if waiting for more.

Iza shook her head. "No, we need to get Cierra back and we've got some repairs to do from that last firefight while we're there." Iza gave each of them a look. "I appreciate everyone coming through for each other. It means more than you could ever know. Let's resupply and get ready for our next run."

Cierra stood there in her pedicured bare feet, watching Iza explain their situation without comment. She would have two hours to take care of necessary business and then they'd be leaving with or without her. She hadn't tried to read Joe's thoughts again, but he kept his mental guards up anyway. The Healer was different. Their first encounter had been more than a little unusual. Instead of speaking her introduction, Cierra chose to use the more intimate form of telepathic communication to reach out to his mind. It had taken him off-guard, but he was able to keep her from probing too deep. Behind her own mental guards, Joe sensed that she was also hiding something and he wondered if anyone else on board knew it.

When Iza finished giving her instructions, she looked at Joe, and that's when it hit him like a shot. It felt like a literal shot of pain aimed at his chest. The impact of her eyes and the sadness behind them told him everything he needed to know. It was as clear as if she were dismissing him from her life. Joe squared his shoulders and followed her off the flight deck.

Iza had made it to her cabin by the time Joe caught up to her.

"Hey, wait up," he said. The temptation to reach out and touch her was strong but he held himself in check. They were bound to each other in a way he didn't quite understand. Since he couldn't read her thoughts, she could be completely closed off to him. But there was something about the way she looked at times where he swore he knew exactly what she was thinking. "You seem off. Is everything okay?"

Iza mustered up a smile for him. It warmed him, but only for the second that it lasted. "Yes, I'm fine. There's just a lot on my mind. Having the H3X was supposed to bring me freedom, but it seems that freedom is only for the rich."

Joe understood that concept. Even back on Earth, the divide between the rich and the poor had grown to unbelievable proportions. Joining the TSS had kept him out of poverty and gave him purpose. Although the knowledge of the universe was something that many back home still didn't have, that was a kind of wealth that he could appreciate.

"You have a ship, a crew, and your life outside of prison," he reminded her. "Freedom is relative at times, but you're freer than many—even if it's not your ideal version of freedom. I used to feel the same when I was with the TSS. There's a lot of education and honing of one's abilities. The problem is that in the end, you still belong to the TSS. Even as High Dynasty, the Sietinens balked at some of their obligations."

Joe didn't know all the details of their careers from memory, but from what he remembered of what he'd studied, there had been some difficult times. Many of them hadn't been pleased to be used in the TSS' agenda. Joe couldn't imagine having to deal with some of the things they'd dealt with, being responsible for the Taran way of life on top of it all. Of course, the poor had their own problems and it wasn't practical to compare them.

This was something different, though; this was about the two of them.

Iza tugged on her necklace.

"What's going on?" Joe pressed.

"What?" She seemed surprised that he'd called her on it. This was becoming a thing with her.

"Are you going to tell me what's going on with you or what?"

"Or what," Iza said, and her eyes dropped to the floor. "Look, I know it's not fair, but I've got some things going on and I just can't give you what you deserve. We can't be together in the way you want right now. Can you just be okay with that?"

No, I'm definitely not okay with that. Joe felt the ground fall out from under him as he listened to her words.

"Can't we talk this through?" He had only just started to

understand the special bond between them, and now she was slipping away before he had a chance to figure out why. "I know there's something wrong and I want to help."

"Something *is* wrong, but you can't fix it." She went inside her cabin and closed the door behind her.

What did I do?

—

With Iza inexplicably avoiding him while they waited for Cierra to gather her things, Joe found himself wandering the ship to clear his head. He eventually found himself in Engineering, where the new jump drive had been secretly installed behind the casings for the original model. The SiNavTech nav console had also been upgraded, but Joe had worked with Trix to configure the interface to match the normal civilian systems.

They no longer needed cool-down stops for the drive, but Trix had agreed to plot courses and wait for the requisite intervals, all the same, to keep the new drive a secret. For now.

It would be there for when they needed it. Stars, they *could* have used it to get away from Karter and the Enforcers in their most recent encounter, but Joe didn't want to reveal their special move to their adversaries until it was absolutely necessary. He trusted Trix to put the equipment to use when it was prudent.

Based on the transit time from Phiris to Leveckis, he was fairly sure that Trix had already taken advantage of the new jump drive's capabilities to get him to the Healer faster, and for that he was extremely grateful. Between that and her keeping his secret about being an active TSS Agent, he was racking up a big debt with the android.

Joe's handheld chirped, and he saw it was an incoming call

from Agent Mandren. *I can't keep avoiding them.*

Since getting the jump drive, Joe had been careful about what information he shared in his field reports to the TSS. Most notably, he'd left out the part about losing an arm and being in the hospital for three weeks. The TSS would have certainly tended to his medical needs, but Joe hadn't wanted to jeopardize staying with Iza; he'd do anything to remain as a part of her crew.

With no one else around, Joe answered the call. "Hello, sir."

"Joe, where have you been? The reports have been a little… sparse."

"Sorry, we've been dealing with a bit of a situation here. The Arvonen Dynasty has inserted themselves into matters. Apparently, they want this ship. They fired on us."

"What do you mean they fired?"

"I mean Mr. Arvonen used his fancy ship to fire on us in an attempt to disable our entire ship."

"I thought he wanted the ship for himself," Mandren said.

"He does, as far as we know."

"Then he doesn't want the ship for what it can do. Perhaps he wants something that's *on* the ship."

Joe's mouth fell open. He hadn't even considered that idea.

"If there's something on the ship that he wants—" Mandren began.

"And we find it first, we'll know what he's after," Joe completed.

"Exactly. I think your mission is clear. Are you having any other trouble?"

Losing an arm, for example? Joe thought of Iza and all the things he was willing to do for her. The way she made him feel. Despite whatever was going on between them at the moment, he wasn't about to give up on her. He couldn't tell his superiors what was really going on, they'd never approve, and he'd be sent straight back to Earth.

"No, nothing. It's been eventful, to say the least, being on a crew like this one."

"I would suggest you avoid any illegal activity in the future. I know you're trying to fit in, but if you go too far, we won't be able to protect you."

Joe nodded his understanding. *Losing life or limb.* At the time, he didn't think. He saw the shot heading for Iza and he acted. When it came to Iza, he knew he'd do it all over again. *Why couldn't she see that?*

"What about this Captain Iza Sundari?"

"What about her?" Joe's question was quick. Too quick. The rush of anger at the sound of her name in Mandren's mouth along with the skepticism made Joe clench his hands in preparation to defend her.

"She seems a bit reckless. I'm not so sure we should be trusting her. She appears to veer from lawful activity too quickly."

"She's an orphan who grew up on the outside of Wardship. If she'd had proper training and care, I don't think she'd have ever gotten in trouble in the first place. Now that she has, she's not afraid of it. That's the only difference between her and someone like me. Besides, without her, I wouldn't have the intel I have." *Or a new arm.*

Mandren didn't say anything for a long moment. "Congratulations!"

"For what?"

"When we sent you out there, I'd hoped you'd make friends in a way you never did here. I'm proud of you for finding a team, even though it wasn't strictly within the TSS. I know it wasn't easy for you."

"Thank you, sir."

"But watch your back. Any time the Lower Dynasties start throwing around their power, it's always a sign of bigger trouble brewing. It might be part of something bigger we're tracking, and we need to be sure. This mission has become my top priority."

"Yes, sir," Joe acknowledged.

"I think we're beyond 'sirs' by now. Ian is fine. If anyone does overhear your conversations, it would be best if you weren't being so formal."

"Yes, s— Ian."

"Better, keep working on it. I'll await your next report."

When the transmission ended, Joe smiled. He'd inadvertently placed himself in the middle of something, and they wanted him to see it through. He couldn't have planned it better if he'd intended it. Not that he had a choice in the matter. When he was being honest with himself, he knew his reasons for staying on board the H3X were more about Iza than it was about his mission. Being near Iza still ignited a part of his soul. She used to feel the same, and he had to believe she'd work through whatever was presently troubling her. And, eventually, he knew he'd have to be honest with her about who he was and how he'd come into her life.

The current distance between them only solidified his need to be around her. He hated feeling so tied to her, and yet, he'd never felt more connected to another person in his life. It was the kind of connection he'd always observed from the outside. Even without the telepathic connection, he knew she felt the same. The longing in her eyes and the sadness when they were apart. She'd have to come around at some point. Didn't she?

WHEN IT GREW close to mealtime, Joe went to see Iza. She'd been aloof all day. Since his return, she'd been different. He hoped she wasn't still blaming herself for his injury. None of them could have known he'd dive in front of her in the last second. He'd been prepared to get her out of harm's way, but his actions told him more about his true feelings for her than anything else.

He knocked on her door, but she didn't answer. He couldn't sense her the way he could with most people, but he was sure she was inside; her movements were predictable. When she wanted to be alone, she sought out the gym or her cabin, and he'd already ruled out the other.

"Hey, I know you're in there," he said softly against the door. "Let's get something to eat."

A shuffling behind the door confirmed his suspicions.

"I'm fine," she said against the closed door.

"You don't sound fine." *Was that a sniffle?*

"Did Karter say something to you?"

"Karter? No. Iza, what's this about? Please know you didn't do anything to hurt me. I'm fine now, and we'll pay off any debt the surgery accrued."

"Karter didn't charge us for it."

He didn't? Joe didn't trust for a second that Karter had covered the expenses out of the goodness of his heart. "He might not have charged us credits for it, but I'm sure he's going to try and make you pay in another way. That's just the kind of guy he is."

When she didn't answer he knew he was right. Karter was a snake. *Is that what she's upset about?*

"Look, I don't know what he told you, but…" Joe paused. What was he going to say? He didn't understand his feelings enough to put them out there into words, but she needed to know where he stood. "You're not alone. I can't speak for the others, but I'm not going anywhere. I don't regret saving you, and I'd do it again. You're going to have to learn to be okay with that. Maybe you regret being with me, but I don't. No matter what, I'm going to be here for you."

Too stalkerish? Desperate? Not enough?

Joe put his head against the cabin door, wishing there was a way to transmit his thoughts to her directly. Telepathy would be a good thing right about now.

"I didn't mean that in any kind of strange way," he tried to explain. "What I want to say is that when you're ready, I'll be here. I think whatever we have is worth fighting for, so I'll do whatever it takes."

She was quiet for so long, he thought he might look a fool still standing there with his head against the door.

Then, in a soft voice, she said the words he'd been waiting to hear, "I could never regret being with you."

—   —   —

Iza knew she was being a coward. Hunger pulled her out of her room sometime around 19:00.

Jovani had been outside her door only a couple of hours before, and she'd stood with the door between them, trying to breathe. He'd been so sure, so present. When was the last time anyone had made such a promise to her? She could only think of her father. That made her think of her mother. The spiral of thoughts forced her to fight off the tears again.

Composed at last, she opened the door and sighed in relief when she found no one on the other side of it.

Iza didn't expect anyone to still be lingering in the galley, so when she heard laughter just outside the archway, she almost turned back. But, her stomach protested, forcing her forward. Whatever they were doing, she'd be in and out before anyone noticed.

The brown rectangle dining table was filled with the crew and passengers, leaving three chairs on the end available. A spread of food prepared by Trix filled the table along with scraped plates. She'd gone all out this time. There was real meat, baked bread, and vegetables. For an android who didn't entirely love the idea of food, she had a gift for preparation that Iza wasn't ashamed to say she envied.

Before Iza reached the cabinet where she'd stashed several protein bars, she heard Trix call out to her.

"Are you joining us, Captain?"

Iza was shaking her head, but Braedon had already abandoned his seat next to Jovani and pulled it out for her to sit.

"Come on, Iz, take my seat."

"Yes, we need another woman at this table," Cierra said with a smirk to both of them.

Unable to resist their encouragement, Iza acquiesced. She sat down in the offered chair beside Jovani. He threw a casual arm around the back of her chair, saying nothing and keeping his eyes on the others. Trix placed a full plate in front of Iza, and she immersed herself in the conversation.

"Who told you that?" Jovani asked in response to something stated before Iza entered.

"Everyone knows. It's like the most obvious thing that you learn in basic Taran education," Braedon said.

"I don't believe it."

"I'm not saying it's right, but it's true. Ask anyone," Braedon asserted, shaking his head.

"How do you like it?" Trix asked Iza before she'd taken a bite of the meal.

Jovani leaned in to whisper in her ear, "Tell her it's amazing or she'll jump up to cook something else."

Iza choked back a laugh. "It's great, Trix. Good job."

Trix looked from her to Jovani but seemed to accept it as she nodded and turned away, moving to stand at the other end of the table.

"If I have to sit here, so do you," Iza said to Trix.

The others hadn't seemed to notice her distance and now agreed as they beckoned Trix to sit. "I do not require food."

"No, but this is mandatory social time, apparently, so sit down and don't be afraid to speak up," Iza said.

Jovani and Braedon agreed while Cierra said nothing. Braedon was pretending not to stare at the Healer from across the table.

Oh no. Iza wasn't sure what they were getting themselves into, but she reminded herself they were old enough to make up their own minds. She couldn't help but think of herself and Jovani. Sitting with him and laughing along with the others seemed right. It was something she'd been missing, and now suddenly it was as if the pieces finally fit. She'd found what she'd been striving for her whole life.

Iza had to choke down her last bite when she thought of her mother and wished she hadn't. The joy she felt was overshadowed by the path her own mother had put before her.

This wasn't the life her father had wanted for her before he'd died. It was simply the life she got after her mother Left. Now, to learn she was alive was something she couldn't comprehend. The questions swirled in her thoughts until she felt Jovani touch her back.

"Hey, are you okay?"

She must have been frowning and she tried to give him half a smile. The concern in his glowing blue eyes was so genuine and so deep she wanted to dive into them. She hoped he'd leave his brown contacts alone for a while.

Her answer bubbled up from her heart, spurred by the sight and sound of her surrogate family around the kitchen table. "I'm not, but I will be." For the first time in her life, Iza believed it.

Overwhelmed with the responsibility of a ship and its crew, she wondered if she had it in her to take it to the end. While her mother was a problem for another day, was it too much to hope that Karter would find another marriage prospect before their dreaded announcement?

"So, Braedon, you never told us how you and Cierra met."

Iza wanted to kiss Jovani for changing the subject so quickly.

Braedon rubbed the back of his neck. "It's a bit of a long story."

I hope so. Iza swiveled in her seat to face him while he started in on his story.

"Look, I'm not going to go into too much detail," he said.

"Since when?" Jovani said with a cough into his hand. They all laughed before Braedon began his tale.

"Q and I had one of the best months ever on that little planet of hers."

"Speak for yourself," Cierra said, glaring at him through narrowed eyelids.

"I am speaking for myself. You'll get your chance, but this is my turn. Where was I? Oh yeah, it's like a nature reserve.

They want it to be just like Valta. She's a third-generation telepath with the ability to heal like nothing I'd ever seen before. She helped keep you stable enough to receive a new arm. When she and I met, I was feeling pretty low, but by the end of the month we spent together, I couldn't have been better."

"So why didn't you stay?" Cierra asked her eyes filling.

Iza felt uncomfortable enough to want to run from the table, but Jovani held her still with his arm around her chair.

"I'll be the first to admit I enjoyed myself, but I knew I couldn't live like that forever. You were content with your peaceful little world and your life. I still had more to do."

"Dragging yourself about the galaxy without purpose, you mean?"

"No, there are people I can help that no one else will. I thought you would understand."

Cierra bit back whatever she was going to say next.

"She's your Maid Marian," Jovani blurted out.

"Who's Maid Marian?" Iza asked.

"There's an old story in Earth's history of a young man named Robin Hood who lived in the forest with his Merry Men, stealing from the rich to give to the poor and pining for the love of his life, Maid Marian."

"He sounds like an idiot," Iza said.

"I like him," Braedon said. "He sounds resourceful."

"You would think that," Iza countered. "How does the story end?"

"Well, there are many variations, since the character is the stuff of legend," Jovani continued. "Sometimes he ends up with Maid Marian living happily ever after, sometimes he ends up dead. I guess it depends on who you ask."

"Wait, dead?" Braedon gulped.

"Yeah, they used to hang criminals by the neck in those times. It was barbaric but it got the job done."

"I prefer prison, for the record," Braedon said as he squirmed in his seat.

"So, I'm told you don't have a name for the ship. I'm not sure that's a good idea," Cierra said, turning her attention to Iza.

"See? It's not!" Braedon agreed. "I've told her to name the ship or we can expect more and more trouble to come our way."

"Tell me you don't actually believe that superstition." Jovani raised an eyebrow.

"The proof is obvious. How many times has this ship been caught?" Braedon asked.

"I think we might have other ways around that, but for purely non-folklore reasons, I'd like to call the ship something other than the H3X-Z500," Jovani said.

Iza grabbed her necklace and pinched it between her two fingers, thinking of the meaning behind it and how it fit her future quest. The one thing she wanted more than anything else in the universe.

"It does have a name," she said.

"Well?" Jovani asked.

"What is it?" Braedon urged.

"The *Verity*."

The table went quiet while they repeated the name in hushed tones. In that moment, Iza knew she'd made real friends. They had powerful enemies, annoying habits, and complicated pasts. But regardless of what lay ahead, as the captain of the *Verity*, Iza vowed in her heart to keep them flying.

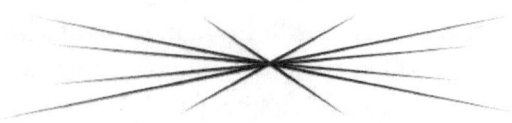

THE STORY CONTINUES IN *DIVIDED LOYALTIES...*

No good deed goes unpunished when you're a crew of criminals.

Agent Joe Anderson finds a home on the *Verity*, but staying true to his TSS mission gets harder every day. With a plot to overthrow the Taran government hanging in the balance, his loyalties will be tested as he's forced to choose between his heart and his duty.

With an eclectic crew of misfits, an alien artifact with unknown origins, and a contractual engagement already competing to ruin Iza's life, things take a dire turn when Trix contracts a mysterious virus.

Iza must come to terms with her unresolved feelings for Joe, save her ship, and her friends from destruction, while solving the mystery of the artifact and her past before everything she's always wanted is lost.

ADDITIONAL READING

Cadicle Space Opera Series by A.K. DuBoff
Book 1: Rumors of War (Vol. 1-3)
Book 2: Web of Truth (Vol. 4)
Book 3: Crossroads of Fate (Vol. 5)
Book 4: Path of Justice (Vol. 6)
Book 5: Scions of Change (Vol. 7)

Shadowed Space Series by Lucinda Pebre & A.K. DuBoff
Book 1: Shadow Behind the Stars
Book 2: Shadow Rising
Book 3: Shadow Beyond the Reach

Mindspace Series by A.K. DuBoff
Book 1: Infiltration
Book 2: Conspiracy
Book 3: Offensive
Book 4: Endgame

Dark Stars Trilogy by A.K. DuBoff
Book 1: Crystalline Space
Book 2: A Light in the Dark
Book 3: Masters of Fate

AUTHORS' NOTES

From T.S. Valmond:

Thank you for reading *Exile*! What did you think? I hope this book was as enjoyable for you to read as it was to write.

This is my first co-authored project and I want to sincerely thank Amy for taking a chance and allowing me to be a part of the amazing Cadicle Universe. As a reader of the books in the Cadicle series, I couldn't have been more excited to be a part of it.

To my beta readers and ARC team, I'm so grateful for your feedback as always and appreciate your support in making the release of this first book in the series so special. Amy and her team were invaluable in editing and polishing this book to a shine and I'm very thankful for all their input.

I wouldn't be able to spend my time doing something so rewarding if it wasn't for my best friend and husband, Matthew. As an artist himself, he truly understands why I need to put my heart on the page. He is the love of my life and my inspiration to create every day.

Those of you who have been with me for a long time know how much it means to me to be able to write stories that show how much finding your family and tribe can enrich your life. Those of you who are new to me, welcome to the TSV family, I'm so glad you found me.

There's much more to come in the Cadicle Universe and I can't wait to share more Verity adventures with you. You're in for a wild ride!

An additional note from A.K. DuBoff:

I hope you enjoyed this book! It's a very special one for me, because it is the first coauthored Cadicle Universe novel to be released. It was a joy to work with Shelina, and I'm thrilled about the ideas she's brought to the universe.

I have to say, I'm still in a constant state of awe that the Cadicle Universe has grown to include coauthors. When I started working on the original Cadicle series as a teenager, it was a fun place to go in my head. For it to now be this big 'thing' out there in the world is surreal.

Many thanks to my exceptional beta reading team—Liz Singleton, Stephen DeBacker, Doug Burnham, Eric Haneberg, Christine Pattee, David Frydrych, Leo Roars, Kurt Schulenburg, Jim Dean, and Troy Mullens—and especially John Ashmore, for making sure that this story was a worthy addition to the Cadicle Universe. I appreciate everything you do! Sincere thanks also to the great proofers who helped add the final polish: Crystal Wren, Bryan Ellis, Diane Smith, Charlie Obert, and Angel LaVey. You are amazing!

Thank you to Mal for inspiring me and showing how great a shared universe can be. And thank you to Nick, the love of my life, for keeping me fed and sane, and for never getting upset when I disappeared into headphone land to write and edit.

I have a *lot* planned for the coming year, and I hope you'll join us on the journey in the Verity Chronicles and beyond! Until next time, happy reading :-)!

ABOUT THE AUTHORS

T.S. VALMOND

T.S. Valmond isn't an author (despite the claims). More like a glorified reporter delivering the news from far away worlds. She'll tell you she doesn't write books she's building a universe but don't believe the hype; she also thinks she's a Jedi. She resides in Canada with her husband and dog in an undisclosed location. One can never be too careful when exposing the secrets of powerful governments, intergalactic worlds, and illegal aliens. (Yes, they're watching.)

www.tsvalmond.com

A.K. DUBOFF

A.K. (Amy) DuBoff has always loved science fiction in all its forms—books, movies, shows and games. If it involves outer space, even better! She is a Nebula Award finalist and USA Today bestselling author most known for her Cadicle Universe, but she's also written a variety of space fantasy and comedic sci-fi. Now a full-time author, Amy can frequently be found traveling the world. When she's not writing, she enjoys wine tasting, binge-watching TV series, and playing epic strategy board games.

www.amyduboff.com